T0274371

OUR SHOUTS ECHO

JADE ADIA

HYPERION
Los Angeles New York

Also by Jade Adia

There Goes the Neighborhood

First Edition, August 2024
1 3 5 7 9 10 8 6 4 2
FAC-004510-24165
Printed in the United States of America

This book is set in Centennial LT Pro / Linotype
Designed by Jessica Nevins
Pen and ink illustrations by Zareen Johnson
Stock images: email 1342573394, emojis 2290021211, lined paper 1566998068, notebook 1718198023, Post-its 212336662, ripped paper 1367983559/Shutterstock

Library of Congress Cataloging-in-Publication Data
Names: Adia, Jade, author.
Title: Our shouts echo / Jade Adia.
Description: First edition. • Los Angeles ; New York : Hyperion, 2024. • Audience: Ages 12–18. • Audience: Grades 7–12. • Summary: Sixteen-year-old Niarah's perspective on life changes when she joins a hiking/camping club and befriends Mac Torres and his wanderlust-driven friends, but as summer draws to a close and her new friends leave, existential dread challenges her new outlook.
Identifiers: LCCN 2023035536 • ISBN 9781368090117 (hardcover) • ISBN 9781368092432 (ebook)
Subjects: CYAC: Friendship—Fiction. • Family life—Fiction. • Summer—Fiction. • Camping—Fiction. • African Americans—Fiction. • LCGFT: Novels.
Classification: LCC PZ7.1.A245 Ou 2024 • DDC [Fic]—dc23
LC record available at https://lccn.loc.gov/2023035536

Reinforced binding

Visit www.HyperionTeens.com

Logo Applies to Text Stock Only

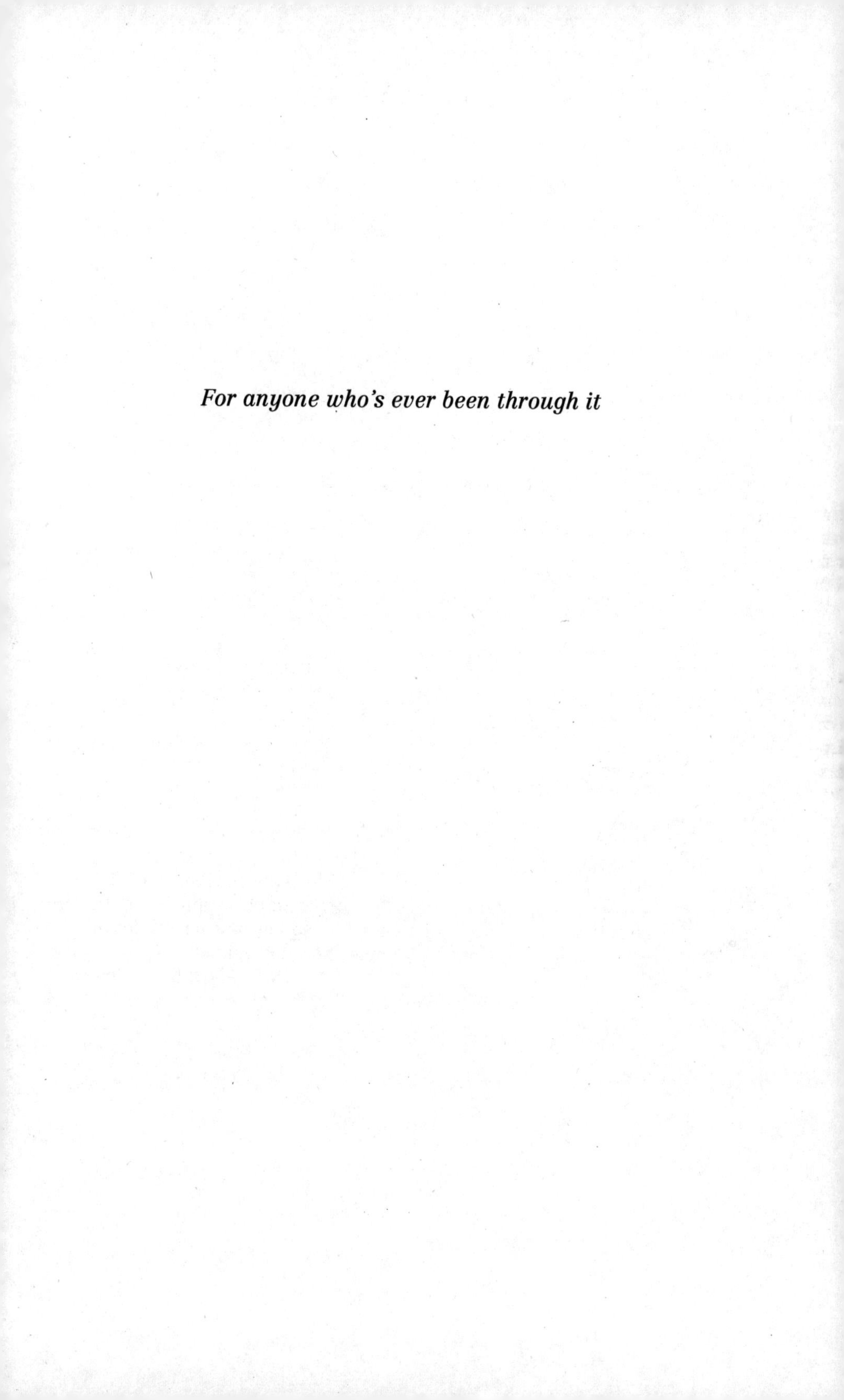

For anyone who's ever been through it

This is a book about being alive. The love and hilarity and mystery of it all.

That said, this story also contains candid discussions about mental health. If you'd like a full list of content warnings, you can find one on my website, www.JadeAdia.com.

But here's my promise to you, reader: This is a book about being alive. The good and the difficult but always, and most importantly, the good.

YEAH, NO THANKS

YEAH, NO THANKS
YEAH, NO THANKS

IN MY CLASSROOM, THERE IS A POSTER THAT epitomizes everything that I hate. A triumphant-looking girl wearing a white bandanna crosses her arms. She nods at me with a vibrant, can-do-attitude grin. Beneath her dopey smile, shiny silver text declares: *You are the future!*

Pathetic.

I don't know if you've noticed, but the world these days is a bit—how you say—shitty.

I like Earth and all. I'm a huge fan of her work. A timeless gem, she is. But these days? Yikes. Ol' girl is tired. I know it, you know it, she knows it. And us people farting around on her surface, dissociating from reality and pretending that we're not hurling toward a giant ocean of flaming garbage? We are merely the overgrown hairs on her freckled chin, waiting any day now to be plucked or lasered away for good.

So, when mass-printed motivational propaganda posters tell

me that I'm the future, or when overeager parents tell me that their generation is counting on mine, I offer up the same response that I give to the cashier at Taco Bell when he hands me a Dorito Crunchwrap without enough cheese: "Send it back."

Y'all can keep your damn future to yourselves.

WELL PREPARED

WELL PREPARED
WELL PREPARED

"EARTH TO NIARAH," MY TEACHER MX. Ferrante repeats, arms crossed as their Dr. Marten loafers tap the linoleum floor. The worst thing about Mx. Ferrante is that they're actually cool, which makes it hard when I consistently mess up every assignment they give me. Today—the last day of sophomore year—is no exception.

"Wh-what was that?" I clear my throat. Ever since I was a kid, I've had the raspy voice of a weary jazz singer smoking their last dying cigarette.

"Time for your final presentation." A menacing *dun-dun-dunnnnn* echoes in the shallow cavity of my brain where my mental preparedness for this situation should be.

"Actually, I already presented," I reply confidently. Naturally, this is a lie. It is a stupid lie because everyone was here, so they know that I'm lying, but it is also *so* blatantly stupid of a lie that it casts just enough doubt to make Mx. Ferrante double-check their notes. They glare back at me, as if to ask if I really thought that dumb trick would work. I shrug, resisting the urge to point out that it almost did.

The front of my notebook is covered in my own half-assed attempt at graffiti and bleak song lyrics. I avoid Mx. Ferrante's eyes, adding another doodle that perfectly captures the essence of my spirit as of late, as well as my general philosophy on love, life, society, and philosophy.

¯_(ツ)_/¯

"Nice try," Mx. Ferrante says. "Front of the classroom, please."

I feel the beady eyes of my over-caffeinated and under-stimulated classmates fall on me. I shrink into my hoodie. Most people hated virtual school during the height of the pandemic, but I loved it. No human interaction required. I was merely one blurry square in a grid of dozens of blurry squares, free from the oppressive burden of being perceived.

"Can I get something from my locker first?" I plead, grabbing a strand of curls and placing it over my upper lip like a mustache. My hair is out in a full mane, Simba-style. A few months ago, I got a new haircut: curly bangs. Cute in theory, until I realized how much maintenance they require. Now my hair is in a constant state of chaos. The only benefit is that the frizzy curls hide my eyes.

"The last time that I let you go to your locker during class, you were found passed out on the lawn after attempting to give blood without parental permission."

The girl seated in front of me turns around, her meticulously waxed eyebrows blending with the swirled baby hair frozen in gel at the summit of her forehead. "You tried to *give blood* to avoid class?"

"Desperate times call for desperate measures," I say. Plus, in my defense, I didn't plan on passing out. I didn't know that I was afraid of needles until then. "I was *allegedly* found passed out." Innocent until proven guilty.

Mx. Ferrante just looks at me and sighs.

I did not prepare for today's presentation. It is becoming clear to me that it is also becoming clear to Mx. Ferrante that I did not prepare for today's presentation. We've spent the entire semester working on the sophomore capstone project: big scrapbook-like things full of essays, art projects, and photographs that are supposed to represent our "vision for the future." For the record, I'm using *we* loosely here. *My classmates* have been working on their capstone projects. I, on the other hand, have been working on establishing myself as a force to be reckoned with in the newest battle royale video game. I'd rather take the bad grade than go through the motions of such a tedious assignment. Take, for example, the topic for today's torture:

Please bring an object that symbolizes where you see yourself in ten years.
Along with the object, prepare a one-page letter, titled "Dear Future Self," to share with the class.

There has been a wide range of presentations. Stacey, the class gunner, showed off a stethoscope because she wants to be a doctor. Nobody had the heart to break it to her that in ten years, when we're twenty-six, even if she goes straight through from high school to college to medical school, she'll probably still be sleep deprived and saddled with hundreds of thousands of dollars of student loan debt, anxiously awaiting the opportunity to work horrible hours as an intern at some hospital that will exploit her labor, still years away from becoming a bona fide doctor. Corey, the class idiot, brought in a music video that he made, which was essentially just three minutes of him and his friends jumping into a pool in slow motion while sinister EDM beats pounded in the background. Xander, the class sex symbol, brought in a pair of tiny baby Nikes because he "wants to be a father." Everyone oohed and awwed, but I know that he only did this as a stunt to boost his potential to sleep with anyone he wants this summer. Hence, my point: This assignment is a joke.

"This is a requirement to pass this course," Mx. Ferrante reminds me in a voice with a surprising level of softness. They like me, for whatever reason. I sense that they were possibly a fellow Weird Kid back in the day, but still. Being liked apparently isn't enough to let me skate by.

I groan in defeat. If teachers are so worried about students failing, then they shouldn't give us grades at all. I unzip my backpack and search for something, anything, to makeshift a presentation on the fly. The main compartment holds a jumble of unread books, a bag of snacks, fast-food receipts, two broken pencils, and a hamburger eraser. The front pocket carries my phone, Metro card, and earphones. Not a lot of potential material. Unless . . .

I plunge my hand deeper into the pit of my backpack, feeling around until my fingertips graze the edge of a Ziploc bag. My saving grace.

Here goes nothing.

The loose nail in the bottom of my desk scrapes the floor as I drag myself up from my seat to the front of the room, special object in hand. Mx. Ferrante gives me one of those now-was-that-so-hard? smiles. I grimace back at them.

The blank stares of my classmates make my skin crawl. I've always hated one-on-one eye contact, let alone twenty-on-one. I open my notebook to a blank page and start bullshitting.

Dear Future Self,

By now, you are twenty-six years old. Congrats on surviving this long. Sixteen-year-old you from the past would like to gift you a necessary item that will encourage your ongoing success. I anticipate that this will be hard to find in your time, so yeah. You're welcome.

Sincerely,
Niarah Simone Holloway

EDC

EDC
EDC

I HOLD UP MY OBJECT. "TA-DAH."

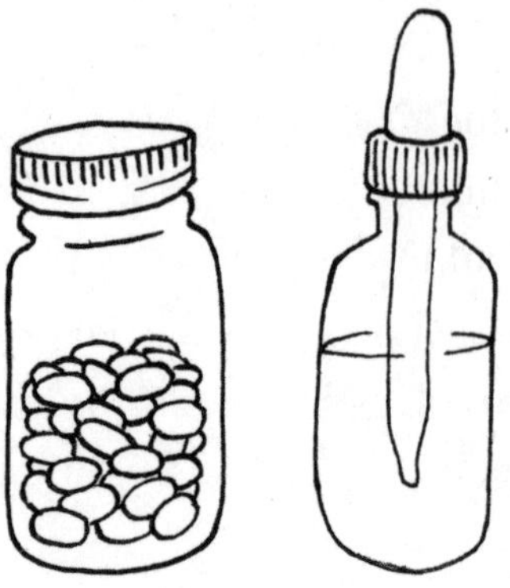

The room is silent as a sensory-deprivation tank. From their desk chair, Mx. Ferrante squints to get a better look. "Niarah, can you please explain what's in your hand?"

I give the plastic bag a little shake. "It's a dual pack of iodine. The dark glass thingy with the eyedropper is liquid iodine, which can be used for purifying water or as a topical disinfectant for injuries. The pills are potassium iodine, which is an FDA-approved nuclear radiation blocking agent."

Corey scratches his head. "Nuclear radiation . . ."

"Yeah. The pills work by saturating the thyroid with stable iodine so it will block the thyroid's absorption of cancer-causing iodine released from a nuclear reactor or nuclear bomb. You know, for when the nukes hit? *Kaboom!*" With my hands, I mime a dramatic explosion. The kids in the front row flinch. "Together, these two forms of iodine will help Future Me survive in the inevitable doomsday scenario when the state fails and there's no clean water and the air's poison and it's every person for themself."

I keep an iodine kit on me at all times. Disaster can strike at any moment, and after months of research, I've concluded that iodine is necessary to keep on hand in my Every Day Carry (EDC) kit. (Well, that and a knife, too, but I can't bring that to school. I'm not tryna get my Black ass expelled for being "armed" on campus.) In a pinch, I can find food and shelter, but if shit hits the fan and the world crumbles while I'm away from my actual emergency kit at home, I'll be thankful to at least have the tools to purify water and prevent nuclear cancer. Doomsday Survival 101, baby.

Mx. Ferrante removes their glasses. "In ten years . . . you see yourself . . . navigating an apocalypse, fighting to survive?"

I pick my nails. "Correct."

"Not law school. Not traveling. Not making friends. Just taking iodine pills?"

I pause. "Well, if the apocalypse doesn't actually involve nuclear threats, then I guess I'd probably sell the pills on the black market."

Mx. Ferrante's mouth falls open, but before they can speak—

"Holy shit, she's actually serious," Corey interjects. Laughter erupts throughout the room. I glance up from my notebook to find Corey's phone out, camera aimed right at me. He's the type of leech who believes that having a minor following online gives him the right to film anyone at any moment. A true visionary, he never misses an opportunity to turn someone else's embarrassment into manufactured social media attention for himself.

I try to laugh along with the class, play this off as a joke, but it's too late. Fingers point. More phones record. Cackles. Whispers. Stares. Time to salvage the situation. "With the pandemic, the increase of severe natural disasters due to climate change, and general unrest throughout America and the world, it's not a bad idea to be prepared for a variety of emergencies."

But there's no use explaining. Corey bolts from his seat, lunging forward to snatch the iodine bag from my hand. I pounce back but miss as he jukes me out. He beams, zooming his camera in on the iodine. "Y'all see this?"

Mx. Ferrante tries to get control of the situation but only makes things worse. The room courses with that feral, last-day-of-school energy when consequences for rowdiness feel impossible. An entire school year of flying under the radar as the Semi-Invisible New Kid, gone in an instant.

"Let me see," Xander yells, arms outstretched to receive the iodine-turned-hot-potato from Corey. But, like the second-string wannabe quarterback that he is, Xander flounders. The shrill wail of the school bell rips through the classroom, startling him. I hiss as my iodine slips from his fingers and shatters on the floor. A mess of sickly orange liquid pools inside the crinkled bag.

Everyone rushes out of the classroom, the moment of my humiliation passing as quickly as it started. Mx. Ferrante begins to say something, but I don't want their pity. My nose crinkles as the harsh metallic scent of the spilled solution seeps into the air. I leave the mess on the floor and make my escape. The last thing I hear before I put on my headphones is the echo of a classmate's voice, dripping with sadistic glee: "Enjoy your summer, Doomsday Girl."

DEFINITION

DEFINITION
DEFINITION

prep·per *noun* \ 'pre-pər \

plural **prep·pers**

: a person preparing for the end of the world as we know it

example : me

THREE TYPES OF PREPPERS

THREE TYPES OF PREPPERS
THREE TYPES OF PREPPERS

PREPPERS FALL INTO THREE LEVELS.

Level One: Light Preppers
The people who know that we live in a dangerous world but don't have the time or money to invest in big preps, so they just do what they can.

Level Two: Diligent Preppers
The ones who believe there is a nonzero chance of something happening that could set society back a hundred years or more, so they invest in prepping but still continue to live their lives, hoping for the best.

Level Three: Online Forum Gurus
The hyperfocused, intense people who believe in government mind control, live off the grid, and are practically praying for the end of the world.

(me on Good Days)
(me on Not-So-Good Days)
1
2
3

PLEASE REPORT TO THE GUIDANCE COUNSELOR'S OFFICE

PLEASE REPORT TO THE GUIDANCE COUNSELOR'S OFFICE

PLEASE REPORT TO THE GUIDANCE COUNSELOR'S OFFICE

THE INSIDE OF MR. GUTIERREZ'S OFFICE LOOKS like an episode of *Hoarders: School Administrator Edition*. Folders upon folders stack and slouch on every visible surface. It smells like printer ink and stale air. The walls are packed tight with framed photographs from school events and his many awards for Teacher of the Year. I notice a new one with this year's date on it.

"Congrats on another win. I'm sure the other teachers are so proud."

Mr. G laughs. "I'm Public Enemy Number One. The math department is plotting a coup to change the rules so that only 'real teachers' are eligible for awards, not us lowly guidance counselors."

If it wasn't for the salt-and-pepper coloring of his beard, the man would look no more than twenty years old. His age—or lack thereof—is one of the many urban myths of this school. On one hand, the sheer number of knickknacks on his desk leads me to believe that he's been here forever, but on the other hand, he's also a sneakerhead with a consistently up-to-date knowledge of rapper internet beef. He could be anywhere from twenty-four to forty-seven years old. There's probably some spooky antiaging magic afoot, so I mind my business. I don't mess with the dark arts.

Mr. G picks up the landline in his office and calls the front desk. "In ten minutes, can you send Mr. Torres in, please?"

I pocket a piece of White Rabbit candy from the bowl by the door. "Who is Mr. Torres, and why is he joining us?"

"Take a seat, Niarah."

"Way to avoid my question."

Mr. Gutierrez flashes me a grin, amused but warning me to watch it. I pick up the chair opposite his desk and adjust the angle so that I can see the door. I don't like having my back facing exits.

"So," Mr. G begins, "Mx. Ferrante tells me that for your Dear Future Self presentation in class this morning, you brought . . ." He checks his notes, his rushed handwriting nearly illegible even to himself. "Iodine to protect yourself from the side effects of nuclear war."

"And to treat water," I add.

"And to treat water," he confirms. "Then, last week, you ditched class to . . ." He checks his notes again. "Donate blood."

"Correct."

Silence passes between us.

I stare at Mr. G. "I'm sorry, was there, like, a question in that?"

He pinches the bridge of his nose and lets out one of his signature Mr. G I'm-a-nice-guy-trying-my-best-to-reach-these-kids sighs. "What are your goals for this summer?"

Ah, the dreaded "goals" question. Teachers love this one.

Fortunately, this is actually a question that I can answer. This summer, I'm going to live out every young girl's fantasy and build the emergency fallout shelter of my dreams.

I shall name it Camp Doom.

To be clear, Camp Doom is not actually a camp. There will be no dorms, no counselors, no activities. It's not a camp like that, more so a station. I'd call it a fort, but that feels either too militant or too whimsical depending on how you say it.

I haven't started building it yet, but in my mind, I imagine Camp Doom clearly: fortified exterior, one wall covered with a pantry full of enough food to last a year, the others boasting a selection of self-defense and survival tools. In an ideal world, I'd build a bunker that could withstand anything. An intense structure, preferably underground. Unfortunately, I don't have the time, money, or skills to execute something like that. I'm not crazy enough to think that I can build a shelter that can protect against a mega-disaster like an asteroid impact. If shit hits the fan that hard, we're all screwed. But I think that I can build something capable of withstanding less-extreme events—the big earthquake, civil unrest, a pandemic-induced zombie apocalypse, maybe—I don't know. So, after weeks of research, I've decided on a more feasible model: the aboveground bunker. Or, in my case, the reinforced, dilapidated wooden detached garage in the backyard. The plan is to begin construction this afternoon.

I tell Mr. G this—not about Camp Doom specifically, obviously—but that I'm working on a Very Important DIY project.

He doesn't seem convinced. I don't blame him.

"Niarah, I want to ask you a serious question." He laces his fingers together like a judge on a daytime television set and leans forward. "Are you depressed?"

I shrug. "Just the normal, age-appropriate amount."

It's hard to know how others feel, but I'm certainly walking around life with a full plate of anxiety plus a side of depression and a scoop of OCD for dessert. And then there are the reoccurring nightmares. I don't know if "normal" sixteen-year-olds still have nightmares. But then again, I don't think that anyone is truly "normal." The concept of "normal" is a tool to either dilute people into complacency or alienate others. If life is a cup of black coffee, "normal" is milk; the more the concept is forced onto you, the weaker you get.

"I know that moving across the country to Los Angeles partway through high school must've been tough—"

"No way. Transferring was actually fine." I may not have any friends here at my new school, but it's better than where I was before. Back in Syracuse, everyone knew my family. Us Holloways were hot gossip. Every day, I'd hear the whispers, clock the nervous stares. Back there, everyone heard about what went wrong in my house. Here in LA, at least, nobody knows me at all. Anonymity is a sweet relief. Or at least it was, until this morning's presentation.

"Was middle school any better?" Mr. G asks.

It takes Herculean strength not to laugh in his face. Being a middle school girl is *terrifying*. One day, you blink and notice that everyone around you is looking at your body and your friends' bodies and you want them to stop. But then you start looking right back. You notice the boys in your class sound different. At a sleepover, you catch a whiff of your classmate's hair and it smells like a cinnamon candle. You're envious, but you also want to stay close enough to smell it all night for some reason that you don't have the words for. You look at your parents and realize that they don't love each other. You learn things in school that outrage you yet you have no power to change, and you start to sweat. A lot. Your mom can't get the funk out of your favorite shirt in the wash. Things start looking up when you discover some depressing music that makes you feel seen until, one night at 2 a.m., you pull off your covers, look down, and find that you're covered in blood. You wobble to the bathroom, toss your underwear in the trash bin, then, in a dark tiled room, slouched against the terry-cloth robe that you've had since third grade, you poke a tampon into the wrong hole. If that isn't the most confusing shit in the world, I don't know what is.

"No, Mr. Gutierrez, I did not enjoy middle school, either."

"Look, I'm only trying to understand what's going on with you. You're a smart kid. Don't you want to go to college? You have so much potential."

Potential. How I hate the word. Potential for what? I'm a person, not a fixer-upper. I don't even know if I can handle more education beyond high school.

Mr. G plops his elbows on his desk and massages his temples. The door opens abruptly and a pair of familiar Dr. Martens stride in.

"Mx. Ferrante?" I ask.

I get the feeling that Mx. Ferrante is avoiding my eyes as they fidget with their messenger bag, staring straight at Mr. G. "Have you told her yet?"

My eyebrows shoot up. "Told me what?"

Mr. G starts to look clammy. "We understand that this year has been difficult for you, but there are consequences to ditching class and not completing mandatory assignments, and none of us want you to repeat sophomore year. . . ."

Hold on.

Nobody mentioned anything about repeating a year. My words fall out in a stutter. "I—I don't understand."

Mx. Ferrante takes a deep breath, then gives it to me straight. "Here's the reality, Niarah: As of now, you've failed sophomore year."

Wait, wait, wait.

I failed sophomore year? Who fails *sophomore* year?

"But I didn't fail your class!" I point to Mx. Ferrante, but they look away.

That's when it hits me: Why they're here. In this office. With us. Right now.

I'm screwed.

CONSEQUENCES
CONSEQUENCES
CONSEQUENCES

"YOU'RE DOING THIS TO TORTURE ME."

"I told you *several times* that you needed to complete your capstone to pass the class," Mx. Ferrante argues.

"I did the final presentation at least." That must count for something.

"No, you didn't. You stood up in front of the class and talked about the end of the world."

"But everything I said was true. That *is* what I see for the future." I don't see myself in the future at all, but when I do, it's in a crumbling world.

"If that's how you feel, fine. But you're going to have to prove it to me. Finish your capstone project this summer. All of it. If your vision for the future is the apocalypse, then back it up. Write something that convinces me that doomsday prepping is a worthwhile activity. Show me why this matters to you so much. Turn in something substantial to prove your point by the last week of summer, then I'll give you the passing grade that you need."

I pull my hood on and yank the drawstrings until the fabric swallows my face. This sucks. Sure, I'm already prepping my shelter this summer, but having to supplement the experience with schoolwork wasn't what I had in mind.

I glare at Mx. Ferrante through my cotton cocoon. "Why couldn't you let me slide?"

Mx. Ferrante smiles like some self-proclaimed hero. "Because I care too much."

I audibly gag. Mr. G claps his hands. "Glad that's settled. Unfortunately, the makeup capstone project alone is not enough."

I groan. "What else could you people want from me?"

"I already spoke to the rest of your academic teachers and convinced them to pass you. You'll receive Cs and Ds, but at least you can go on. From what I've heard, you understand the material when asked, you just refuse to turn in any work. However, that still leaves the matter of PE. . . ."

"Physical education is a scam." First off, the school campus is big as hell, so I already walk enough from class to class. Second, there is no "learning" happening in PE. All we do is participate in forced group activities or mindlessly sulk around the track. I technically show up to PE, but I never stay, except when it's raining and the sports teams are using the gym, so we watch an ancient '90s movie in an empty classroom instead.

"Do you know how many times you've missed PE this semester?"

"No."

"Forty-four."

Nice.

"Do you know the total number of PE classes per semester?" he asks.

I stare at the ceiling. "I'm going to guess at least forty-four."

"Forty-six." He pulls out one of those TI-89 calculators that our teachers insisted we purchase even though we have phones and thus will literally never use a physical calculator in our lives. "You've managed to miss 95.65217391 percent of your physical education."

"Cool. Do I get a plaque like you now?"

Mr. Gutierrez bites back a chuckle, but the expression is fleeting. "You have to make up those lost PE hours. There's no other way around it."

"How?"

There's a knock at the door.

"Come in!" Mr. Gutierrez chimes.

Great. More guests to pile onto my punishment. The heavy wooden door creaks as it slides open on ancient hinges.

"Mr. G, I'm sorry I slacked off this semester, but, like, the world is literally on fire, so I don't see the point in coming to school every day and—"

Whoa.

The rest of my sentence vanishes.

A boy with wavy brown hair tucked beneath a faded Dodgers cap hovers by the door, a neon-pink Post-it note stuck to his forehead.

His eyes scan the scene, taking in Mx. Ferrante's crossed arms, Mr. G's worried grimace, then my face, a heart-shaped canvas of brown skin, partially hidden behind my worn-out sweatshirt. Recognition spreads across his face as he finds my eyes. He lets out a soft chuckle.

Coming from anyone else, his next words would've hurt, but his tone is gentle. The boy tosses me a small, amused smile. "Hey, Doomsday Girl."

LITERAL COERCION

LITERAL COERCION
LITERAL COERCION

"COME IN, COME IN, MR. TORRES," MR. Gutierrez says.

The boy shuffles into the room, his eyes bouncing between me and the teachers until he settles on leaning awkwardly against the wall. He's wearing a dark blue flannel shirt that looks pulled straight from a thrift store. On a mannequin, those shirts tend to look dorky, but on him . . . Well, he wears it differently.

"I saw the video of your project this morning," the boy explains.

I say nothing.

"Your classmates suck," he continues. "I thought that you were interesting."

Interesting. He could've said that he thought that *my presentation* was interesting. Instead, he said that *I* was interesting. I must've heard him wrong. I must be misinterpreting. But then he seals his comment with another soft smile. I flinch.

"Meet Marco: student leader of the Color Outside group," Mr. G announces.

Marco gives me a small, almost-imperceptible nod.

I steal more glances at the intruder. Frizzy waves, brown skin, a mellow smirk, faded Old Skool Skate Vans, a little green Earth patch sewn over a tear in his jeans . . .

"Andddddd this is for you, Niarah." I hadn't realized that neither of us has said anything until Mr. G pulls a flyer out from underneath a stack of manila envelopes. He places the paper in front of me and gives it two quick taps with his finger. "Marco volunteers with a group dedicated to helping people of color access outdoor activities. Hiking, rock climbing, and whatnot. Real nice mission. Other kids from school do it, too."

I am what you call an Indoor Kid. The wonders of my natural habitat include MMRPGs, conspiracy theory videos, and copious amounts of doom scrolling. Normal, reasonable-person activities. Not trees.

I slide the flyer toward Mr. G. "I don't hike."

"Well, this summer, you do." Mr. G pushes the flyer right back. "The first Color Outside meetup of the summer is Tuesday morning. If you attend the activities, I'll have Marco sign off on your hours. Then I can convince the school to give you the necessary course credit."

I give the boy another quick look. "Did they force you into this group as well?"

He bobs his weight from his heels to toes. "At first."

I raise an eyebrow. "A fellow delinquent?"

"Former delinquent," he corrects with a smirk.

That's interesting—that he had once been in trouble, too. We make eye contact again, briefly, before his eyes flit away, head turning straight up toward the ceiling. His movements are a little erratic, a little shy.

"Umm." I strain to keep my thoughts on track. I cross my arms and face Mr. G. "Isn't it messed up that another student is surveilling me? Isn't that, like, a conflict of interest?"

"Surveilling is for narcs. Do I look like a narc?" Marco holds his arms up and examines his outfit theatrically. I ignore him and turn back to Mr. G.

"There's got to be another way. Please."

"It's either Color Outside or summer school," Mr. G repeats.

The thought of being stuck here in this prison over the summer without air-conditioning when it's all hot and sticky makes me gag. The only teachers here during break are the exhausted ones who want to take time off but can't afford it because they're so underpaid. Or, even worse, the temps who only teach during the summer, so they're way too eager to "change our lives" or whatever. It's really bleak, if you think about it.

Marco tries to hand Mr. Gutierrez the Post-it note that he carried into the office, but Mr. G points at me instead. "That's for the newest member of your group here."

"I have not agreed to anything yet," I remind Mr. G.

"Yet," Marco repeats with emphasis.

The boy is decidedly hard to read. Sometimes shy, sometimes confident.

When he steps closer, I catch a better glimpse of his eyes, a shade of brown so deep that it almost blends with his pupils. His eyes have a way of crinkling at the corners, exuding the aura of someone perpetually on the brink of cracking an inside joke with you. Except inside jokes are for friends, and we are strangers. I shrink away. Still, I detect a hint of hope in his glance as he hands me the Post-it. I peel it from his fingers, careful not to touch him.

8 a.m., Elysian Park,
southeast entrance.

Bring water, walking shoes,
and a growth mindset

:)

Growth mindset?

"Jesus Christ," I mumble.

I stick the Post-it onto the flyer and shake it in Mr. G's face. "To be clear: This is literally coercion."

"It quite literally is not." Mr. G waves me off, returning his focus to his planner. And suddenly, the whole meeting is over.

Mx. Ferrante tries to shake my hand on my way out, but I brush past them, past Marco, out of the office.

"Have a good summer, Niarah." Mx. Ferrante's voice fades down the hallway. "And try to engage with the world."

Sure. Will do. Can't wait. Thank you so much.

TREE HUGGER

TREE HUGGER
TREE HUGGER

"WILL I SEE YOU AT THE HIKE ON TUESDAY?" Marco asks.

I try to walk as fast as possible to lose him, but he's either deeply committed to his new role as Hike Club Recruiter, or doesn't take the hint that I'm trying to escape, or both.

"Doubt it."

"Will you think about it?"

"Doubt it."

"You're tough."

"I know."

He's taller—easily at least 6'2" to my 5'7"—so every two steps of mine are one of his. His stride is swift yet peaceful, with the solidity of someone who has nothing to prove. When we finally reach the bus stop out front, it's completely empty. Most people are riding home with friends or walking to one of the nearby cafés to celebrate the end of the year. Only the antisocials without plans take the bus on the last day of school, which is precisely why it's my favorite time. Sweet solitude.

I wait for Marco to peel off, but he lingers, leaning against the light pole. Again with the leaning. When in motion, Marco gives off a relaxed energy, but standing still, he's practically buzzing. On each hand, he wears dark black rings—one on his middle finger, the other on his pointer. One ring has a thin chain running through the middle, the other a wheel of spikes. Mindlessly, he uses his thumbs to twirl each piece around and around. I've never seen wearable fidget spinners before. The spinning rings make a faint humming sound that almost puts me in a trance before I remember that we're still mid-conversation.

"No offense, Marco, but—"

"Actually, it's Mac," he corrects. "My government name is Marco Torres, but everyone calls me Mac." He uses a finger to draw his name in the air, then crosses out the *r* and the *o*. He completes the gesture but then winces, as if he immediately regrets it. He shoves his hands back into his pockets. I say his nickname a few times over in my head. The brevity of it feels like a clap of thunder, or perhaps the pop of a soda can when you break the seal.

"You got some other big plans for summer, then?" Mac-not-Marco asks.

"Sort of."

"Like what? Getting into more trouble?" He smirks.

I kind of like his voice. It reminds me of a walkie-talkie—raspy with a hint of static; right in front of me yet, inexplicably, still seeming far away.

"I'm not *in trouble* now, it's just academic probation." Not like *academic probation* sounds much better, but you know. A girl's gotta defend her honor.

Mac raises a questioning eyebrow at me, and I roll my eyes. "I'm working on a project. A DIY construction thing." I leave out the details of Camp Doom, the prepper journey, and my general descent into madness.

"Sounds cool. Maybe I can come check it out sometime after our hike," he says. He seems to mean it.

"No *our*," I correct. He holds back a grin at my reaction. "I'm not into hiking."

"The point of this group isn't to force everyone to get super into hiking. It's to encourage a connection to our environment." He offers a small smile.

"Then you must be bummed that climate change is going to destroy everything," I say, curb-stomping his little ray of sunshine.

This is what I mean when I say that I'm out of practice with social interaction: I have no filter. Still, I mean what I say. Mac is cute, but naive. I almost feel bad for the environmentalist saps. When it comes to global warming, we're all on a sinking ship. Taking people on a hike isn't going to change that.

"Climate change is a real threat, but the fight's not over, Niarah." He rolls up the sleeves of his flannel, revealing a long line of brown skin stretched across lean muscles. It's only his forearms, but you'd think it was something more obscene by the way that I instinctually look away. Have I officially reached the stage of severe social isolation where I can't even look at someone's arms without flinching?

I clear my throat. "The fires are getting worse. The seas are rising. There was a time to fight, but that ship has sailed. I don't see the point anymore."

"Humans have lived in harmony with nature in the past and

we can do it again. The era of overconsumption and unchecked capitalism is still relatively new and short-lived in the grand scheme of history," he says, voice sincere as Greta Thunberg herself. "We can find new, sustainable ways forward."

The late-afternoon sun shifts out from behind the tree line, showering him in early summer light. He holds a hand above his eyes to block the rays as he casts me a playful smile, challenging me to keep the debate going. From this angle, I notice the splash of tiny freckles that dot his skin.

"I don't know if I want to entrust the fate of my high school career to a hopeless Tree Hugger."

A thin gold chain with a Virgen de Guadalupe pendant scatters rays of sunshine like confetti as he shakes his head in laughter. Against my best judgment, I watch his reaction and feel a foreign emotion at the fringe of my consciousness: the desire to make him laugh again.

I see a better view of his face beneath his hat. His eyes are intense—narrow and deep set with heavy eyelids. His thick eyebrows run in firm, straight lines across his forehead with only the slightest bit of arch at the end. Resting, his features are sharp, but the way that he smiles nervously, awkwardly shuffling his hands between his pockets and behind his back, softens the overall effect.

I get a little lost looking at him, and when I pull myself together, I realize that he's looking right back at me. His eyes travel slowly from the sweatshirt that I wear every day no matter the weather, to my basketball shorts, down to my unfashionable yet functional running shoes. You never know when disaster will strike, so I only wear comfortable footwear. Nobody wants to flee the apocalypse in flip-flops. Still, today, I have the slightest wish that I wasn't looking so much like . . . I don't know. Me.

I'm grateful when the moment is interrupted by a scrawny dog rustling in a bush a few feet away. It's an ugly little thing. Long, matted fur and scabs on its joints. No collar. I pull my backpack forward and feel around until I find my snack bag. It rips open with satisfying whiz as I grab a handful of high-protein dog treats wrapped in a napkin. I toss a couple toward the bush—close enough so that the dog can smell them, but not so close as to freak it out. It takes a second for the dog to finish its investigation of the treats, sniffing and rolling one around with its nose, before devouring them all. I toss over one more.

"You keep dog food in your backpack?"

When I look up at Mac, his expression is difficult to read. I freeze. After today's class presentation, I've learned my lesson about disclosing my EDC. I rack my mind for the least weird explanation. I settle on the bare minimum of truth. "I have a dog at home," I say plainly. But what I really mean is *of course* I carry around freeze-dried, grain-free pork biscuits in case of emergency. My dog, Bruce, trusts me to take care of him, no matter what. In all my earthquake kits, in every EDC, there are always materials for Bruce, too.

Mac's brows knit together. "So, you give your dog's treats to strays?"

I shrug. "It's hard enough to survive."

A group of freshman girls walks by and does a shameless double take when they see Mac. He either doesn't notice or doesn't care. He keeps his eyes locked on mine as he leans away from the pole, taking a large step toward me. I panic, urgently needing something else to do with my hands. I reach into my backpack to fish out my water bottle, but it's empty. Mac pulls his own bottle out of the backpack slouched on his left shoulder. He hands it to me and motions for me to drink. I take a sip from the wide rim, but my hand's shaking, so I spill a little. A tiny splash of water falls ungracefully down the side of my face. I frantically abort mission, wiping my chin and shoving the bottle back toward his chest.

Mac watches me with amusement. He bites his bottom lip as he restrains a smile. "How come I've never seen you before, Niarah?"

The bus appears from around the corner. We watch it lurch toward us, and as we do, a very good reason to avoid Mac flashes right at me. As he shifts his weight from one foot to the other to get a better look at the bus, I see the text on the T-shirt hiding beneath his flannel: *University of California Davis Incoming Class.*

My heart sinks.

He's a senior. Of course. He's graduating tomorrow.

I have two reactions to this new information: First is jealousy. I'd do anything to get out of high school, meanwhile he's getting ready to walk across a stage and leave this place forever. Come August, he'll be on his way to UC Davis, seven blissful hours away from LA. The second emotion is harder to place, but it feels suspiciously like disappointment.

The bus wheezes in front of me. I step aboard without saying goodbye, but Mac rushes forward to stop the doors from closing. He nearly trips over his own feet but catches himself before he falls. He curses beneath his breath and cuts me a self-aware look. One of those silent laughs that only lives in the eyes passes between us. "I really think you should join Color Outside, Niarah."

He says my name a lot. Too much.

I like the way it sounds. Too much.

What's the point in getting to know someone who's about to pack up and disappear a few months later? All relationships are temporary, and someone's always going to leave, often sooner than you want them to. I happen to know a thing or two about abandonment.

I climb the remaining stairs on the bus and wave at the driver to let the doors close. "Enjoy your last summer before college, Mac."

And I'll enjoy mine. Alone, as intended.

AN APOCALYPTIC AWARENESS

AN APOCALYPTIC AWARENESS
AN APOCALYPTIC AWARENESS

ON MY VERY FIRST DAY IN LOS ANGELES, I nearly died in the shower. Bottom three non-murdery ways to go out. I was several minutes into a sinfully long soak, water pummeling the back of my neck at full power, trying to drown out the memory of a recent PSA about the importance of conserving water during the drought.

Whatever, I thought. *The planet's dying anyway.*

I adjusted the water pressure and began preparing my vocals for the next screamy song on my playlist.

A second later, the earthquake hit.

As the tiles rumbled beneath my soapy feet, I cursed the fact that I wasn't a Never Nude who showered in a bathing suit. We all will die someday, but I always prayed that when my time came, I wouldn't be naked and listening to Slipknot.

I didn't die, though. After clutching onto the shower curtain like a startled cat, the ground chilled out. The earthquake was only a 4.2—a minor hiccup compared to the giant belch that will one day send the city plummeting into a fault in the planet's crust—but still. The whole situation pissed me off. The prospect of dying in the shower was precisely why I did not want to move to the danger zone commonly known as Los Angeles in the first place.

Prior to my near-death-experience-lite, my mom and I lived in Syracuse, New York. Even though Syracuse gets hit with heavy storms and snow, it's often at the top of the list of urban areas safest from natural disasters. Los Angeles, on the other hand—with its absurd population density and high frequency of earthquakes, wildfires, and flooding—is a city poised for imminent destruction.

And if that wasn't enough, my mom decided to move us into a house that is quite possibly the stupidest structure I've ever seen in my life. It's essentially a fish tank, full of floor to ceiling windows like we're in some sociopath-directed sci-fi horror film. I tried to tell her that a glass house is impractical for when disaster strikes and the streets descend into anarchy and we need to hide, but she didn't listen. Mom said she wanted to move somewhere to feel "safe" after everything that went down with my dad, and yet, she chose this hellhole. Another example of her questionable judgment.

After the earthquake scared me within half an inch of my inconsequential life, I stumbled out of the shower, wrapped on a towel, and immediately googled how to make an earthquake kit. I filled my old *Sesame Street* lunchbox with Pop-Tarts and canned tuna, peanut butter and bags of water. And when I finished, I actually felt better. Momentarily sedated.

Ever since we moved, ever since the Bad Things happened that made us move in the first place, my hands are always lightly shaking. It's gotten so bad that I stopped wearing bracelets because they draw unwanted attention to the tick, creeping out onlookers.

But the first night that I assembled that earthquake kit—the first night that I felt prepared—my hands stopped shaking.

So, I started watching even more videos about preparedness. It honestly started off as a joke. A documentary on the collapse of global food systems here, a thread on the threat of an AI uprising there. A vividly detailed post about how if aliens ever make contact with Earth, it'll be to harvest our sun and leave us to die.

I understand why mainstream culture thinks that prepping is insane. Why I got laughed out of the classroom. I read the comments from the incels and neckbeards online, and I know that lots of the "facts" that they're spewing aren't real. I see how some people take it too far. Still, I enjoy prepping. I find it fun. And more importantly, I can't help but feel attached to my own, low-grade version of a prepper's worldview. One that takes into account the fact that as a young Black girl in a single-parent household in post-pandemic, post-spending-my-formative-childhood-years-quarantined, post-overturning-abortion-freedom, post-more-mass-shootings-than-I-can-count America, I certainly have a reason to be suspicious of things getting better. In fact, I have more than enough reasons to believe that the state of the world is only getting worse.

So, one day, it all clicked: Maybe this *is* the beginning of the end.

Things aren't getting better, and neither am I.

A PREPPER'S GUIDE TO THE BEGINNING OF THE END OF THE WORLD

Niarah Holloway
Mx. Ferrante
Sophomore Capstone Project
June 2
Dear Mx. Ferrante,

For my makeup capstone project, I am going to make a survival guide.

If Yamile can get away with turning in a scrapbook of selfies of all her outfits from sophomore year as her capstone, then I think you can let me turn in this.

I was already planning on spending my summer prepping, so despite your attempts to force me to "engage with the world," this assignment is merely reinforcing my doomsday plans. So, yeah, nice try.

That said, I do not want to be in your class again next year (no offense), so here it goes:

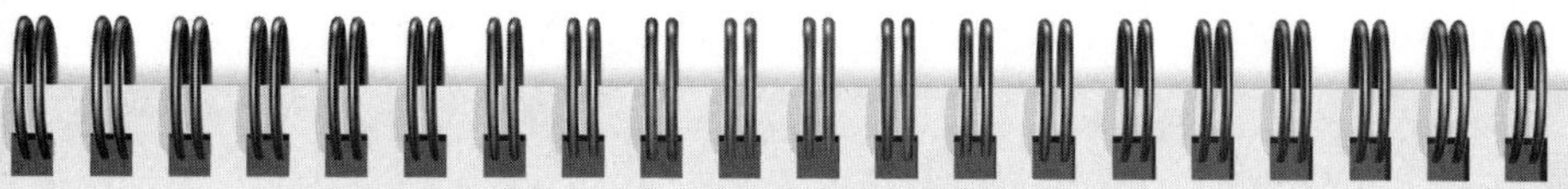

DOOMSDAY PREPPING 101

According to the internet, there are eight steps that you must take to start prepping to survive the apocalypse, doomsday, or any other SHTF (Shit Hits The Fan) scenario.

Step 1: Develop a survival library.

The goal of the survival library is simple: Gather all your favorite articles, survival tips, instructions, and checklists in one place. No one can remember every single detail about every single subject when it comes to prepping. Hence this notebook. Shout-out to Mx. Ferrante for giving me an excuse to get a head start on this.

Step 2: Build an emergency shelter.

(see next page)

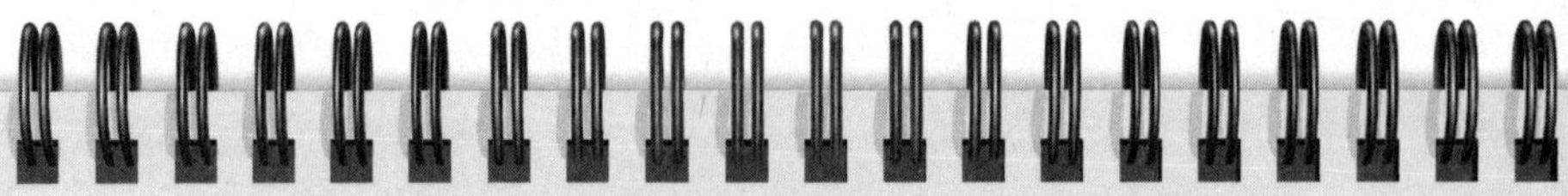

HOW TO BUILD AN EMERGENCY SHELTER, PART 1

Identify the space: Location, location, location! That's what a real estate agent emphasizes when you're picking your first home. The same principle applies to prepping. Pick the least crappy location you can manage.

Develop a water source: Imagine surviving the apocalypse only to die three days later from thirst. Humiliating. Do better.

Strengthen the walls: Put all those hours spent on *Minecraft* to the test. Make sure that your shelter can withstand an attack.

Stock up on supplies: hot chips, toilet paper, ninja stars, etc.—compile the essentials that you'll need to survive.

Make it comfortable: You may need to bunker down in your shelter for an extended period of time. Be sure that your space is cozy enough, so you don't lose your mind. Don't go too crazy with interior design, though. Function over form, always.

DEVELOP A WATER SOURCE

DEVELOP A WATER SOURCE
DEVELOP A WATER SOURCE

I'M DIGGING A HOLE IN THE GROUND TO FIT A fifty-liter water tank beside Camp Doom. It won't be enough water to last forever, but in a pinch, this can carry me through the first days after an emergency. I stab the soil with the rusty shovel that I got from Goodwill. The ground hardly moves. I try again, jumping on the shovel this time for more pressure. Still not even a dent. It's like there's an invisible forcefield guarding the soil to mock me. I pull out my phone to watch another video to find out what I'm doing wrong. After a second watch, I realize that I'm not doing anything wrong, I'm just weak as fuck.

This shit is harder than it looks.

Right as my hope is starting to wane, Bruce rushes out from the doggy door leading from the kitchen to the backyard, sprinting toward me with reckless abandon. Bruce is a Pomeranian, but he has the personality of an airport security dog—a German shepherd, a Rottweiler, maybe even a hundred-ten-pound cane corso. The heart of a guard dog in the body of the fluffy end of a Q-tip. For Halloween last year, I got him a Batman costume to live up to his name. He hated the mask but fell in love with the cape. Now, nine months later, he refuses to leave the house without it. This afternoon is no exception. A silky black cape the size of a napkin ripples in the wind as he runs. A tiny man of justice. Vengeance with a snaggletooth.

He stops centimeters short of barreling into me, snapping upright to attention. I greet him with an obligatory ear fluff before returning to the task at hand. Niarah versus Impossibly Hard Soil. I fill a bucket with water from the kitchen sink and bring it back outside to wet the soil. This time, I manage to unearth a teaspoon of dirt. I pump a fist in the air. *"Victory."*

Bruce barks encouragingly.

"Hey you," my mom calls out from the back door. "Why don't you use that shovel to build your mom a flower bed?"

"I'm building us an emergency shelter, not a space for you to plant nonedible flowers that will inevitably die from this drought."

I did ask Mom's permission to build Camp Doom. I said it was for school, which was a lie back then but is now sort of true given that I'm using it for my capstone. She wasn't thrilled with the idea, but considering that I usually spend every weekend indoors yelling at gamers on the East Coast through my headset about their sloppy attack formation, she figured that absorbing a minimal amount of sunlight each day would be a pleasant change. That's the perk of setting a low bar for yourself: If your parent only expects you to be a loner, then they'll be surprisingly chill when you build a doomsday shelter in the backyard.

"Roses are pretty, though," she says.

I bite my lip. She doesn't get it. I keep digging, trying not to walk into yet another argument with her. Uneasy silence settles between us. Our typical rhythm these days.

"Let's go to the store. Get your jacket," she says after a long pause.

"Nooooooo. I literally just started working."

She scoffs. "Working?"

"Yes. *Working.*"

She looks at Bruce, panting at my ankle, then back over at the pathetic dent in the dirt beside me.

"It's harder than it looks."

"I'm sure it is," she says with a grin. She starts toward the gate that leads to the driveway in front of our house. "Get in the car."

"Wait. My backpack." School may be over, but I carry my EDC everywhere. To the living room, to the store, to restaurants. Doesn't matter. I can tell she still thinks the backpack thing is weird, but she stopped commenting on my habits a long time ago. Too bad she hasn't also stopped forcing me to go to the grocery store with her every Friday, even though she doesn't need my help. I suspect that she likes to drag me along in order to oppress me.

CHICKEN LITTLE

CHICKEN LITTLE
CHICKEN LITTLE

THE ONLY THING THAT I LIKE ABOUT THE grocery store is that beside the sliding doors at the entrance, there's a tiny picture of Bruce. He was banned for life for terrorizing other customers. I tap his lopsided, google-eyed Wanted poster for good luck as I step inside the capitalist wasteland.

Air-conditioning has transformed the store into a walk-in refrigerator. I tuck my arms into my sweatshirt for warmth as I trail behind my mom. Shopping with her is the worst because she insists on going down every single aisle, including the baking supplies section, even though neither of us could bake a cake to save our lives.

"Ox likes these," she says, holding up a bag of sweet onion potato chips.

"Ox," I mumble because I can't think of anything else to say. "Hm."

Ox is a giant man from Toronto who used to be a D-league

football player who never went pro and now owns and operates a furniture shop nearby.

Ox has the entire scene from *The Last Supper* tattooed on his chest.

Ox is my mother's boyfriend.

Before I was born, Mom dated Ox for a year when she was in college and he had an internship in New York. Apparently, it was this big, epic love thing, cut short only by the fact that Ox moved to LA and neither of them were ready to relocate for the other. They fell out of touch, but after my mom left my dad a couple of years back, Ox ran into one of their old mutual friends and asked for her number. He called her up that night to check in. That first call lasted eight hours. They've been dating ever since, picking right up where they left off. Which would be sweet if it wasn't deeply annoying. My mom's known this dude forever, but I only ever learned he existed just over a year ago. Even though *they* go way back, I hardly know the man.

"He's coming over for dinner tonight." She says it as if he doesn't come over for dinner every night. He's over all the time now, ever since she gave him a key. Mom and I have fought about Ox before, but I don't have it in me to complain right now. I pretend that I didn't hear her. She pretends that she doesn't mind. What good actors we are.

"Hey, Chicken Little," she shouts from the end of the aisle, breaking the silence. That's been my new nickname from her ever since I first explained Camp Doom. She thinks it's funny, you know, like I'm running around yelling that the sky is falling, creating mass hysteria. But if that chicken nugget were around today and if he believed in imminent climate disaster the way I did, he'd probably be building a shelter, too, and he'd be right to do so.

“Please stop calling me that,” I mumble, sneaking a couple cans of vegetable soup into the cart for the Camp Doom supply closet.

“If this pack of chicken thighs is $14.99 but today there’s a sale for twenty percent off, how much is the chicken?” She smirks as she wields the raw meat menacingly above her head.

“Why must we do this?” This behavior is yet another reason why I dislike our grocery store errands. The woman is incapable of buying anything without quizzing me first.

“We must do this because somebody here apparently does not attend class. I have to make sure you’re learning something.”

“I don’t have to go to class to learn things.” What I hate the most about high school is how the entire setup illuminates how society sees me: as a future resource. I spend all day being molded into whatever they need me to be—a worker, a consumer, even a savior. It’s like us students are the spare tire in the back of a van being joyridden by older generations, but instead of actually changing the way that they’re driving, the adults keep speeding straight toward a pit of nails, knowing that us youngins will be there to clean up their mess. I hate it. I hate the factory that we call school.

“Agree to disagree.” The pack of chicken, removed from its refuge of refrigeration, has started to sweat. A fat bead of moisture drips from the package onto my mom’s shoulder. I gag a little, but she doesn’t notice. Instead, with her free hand, she grabs the grocery cart and climbs up onto the back bar where toddlers ride.

“Mom, what are you doing . . . ?”

She raises her voice teasingly, her New York accent elongating the vowels. “How much is the chicken if it’s twenty percent off?”

Great. People are staring now. “It’s summer vacation. I don’t need a test.”

"Shoulda thought of that before you jeopardized your high school career." She shimmies her shoulders as she starts to chant, "Chick-en. Chick-en. Chick-en."

Shoppers on the ends of the aisle slow their pace to observe the spectacle. Another Black woman walks by with her young son. I reach out to them and desperately whisper, "Please, take me with you." The woman glares at me and pushes her son along, hurrying out of the way.

It is then that my mother begins to cluck. Like a chicken. At full volume. In the middle of the frozen food aisle.

"Mom."

"Bock."

"You're making a scene."

"Bock. Bock."

"Please. Don't—"

"Bock-bock-BOCKAHK."

"$11.99! It costs $11.99."

"Winner winner, chicken dinner." She dismounts from the grocery cart, setting the meat down to clap. I cross my arms as she cracks up, deeply satisfied with her stunt. She has this insane laugh where she throws her head back and places a hand on her clavicle like some vintage Hollywood starlet. No wonder she uprooted our lives and dragged us out to Los Angeles, of all places.

Amused shoppers around us smile affably, as if my mother isn't a complete nut. That's one of the curses of living with her. She's constantly stirring up batshit crazy hijinks that observers find endearing, but to me—the person forced to stand next to her while she proves to her friends in the middle of a TGI Fridays that she can do the splits—it is maddening.

"Glad to know that you've retained at least some of the public education that my taxpayer dollars work hard to provide you," she says.

I ignore her and keep walking.

"Hey, listen." Her voice is calmer now. "The new school, the new house—this was supposed to be a fresh start for us. But it's been a year and you're more distant than ever." I quicken my pace, but she speeds up alongside me. "I worry that you're still feeling on the defensive. After everything with your father—"

"I don't want to talk about him." Not now, not ever. Before everything went down, I tried to talk about him with my mom. A lot. Several times. Every night, even. But she didn't want to talk then. So excuse me if I don't feel like talking about it now: after the chaos, after the pain, after the shit hath hitteth the faneth. It's too late. *She* is too late. I opt out.

"Fine," Mom says with a sigh. "But this summer, I don't want you spending so much time alone."

I like to spend time alone—is that a crime? I prefer my own company to that of all the delusional, horned-up cretins around me.

We reach the checkout line, the freedom of escape in sight at last. I load the items onto the conveyor belt as fast as possible.

"Are you going to join the outdoors group that Mr. Gutierrez suggested?"

I nearly drop a can of chili. "He told you about that?"

"Of course he did. Niarah, almost being held back a grade is a huge deal. You're going to that hiking group. You need the credit and you need the social interaction."

Social interaction. She says it like it's a tiny little pill that I can take then magically feel better.

"I'm doing summer school instead." At least summer school is only ninety minutes a day, twice a week; the outdoors thing would take up basically the whole day. Plus, there's the whole Mac issue. He makes me feel . . . nervous. I don't like it.

"Getting outside will be fun. It'll help with your anxiety."

I know I'm anxious as hell, but I hate it when she puts it all on me, as if she's totally well-adjusted herself. She has this whole whoo-hoo-I'm-so-fun disposition in public, but I live with her, so I know the truth. Inside, she's anxious, too. During the day, she's all goofy bits and sunshine. But nighttime is interspersed with *What's that?* and *Hello??* and *Are you okay?* and *Who's there?* I can't even turn over in my bed in the room next door without her bolting upright, checking to make sure that the front door is locked for the fifth time. No wonder I'm so paranoid. Are the issues that I struggle with actually my own, or did I just inherit her fear?

"Well, if you don't want to do the outdoors group, maybe you and I can go to the park together? After summer school in the afternoons?" She offers me a sheepish smile. I avoid her eyes.

The cashier rings up our groceries and asks Mom to input her phone number for the coupons. My mother's cobalt-blue nails stab the little machine until the sales start rolling. I watch the discounts tumble across the checkout screen. Even though digital coupons are nothing but a cleverly designed marketing scheme, it's still satisfying in that soulless, capitalistic way that I can't deny. At the end, it chirps and the screen reads, *Congratulations! You've saved $6.17.*

The cashier rips a receipt as long as a winter scarf and hands it to my mother. "Thank you for being a loyal customer, Ms. Dixon."

A sudden burst of pressure slams my chest.

"Ms. Dixon?" I whip around to face my mother, hands gripping the cart so tight that it burns. "Who is Ms. Dixon?"

Mom stuffs the receipt into her purse. “You know that’s my maiden name.”

“Since when do you use it, though?” I’ve been Niarah Simone Holloway for my whole life. My mom has been Carmen Tracy Holloway for my whole life. But now . . .

She stares right back at me, calm and collected. “Baby, it’s just a name. I figured it was time.”

I grit my teeth. “When were you going to tell me?”

The awkward cashier gulps. “If you, uh, don’t mind, there are customers behind you—”

“I’m telling you now,” Mom says, disregarding the cashier’s nervous attempt to move us along.

I’ve always resented the fact that I carry around my father’s name. It’s been my own personal scarlet letter for years. The only thing that made it not so bad was the fact that I didn’t have to lug it around alone. But not anymore, apparently.

The chasm between us grows another inch.

BULL IN A CHINA SHOP

BULL IN A CHINA SHOP
BULL IN A CHINA SHOP

"HOW'S IT GOING IN HERE?"

"Fine." I study the mess around me. Ever since we moved to this house, the room at the end of the hall has been a shared office for me and my mom. Technically, it's *her* office, but she works in person every day and never uses it, so it's mostly mine. Here, I have my second computer monitor, my bookshelves, and my notebooks. There's only one small window, so it's dark in here, which is perfect (no screen glare). And unlike in the living room, there's a door that I can close to be alone. This has been my favorite room, but now it's being ripped away from me. Go figure.

"Maybe you should leave one of your bookcases in here for Ox," Mom says.

Absolutely not. Ox is the reason why I must give up my lair. He's a carpenter or whatever. He makes furniture, and apparently, he needs space here to do so this summer while his workshop is being renovated. Or at least that's the official reason. I suspect that this is actually a trial run for a future move-in. Mom made me choose between whether I keep the garage or the office for myself. I need the garage for Camp Doom, obviously, so the choice was easy, but that doesn't mean I'm not pissed.

"I think you two are going to get along," Mom continues. I stay silent. Ox and I most definitely do not, and will not, get along. "He's looking forward to spending more time with you."

I pick at my nails. I refuse to spend any more time with either of them this summer than absolutely necessary.

"Say something, Niarah," Mom begs. She's always hated the silence, but I can't help but notice that she seems to hate it even more now that it's me and her alone.

I want to say that I don't get why she'd go for such a stereotypical macho dude. He's built like a refrigerator. A Samoan gladiator with a mustache like a walrus and a voice like Formula 1. But I settle for saying, "I don't get Ox."

"I like him and I want you to get to know him."

I stack a few more books. "Yeah, but do you even know him?" The first time I met Ox, he came over for lunch after attending an Alcoholics Anonymous meeting. He brought it up himself and explained that he's four years sober. Four years doesn't seem that long to me. What makes her think that in such a short stretch of time a person can change?

"Not all people are inherently untrustworthy. Plus, Ox is special. He's kind. Nothing like your father."

And that's my cue to mentally check out.

I hate the way that she forces him onto me—Your Father this, Your Father that. As if he wasn't *Her* Husband. As if she wasn't the one that chose him. I didn't have a say in the matter of who my biological parents would be. If I did, I sure as hell wouldn't have chosen him.

"Dinner will be ready soon. Come downstairs in thirty."

She leaves and I don't feel like packing anymore, so I head downstairs to try and sneak a cup of guava juice while my mom is setting the table. I peek my head inside the kitchen to make sure that the coast is clear before storming the fridge.

"That you, Niarah?" a voice calls out from behind the spice cabinet door.

I stomp across the room with the intention to ignore his giant 6'5" shadow, but when I see him in the light, I stop short.

"Wh-what are you eating?" I clench my fists.

"Made a lil tuna salad. An appetizer. Want some?" Ox's large brown hand holds out a cracker with tuna to me, but my eyes are locked on the army surplus store duffel bag sitting half-open on the table. Aka our earthquake kit. The one that I just restocked.

I survey the damage. In addition to the tuna, it appears that Ox has torn into the M&M's, the shrimp-flavored instant ramen, and the Pop-Tarts as well. His reckless disregard for mixing flavors is almost as chilling as his idiocrasy. I snatch the bag from the table. "Where did you find this?"

"In the closet?" Ox's face has a cartoonish quality where his mouth tends to fix itself into dramatic, crescent-shaped smiles or frowns as if drawn by a child. Right now, I'm locked eyes with Worried Ox: furry brows knit together, visibly baffled as to why I currently look like I want to tear the tattoos off his greasy knuckles.

I simmer, speaking through my teeth with forced restraint. "Why would you enter an entire, fully stocked kitchen and still choose to eat the nonperishables in the earthquake kit *from the closet*?"

Ox nibbles at the corner of the cracker. "I had a craving for tuna," he says simply.

I feel a headache coming on. I press my fingers to my temples, but it's no use. "What if there was an earthquake? What would we have done if you ate our rations because you were, what, craving a snack?"

Ox wipes his cracker-crusted hands on his basketball shorts. A grown-ass man yet he's always wearing basketball shorts. Unreal. When he reaches for a napkin to finish the job, his massive tattooed arms catch the light. I notice a new one—a dolphin wearing sunglasses—and add it to my internal list of red flags about this man.

"Look, Niarah, I'm sorry. I should've asked permission. But . . ."

"But *what*?"

He opens his mouth but stops himself. I can tell what he wants to say—something about how the world clearly didn't end in the past few minutes since he ate the kit, but that's not the point.

"Something bad could have happened," I say. I nearly pull my hair out from the roots as Mom walks into the kitchen. She's carrying a bottle of nonalcoholic wine, which she now buys since Ox is sober, though it seems like a waste of money to me.

"They didn't have any white, but I got an interesting-looking red—" She stops when she sees me. "Niarah! Great. We're about to watch *Jeopardy!* before dinner, wanna join?"

"Absolutely not."

"Where are you going?"

I swipe the duffel from the table. "To refill the emergency kit."

ALWAYS HAVE A GO BAG

ALWAYS HAVE A GO BAG
ALWAYS HAVE A GO BAG

IT ALL STARTED WITH A GO BAG, OR RATHER, the lack thereof. Four years ago, my mom raced into my bedroom in the middle of the night and shook my shoulders out from underneath the quilt. Her eyes were wide, completely bugged out of her head, and there was an urgency in her voice that I knew not to question.

"Grab a jacket," she said.

I didn't move.

She tried again: "I said—"

A glass window broke down the hall. That snapped me out of it. I climbed out of bed, swiped my phone and jacket. I tried to gather other things—my laptop, some books—but she stopped me.

"We have to go *now*."

I slipped on some shoes. She pulled my arm, and we sprinted out my room, out the back door into the night.

It would be three weeks before I'd get to return to my room. Three weeks of discount underwear from Target, wearing the same jeans. One night sleeping in the car, one night in a motel, then nineteen days staying on my aunt's couch in an unfamiliar house in an unfamiliar city without any of my belongings. Not that long, but also an eternity.

We didn't flee that night because of a natural disaster, but one of a human variety. Nevertheless, the lesson was learned: Never be unprepared. Always be ready to leave. Always have a Go Bag.

SUMMER SCHOOL ORIENTATION

SUMMER SCHOOL ORIENTATION

SUMMER SCHOOL ORIENTATION

I DON'T ASK FOR PERMISSION BECAUSE I KNOW that he'll say no. I don't want to be here, but nobody cares. Nobody ever cares about anything at school except for when you try to escape. The adults are always restricting our movement. It's like we're cattle. Or mold.

"Where do you think you're going?" Mr. Brady's voice booms throughout the gymnasium, right on cue.

I wince as I'm caught, moments before slipping out the back door.

"Haven't you heard?" Morgan interjects. Morgan is another sophomore. Morgan always smells like Cheez-Its. I hate Morgan. "The sky is falling, so she has to go stockpile seeds with all the other delusional incels."

Mr. Brady raises an eyebrow, confused. Everyone else laughs.

It's Preview Day at summer school. Everyone comes to campus to "shop" potential courses before the registration deadline as if we aren't trapped here against our will. To say that I can't bring myself to participate in the dreaded Sports Camp class right now is an understatement. The air in here is stale and humid. Everything smells like melted sunscreen and unwashed gym shorts. If I stay any longer, I will projectile vomit all over Morgan's egg-shaped head.

"I'm going to the restroom," I say. I send Morgan a personal death glare and cut Mr. Brady off before he can protest. "A teacher can't deny access to the bathroom. Doing so would be a human rights violation. I think."

He rolls his eyes, too bored to fight. "If you're not back in five minutes, I'm sending Yamile to look for you." From the other side of the room, Yamile—the class snitch—gives me a menacing grin. I curl my lip at her.

"I promise I will be right back," I say, slouch-pushing against the wooden door. I slip my backpack on quietly and breathe in the silence of the empty hallway. I exhale.

There's no way in hell I'm going back in there.

I catch my reflection in the mirror lining the main hallway. I've been cursed with a perpetual baby face and an underdeveloped body to match. Knock-knees on the bottom, bony shoulders sharp enough to cut through titanium on top. Overly round in the jaw region, overly flat in all the places that count. Big brown eyes that once were described by a neighbor as "excessively alert" and an unsettlingly long torso inherited from my grandfather.

I'm not saying I'm ugly or anything, but I can be real about the currently subpar situation going on here. To be honest, I think that I'll probably grow into myself decently. But by the time I do get hot—around twenty-nine years old, maybe—the world will probably be in such a state of horror that nobody will even notice because the icebergs will have melted, making physical hotness a much less desirable trait than the ability to fashion fish hooks out of old iPhone parts.

I turn a corner and find an empty bag of hot chips on the ground. I crumple up the plastic and yell, "Kobe." The makeshift ball hits the rim of a tall bin and falls to the side. I shuffle over to retrieve the chip ball to try again, but when I reach behind the metal container, I jump.

Corey and Xander from Mx. Ferrante's class glance up from their spot on the laminate floor. Their eyes skim over me lazily as they each take a pull from an e-cigarette that's definitely not allowed on campus. They look sort of stupid sitting there all scrunched up, hiding in a corner like elementary schoolers. But once they notice that I'm alone without a teacher, they stand. The energy shifts. I back away.

"Your video got a lot of views, you know," Corey says. He's got a new buzz cut that makes his ears look big. "Everyone's been commenting asking for an update on Doomsday Girl. Should we do a little interview now?"

Corey wraps his bony fingers around his phone and points the camera at me again. I smack his claw hand away. "Get out of my face."

"Oh, ho, ho," Xander jeers. He slips his phone out and holds it up like a fake microphone. "We're here live with Doomsday Girl of Los Angeles. So, tell us, what's it like being a sixteen-year-old incel?"

I keep my head down and walk toward the door. I hear their footsteps following me.

"Is your dream home an underground missile silo bunker or a cave?"

"Shut up."

"Are you in a cult?"

"What? No."

"Fuck, marry, kill: your precious iodine, your gas mask, your weapons stash. Go."

"Leave me alone."

"When the apocalypse comes, how far would you go to—"

"I SAID LEAVE ME ALONE."

I spin around, ready to threaten the idiots within an inch of their lives, but I freeze when I see the wide smiles plastered across their dull faces, hiding behind the security of their stupid fucking phones. How brave. Cowering behind their cameras. The last thing I need is to provide more material for Corey's little show. My hands are shaking, but I take a deep breath and gather myself. Everyone's so full of shit.

"Oh my god, wait, what's that?" I point up above their heads. The boys' eyes and phones follow my direction and I take the opportunity to purse my lips and spit on Corey's precious Air Jordan 1s. The wetness slaps his Nikes with an audible *splat*. He gapes down, scowls, then cranks toward me, a fierce red creeping up his neck.

"You're so fu—"

"HEY."

All three of us spin at the sound of a voice at the end of the hallway.

Yamile's face creeps into a smug sneer as she strolls down the corridor like it's a runway. "I knew you were trying to ditch."

I cut my eyes over at the barbarians. They cross their arms and snarl at me. The danger of unfinished business simmers behind their glares.

"Time to go," Yamile says, grabbing my arm like a cop.

"Power-hungry psychopath," I whisper.

“Delinquent freak,” she replies.

I rip my arm free but let her steer me back toward the gym.

“We’re going to have a greaaaaat time at summer school, Niarah,” Corey drawls. “Wait and see.”

I flip him off for good luck.

FIRST IMPRESSIONS

FIRST IMPRESSIONS
FIRST IMPRESSIONS

THE EARLY MORNING AIR FEELS COOL AGAINST my skin, slick with a film of overpriced sunscreen that smells of Rich White Girl and formaldehyde. My lips chap and crack from the barren air.

Summer school managed to suck even more than I could have imagined, so now here I am, walking 1.2 miles to the nearest park to see if Mac and his happy bunch of hikers are less horrendous than the alternative.

I haven't explored the neighborhood much since we moved, but I pass by the few sights that I've become accustomed to: the elementary school with pillars painted like pencils, the auto shop that's inexplicably open 24-7 and constantly bumping ranchera music, the pink liquor store, the pottery studio always occupied by the same three people covered in clay, seemingly never speaking to one another.

Somehow, I arrive early, which is pretty much my nightmare.

Up ahead, a guy in a bandanna holds up a sign: *Color Outside*

Meetup Here. I hesitate, trying to pick which tree to hide behind, but the dude sees me.

"Good mooooorning." He beams, waving at me wildly like one of those inflatable car-wash air dancers.

I give him a tight-lipped smile and head over against my will.

"You must be Niarah," he says as I get closer. He's not tall, clocking in at around my same height, but his presence is large. Or maybe, more accurately, his presence is *loud.* Never in my life have I seen someone dressed with so much spirit at nine a.m. His tan skin glistens with what looks like a shimmery sunblock or highlighter of some sort. Silver eye makeup draws ornate lines around his dark brown eyes, framed by impeccably maintained eyebrows. The bottom half of his hair is shaved in an undercut with sharp lines cutting across the back. Bleached-blond tips spike up above the black bandanna on his forehead.

"You are Niarah, right?" he asks again.

"Yeah, sorry." He's wearing baggy, bright red parachute pants paired with a sleek black muscle tank. Ornate silver rings and cuffs adorn his wrists and fingers. The outfit walks a fine line between hiking versus attending London Fashion Week. I try to stop staring at the dozens of details that take his look over the edge. "I didn't expect to be the first one here."

"You're right on time. Now, consume a pastry," he insists. He motions at the blanket on the grass behind him. Several platters carry spiral formations of fragrant, flaky baked goods. I just ate breakfast, but the way that he's staring at me is too much to shoot down. I grab one and prepare my best rendition of a "wow!" face to be polite, but I don't end up having to pretend: This is *good.*

"Holy shit," I moan.

"I know," he says proudly. The tiny buttery pastry melts in my mouth, giving way to a soft, tropical flavor. "Guava and cream cheese pastelitos. The salted honey drizzle is my own touch, though."

"You made this?" I can't even reheat pizza rolls without burning them half the time.

"You're welcome." He laughs as he whips a napkin out of nowhere and hands it to me as crumbs gather on my lip. "I'm Andrew. Mac told me about you." I don't know if it's a trick of the morning light or not, but I think I catch the hint of a smirk. "Speaking of . . ." Andrew points over my shoulder.

Taking a deep breath to steady myself, I fix a polite smile on my face as I watch Mac stride toward us.

"You made it," Mac says, breaking out into a wide smile for a second before reining it in to a much chiller grin. He stops right in front of me, hands awkwardly curled into the pockets of his dark brown pants.

Andrew sprints toward Mac and jumps on him like a koala. You'd think that these two haven't seen each other in years.

"Andrew Pha, you can't be doin' this every morning, man," Mac says through laughter as he stumbles to prevent himself and Andrew from falling over.

"I will greet you like this every single day until you go off to college, sir," Andrew says before finally letting go, slipping onto the grass. "Ugh, your hair is still wet."

"Sunrise ride. Thought I'd bring some of the ocean back for you." Andrew ducks for cover as Mac shakes his head like a dog, sending beads of water flying everywhere.

He's not wearing a hat today, so his hair hangs in a curly curtain, parted in the middle with renegade wisps that fall over his eyes. His hair is a deep shade of brown, but when the sun hits it, I can see a touch of auburn in the mix from an overdose of sun or sea or both.

"You surf?" I ask. *Of course he surfs.*

"I surf indeed." He tosses an overly familiar smile my way. I make sure not to react.

"I like your shirt," Mac says to me.

It's a dark gray tee with black writing that says *I do not think therefore I do not am.*

"Thanks," I reply, smoothing the shirt out. "I like to wear this one when I'm dissociating."

Mac chuckles and tries to catch my eyes for a little too long. I shift away and he responds accordingly, clearing his throat. Andrew watches us, grinning widely.

A person carrying two giant water bottles strolls up beside Mac. Andrew reverts back to koala mode and storms his next victim. "Good morning, good morning, selamat pagi, sunshine!" Andrew plants a wet kiss on the cheek of the new arrival.

They grunt as they push Andrew off, but beneath the sneer, there's an obvious glimmer of amusement.

Andrew giggles. "Niarah, this is Sage. They are not a morning person."

Andrew tries to shove two pastries directly into Sage's mouth, which they promptly swat away. Instead, Sage silently outstretches a hand to me. Their handshake is firm. Smile genuine yet reserved. Sage looks like a motorcyclist who doubles as a bouncer at an exclusive underground bar in Berlin. They're dressed in all black: black hiking boots, black over-the-knee socks, black shorts, and a black button-down shirt. A clean buzz cut. Big Don't-Mess-With-Me Energy.

Weirdly enough, I've actually seen them before. "Hey, you were the class valedictorian, weren't you? You won some big scholarship, right?"

Every year, first in the class gets a hefty check to the school of their choice. A photo of Sage's face, fixed into the firm, almost smirk of a future Black leftist leader, has decorated a banner lining the school's hallway for the past few weeks. "Do you know where you're going to school in the fall?" I ask.

Sage shakes their head.

"They're doing a gap year," Mac explains.

Whoa. As much as I hate school, I don't think I'd know what to do with an entire year off. "That's crazy. Win a big scholarship, then put it off?" As soon as the words leave my mouth, I know I said the wrong thing. I was aiming for my tone to sound impressed, but by the way that Sage crosses their arms and frowns, it's clear that I missed the landing. "Right, no, I know, I didn't mean it like that. I meant crazy as in, like, bold?" I stammer. "It's just a big opportunity—"

Sage remains silent, their frown only deepening as they tilt their head to the left, studying me. They haven't spoken a word throughout our entire interaction.

Andrew and Mac shift awkwardly beside us. Mac leans over to me and says, "Sage is kind of quiet."

I glance back at Sage, who's looking at me with an expression of absolute boredom. "Got it."

"Sage is trying to convince me to join them for a leg of the gap year trip," Andrew says, jumping in to salvage the conversation. He tugs Sage's collar and they uncross their arms at last.

"You're not going to college either?" I ask Andrew.

These people are getting ready to start their lives, meanwhile I still have two more years left of high school. Or three years, I guess, if I don't get my act together this summer. Fucking hell.

"I'm doing a one-year culinary school program," Andrew explains. "Trying to win the Next Best Chef in America award and put Malaysian food on the map out here. The culinary school's schedule is pretty nontraditional, though, so I'll have some time to move around." He shakes his hips a little and winks at Sage on the *move around*. I can't tell if those two are close friends or something more.

"And Mac is going all the way up north for four years. Abandoning us. What a crime!" Andrew wails.

"I'm aware," I mumble.

Mac's eyes meet mine with a shy shrug, but he's quickly distracted. "Andrew, c'mon, man. You said you'd quit after graduation."

Beside Mac, Andrew discreetly takes a long pull from a vape pen.

"I said I'd *consider* stopping," Andrew says. "At least it's not tobacco."

"You're obsessed with that shit," Mac grumbles.

"I'm not obsessed, I just like it. It's a beautiful day. This makes everything a little more beautiful."

Mac clearly has more to say, but he's called over by some of the other counselors. He frowns as he walks away.

A group of participants of all ages start to gather around. Over by the tree, Mac whips out a clipboard and checks everyone in. His outfit is neat yet simple. Some Dickies pants, leather hiking boots, and a green work shirt. While the vibe of the look is relaxed, each of the items were clearly ironed before he put them on—crisp lines without a wrinkle in sight. As he works, smiling warmly at each hiker, he occasionally uses the tip of the pen to brush a rogue strand of hair out of his eyeline. It's not the cut of his hair, it's the shape of it. Or lack thereof. It's like an illustrator took a piece of charcoal and sketched it across his head, except there's a softness to it, so maybe it was more like a crayon or an oil-based pastel. He seems to put a decent deal of effort in the rest of his aesthetic but draws the line at caring about his hair. Maybe it's balance? Or restraint. Or apathy. Who knows.

Mac catches my stare. He puffs his cheeks in and out like a blowfish. He does it fast while no one else is looking. So swift that it seems like a glitch. A surprised laugh leaps from my throat. Mac beams, seemingly satisfied to have elicited a reaction, but I force my lips back into a tight smile. I know exactly how this goes: Boy flirts with girl, girl catches feelings for boy, boy dumps girl at the end of the summer for older, hotter college girls and/or boys. A tale as old as time. I can't go down this easy. No, ma'am.

I turn away toward the trailhead. I'll hike, log some participation points, then leave. Nothing more.

PREPARE TO BE UNDERWHELMED

PREPARE TO BE UNDERWHELMED

PREPARE TO BE UNDERWHELMED

HIKING IS JUST WALKING WITH UGLIER SHOES. I don't get the hype. We're in the middle of Los Angeles, farting around a dusty park dotted with gopher holes and coyote droppings, and everyone around me is like, *Wow, nature!* as if we can't hear the rush of street traffic beyond the trees. Pure nonsense.

1.6 MILES INTO THE HIKE

1.6 MILES INTO THE HIKE
1.6 MILES INTO THE HIKE

"I'M NOT GOOD AT THIS," I DISCLOSE TO MAC. "Whatever is the lowest bar of expectations, I need you to set it twenty feet lower than that for me." Believe it or not, spending years inside playing video games hasn't left me in the best shape. We're only thirty minutes into the hike and my legs are already searing.

As we walk, Mac runs a hand through the thick waves of hair that fall right below his jawline, made even denser by the hint of a loose curl pattern. With each step, the waves swish. A flutter in my chest of unknown origin swishes along with it.

"Don't worry, I'm a slow hiker, too," he says. He tucks his hands into his pockets, kicking a rock out of our path.

"You don't have to wait for me," I say, motioning toward the people twice my age moving three times as fast.

"Nah, for real. Look." Mac fishes an inhaler out of his back pocket, holding it up with a quick shake. "Bad lungs."

"Oh." Wasn't expecting that. Guess I forgot to check my ableism at the door.

"Slowing down is good, though." Mac stops abruptly in the path, almost knocking over the hiker behind us. "When you go slow, you can pay attention. You see that?" He points at a tree.

"Uhm. Yes. It's . . . a tree." I should've known this beautiful boy would be stupid.

Another hiker from a different group frowns as they have to make their way around us. I give them an embarrassed shrug, apologizing for stopping in the middle of the trail.

"No, no. Look *in* the tree. You see that bird?" I don't at first, but then a little, pale blue head pops out between two branches. "That's a California scrub jay. My dad started teaching me about birdwatching to help improve my focus. Oh, and that bird over there . . ."

The boy keeps pointing at glorified pigeons and I check my phone. How long must I stay here to get him to sign off my PE log sheet?

Sage and Andrew notice us lagging. They break off from the group ahead.

"Y'all good?" Andrew asks.

"Yeah." Mac nods, locking his eyes with mine. "Just enjoying the company."

He winks and I stare back at him, speechless.

Sage rolls their eyes and pulls out their phone. They open a blank note and tap out a quick message, faster than I've seen anyone type before. When they finish, they hold up the phone to Mac, but I can read Sage's words over his shoulder:

You don't have to flirt with everyone.

Right. My ego is swiftly knocked down a few pegs. Mac looks like he's about to protest Sage's accusation, but he's interrupted by the bellowing serenade of a salsa singer echoing in the wind.

"Wait, do you hear that?" I ask. Perhaps the heat has finally gotten to me and I've started to hallucinate the ghost of Celia Cruz in this godforsaken urban park.

"You see that line of palm trees in the distance?" Mac points with one hand and places the other on my shoulder to steer me in the right direction. Goose bumps activate across my body in waves radiating from the site of his touch. "That's Dodger Stadium right over that hill. There's a home game later, people are tailgating."

The music gets louder as we round the bend of the trail. We catch up to the rest of the Color Outside group, the energy of the hikers igniting at the sound of the barbecue pits and picnic tables below.

"I love this song." Andrew screams along to the music and yanks Sage by the arm as they run-tumble down the hill toward the action. The rest of the group follows their lead, frolicking along like a herd of unicorns. I wait for Mac to rein everyone in, but he just stands there, swaying slightly to the music and twirling his rings as he waits for the others to make it down the rocky trail safely.

"What about the rest of the hike?" I don't want to tell this guy how to do his job, but I doubt that he's supposed to let everyone run off into the proverbial sunset mid-hike.

After the last person ahead of us makes it down the hill, Mac waves me forward with a grin. "This is part of it."

1.7 MILES INTO THE HIKE

1.7 MILES INTO THE HIKE
1.7 MILES INTO THE HIKE

WHEN WE DESCEND UPON THE PICNIC AREA, THE scene is electric. Lowriders line the parking spaces where different generations of car aficionados admire one another's wheels. The smell of carne asada blends with the sweetness wafting from the soft-serve truck a few yards away. Amateur athletes sprint around in a sweaty game of pickup soccer beside a bounce house that trembles as hordes of kids jump, flip, and spin inside its colorful rubber walls. Every single person is decked out in Dodger blue.

"You look perplexed," Mac says, breaking my trance.

"What happened to all the connect-with-nature stuff? How does crashing a tailgate count as a hike?" The Color Outside group has fully disintegrated across the picnic area. Andrew bolts straight for the grill, befriending the cook. Sage finds a shady spot beneath a tree and pulls out a book.

"Of course this counts," Mac says. "We're outside, right? And we're in a park. And we're relaxing. Why wouldn't it count?"

I point to the people who've turned their T-shirts into blankets, preparing to do nothing but nap in the sun. "Does that count?"

"That definitely counts."

"What about that?" One of the tailgaters passes out Tecate beers, which the older hikers take gladly.

Mac laughs. "For sure counts."

"How am I going to meet my PE credit requirement if when we go hiking, we barely even hike? We walked for, like, forty minutes, now we're sitting."

"Don't worry. I'm logging your participation by the hour, not the mile."

"Is that allowed?"

"Probably not." He throws me a smile.

"Mac. ¡Mijo! ¡Ven acá!" A chorus of older women erupts from the edge of the park where the lowriders are parked. A group of about ten people in matching shirts lounge around three cars, each one custom painted and hooked up with hydraulics.

"You know them?" I ask.

"My uncle is in one of the car clubs. Now that I've been spotted, I should go say hi, otherwise my parents will kill me if they hear I was being rude." He stands up from the grass. "Wanna come?"

Honestly, not really, but Andrew is off mingling and I don't know anyone else here, so it's not like I have another option. Mac extends a hand to help me up. I decline, getting up on my own instead. His hand retreats and tucks behind his back.

"Wassap, nephew?" A large, burly man with a goatee pulls Mac into a fierce hug. They speak in Spanish to one another, but I got a D in Spanish, so I have no idea what they're saying. There's a strange comfort in standing with friendly strangers speaking another language. Even if I wanted to contribute to the conversation, I wouldn't be able to. All social expectations to be proficient in basic small talk are blissfully gone.

"Nice to meet you, sweetie," a woman says, enveloping me in a surprise hug from the side. I get a little nervous, mumbling back a soft "Nice to meet you, too." I've never been great with meeting new people.

"Oye, mijo, how come you've never introduced us to this girl before?" another auntie says.

Mac cringes. "Because I literally just met her."

Auntie #1 squeezes my shoulder. "You're so pretty. Mira, estos ojos." I freeze like a possum. Maybe if I do or say nothing at all, this interaction will end as quickly as possible. "Wow. Mac, isn't she so pretty?"

Mac grimaces. "Tía Rosa, please, relax."

The woman releases her grip on my shoulders to scoot toward Mac, running a hand through his hair. She lowers her voice to a conspiratorial whisper. "¿Pero ella es tan linda, no?"

Mac's entire body stiffens. He looks like he's about to pass out or run away. "Tía, porfa—"

"¿Sí o no?"

Mac grumbles. "Sí."

The woman releases her grip and smirks. "That's all I was trying to say."

A fierce blush warms beneath Mac's cheeks. "We are leaving now." He barrels away, motioning me to follow. "This is why I avoid y'all in public."

"Give your little brother a hug for me, okay?" someone says.

Mac's posture becomes rigid. He glances quickly back at his relatives, then looks away and keeps walking in long strides.

"You have a brother?" I ask, struggling to keep up with this suddenly quick pace.

Mac fiddles with his rings, his eyes wandering around the park. "Uh, yeah. I have two. One older, one younger. Gael and Daniel."

I'm about to ask more about them, but Mac clears his throat. "Want some fruit?" he asks.

"I didn't bring any money."

"That's okay, I got it."

"No, I'm good." I don't like other people paying for me. I don't like debt.

"You sure? We can share?"

I also don't like sharing. "No thanks."

He shrugs, but I follow him to one of the many fruit carts that decorate the streets of LA. The ice-filled glass window showcases vibrant slabs of summer fruits. Mac slips seamlessly into Spanish as he orders a cup of mango, papaya, watermelon, and cucumber. The vendor chops away at the fruit with a satisfying rhythm.

"¿Chile y limón?" the vendor asks.

"Claro que si," Mac says.

The vendor squirts hefty bursts of Tajín and lime juice over the cup before handing him the massive vessel with two forks sticking out from the top.

I point at the two forks. "I said I'm good."

"If you say so." He carries the giant container of fruit to an empty spot of grass.

I sneak glances at Mac as he relaxes onto the ground. It's hard not to.

"I never add the lime and chile," I admit once we're seated. I'm not opposed to it, it just never occurred to me to try it. Fruit is fruit; it's good on its own.

"Once you go Tajín, you'll never go back." He turns his fork into a skewer, piling several slices on top of one another before devouring it all in one excessively big bite. Never have I seen someone so excited to eat fruit in my life. Juice blended with the hint of chile spills from the corners of his mouth onto his shirt. He uses the back of his hand to wipe his mouth. “Sorry. Messy eater.”

“I can tell.”

He offers me the second fork again. I’ll admit that he does make the fruit look good. I pluck the fork from his hand and pick out a slice of Tajín-coated cucumber. He smirks as I take a bite.

A gust of wind blows, carrying the distinct smell of soot. All week, there’s been a fire ravaging Northern California, and the smoke-filled air is finally making its way down to LA. I cough into my elbow.

“I hate fire season,” Mac says. He does a little toe-heel tapping thing against the grass.

“It’s not fire *season* anymore. It’s just fires. All the time.” I stab a piece of mango.

“Things will get a little worse before they get better,” he says, maybe to himself more than to me.

“Or things will . . . get worse.” I grab a chunk of papaya next. “Do you really believe that we can save this planet?”

He pauses before answering, crinkling his brow. He shoves another too-big bite of fruit into his mouth and observes the sky. An airplane flies overhead, drowning out the sound of the birdsong in the trees. Out on the horizon, we can see the tips of downtown LA and the layer of smog covering the city. A horn from one of the millions of cars on the planet spitting poison into the air blares in the distance. And yet, when Mac looks back at me, he just smiles and says: “Yes. A new future is possible.”

“Maybe if doomsday doesn’t come first,” I mumble.

He laughs, even though I didn't mean it as a joke. "What would you do?" he asks. "If you knew the world was ending?"

"Again, I maintain my position that it's not *not* already ending. . . ."

"But what if you knew that in seven days, a zombie apocalypse would begin. What would you do then?"

I've thought about this a lot. First, I'd decide if it was a situation that requires me to bunker in at Camp Doom or Bug Out (aka pack my shit and leave town). Depending on how things are looking, I'd solidify my location, then prepare to defend myself. I wouldn't go down without a fight. I give Mac a minimalist version of my zombie apocalypse plan before tossing the question right back.

He pauses, bringing his thumb to his chin. "I've never been to Yellowstone," he says at last.

"The national park?"

"Yeah. It's supposed to be beautiful. I guess I'd go there."

"To make a doomsday camp?" I don't know if I'd want to bunker out in the middle of nowhere without any solid shelter around for miles. He'd probably die a slow painful death within the first wave. And that's only if the bears and wolves didn't kill him first. Poor guy. He'd never make it. But I'll give him two points for creativity.

"Nah, to like, see Yellowstone. Hike a bit. Enjoy it while I can." He pauses. "But if it happens during the winter, I guess I'd go somewhere with better weather. Like Big Sur. They have cool tide pools up there. And I'd wanna see those cypress trees. Did you know that in Patagonia there's a cypress tree that scientists believe could be up to five thousand four hundred eighty-four years old?"

My brain struggles to wrap around his thought process. "You wouldn't, like, do anything to try and survive?"

He shrugs. "I guess if I knew things were going south, I'd rather spend my last days living than surviving."

"Surviving and living are the same thing."

Mac smiles. "Not really. Not at all."

Physical Education Activity Log (page 1 of 3)

Student Name: Niarah Holloway

Date	Activity	Duration	Supervisor Signature
June 14	Forcibly walking uphill in the heat	~~Too long~~ 2.5 hours	Marco Torres

Hours Complete / Number of Hours Required for Completion: _____/ 80 hrs

TOO CURIOUS

TOO CURIOUS
TOO CURIOUS

WITHIN MINUTES OF CLIMBING INTO THE SHOT-gun of Mac's massive, 2007 forest-green Ford Explorer, I regret my decision to accept a ride home. First off, Mac is not a good driver. At all. His skills behind the wheel are that of an over-caffeinated squirrel with opposable thumbs. Second, what he lacks in driving ability, he unfortunately makes up for in aesthetic. Mac has this way of leaning back when he drives that makes the muscles in his arms flex a bit as he grabs the steering wheel, so I spend the entire drive forcing myself to stare out the window instead. Third, Mac drops Andrew and Sage off at home first, so for the end of the drive, it's just the two of us. I try to ignore the cutting glance that Sage gives Mac before they get out of the car.

"Does, uh, Sage talk at all?"

"Sometimes. If they like you, they will."

"They didn't say a word to me all day." I can do that math.

"Give 'em a minute to warm up. Don't take it personally."

I didn't necessarily get off on the best foot this morning. I'm not sure if this is just a matter of warming up, but whatever. I let it go for now and keep observing the details of Mac's car. I won't count this against the boy, but it is worth mentioning that the inside of this vehicle is a mess. It's covered in receipts, sand, and wrinkled Post-its. There's a neon-green sticky note smushed onto the dashboard with today's date. It's a to-do list, scrawled in haphazard handwriting, reminding him to show up for this morning's hike on time, brush his teeth, drink water, and get gas.

Mac notices me reading and lifts the note from the dash, crumpling it and tossing it into the cupholder. "I'm kind of forgetful."

"Forget-to-brush-your-teeth forgetful?" I ask.

At a stop sign, he leans over my lap to open the glove compartment and pulls out a travel toothbrush. "I always remember eventually." He laughs in a slightly nervous way that comes out sounding more like a cough. "There's a lot of thoughts competing for airtime in my head before I take my Adderall. The Post-its help."

He stiffens up as he keeps driving and taps the steering wheel awkwardly. I retrieve the discarded sticky note, smooth out the wrinkles, and return it to the dashboard. It doesn't stick as well as before. "I'm a big fan of checklists, too."

He keeps his eyes on the traffic ahead, but I catch him biting back a smile.

There are no open parking spots in front of my house, so Mac pulls into the driveway. He fumbles with the car, first forgetting to put it in park, then remembering only when we start to roll backward, then slamming on the brakes, then trying to prevent the little dancing Gundam figurine on his dashboard from falling over, then knocking the figurine over into my lap, then frantically apologizing while trying to retrieve the figurine, then realizing that his hands are completely in my personal space, then apologizing again, toppling over the half-empty cup of water in the cupholder, then saying, "Okay, I am stopping now."

He tucks his hands underneath his legs and leans his forehead against the steering wheel, hiding his face. "Sorry."

What a train wreck. "It's okay," I say. It's actually kind of endearing.

We sit in silence for a moment before I gather my things and prepare to hop out. "Well, it was nice knowing you," I say.

He cocks his head to the side. "What do you mean?"

"I don't think I'll come back to Color Outside."

He sits up straight now. "Why not?"

"I don't know how a climate optimist will feel having a climate doomist around raining on everyone's parade."

"Nah, you gotta keep coming. If you stick with us for the summer, I promise that you'll see the light."

I raise an eyebrow. "And what if I don't?"

"Well, then you know what they say." He reclines against the side window. "Opposites attract." Mac rubs the back of his neck as he casts me a sly smile, laced with an unexpected level of boldness that makes my face burn.

My soul exits my body, leaving my brain scrambling to find an appropriate response to this boy. This cute boy. I can't believe this is happening. What am I supposed to say now? Seconds pass, and in the end, all my mind can come up with is a vague and nonengaging "Hm."

Mac fiddles with the window, moving it up and down a few times. "Well, I'm still happy you came today," he says.

"Oh. Um. Thanks." His hand—resting on the cupholder between us—is very close to mine.

"Can I, uh, maybe have your number? If that's all right?" His voice cracks a little with nerves.

I nod. Whoa. I am unconvinced that this is actually happening. He fumbles his phone out of his pocket and passes it to me. In the handoff, our fingers brush and I try not to act like that one touch alone doesn't make my chest pound. My brain immediately launches into a fantasy montage of him holding my hand. How pathetic. The hottest thing I can imagine is some dude holding my hand.

I stare at the phone screen for a moment, unable to recall my phone number. It's the way that he's looking at me. How am I supposed to remember how to do anything when a boy like that is looking at me? Eventually, I pull it together and enter a number that I'm 97 percent sure is mine. When I return his phone, his hand lingers on mine. For real this time. Holy shit.

"See you soon?" he asks. A hint of anxiety persists in his voice, even though I gave him my number, so he's in the clear.

"Maybe," I say. I was going for aloof, nondesperate, and mysterious with that response. Unclear how it landed.

I'm about to jump out of the car before I make everything weird, but Mac suddenly points out the window over the dashboard. "What's that?"

I follow his line of sight down his arm until I see what he sees.

Oh no.

JUST LIKE EVERYONE ELSE

JUST LIKE EVERYONE ELSE
JUST LIKE EVERYONE ELSE

"NOTHING," I LIE. BUT IT'S NOT NOTHING. IT'S the elaborate pile of sheet metal, dirt, and wood stacked beside the detached garage in the backyard that is the beginning of Camp Doom. Mom left the yard gate open, so the whole mess is visible from our parking spot in the driveway. I attempt to slip out the car, but my hand is shaking too much. I fumble with the door handle, unable to defeat the child lock.

Here's the thing about Camp Doom: I'm legitimately excited to build it. I have so many ideas, so many plans. But after my class's reaction . . . perhaps I should keep some things to myself.

Mac clocks my jumpiness, raising an eyebrow. I let out an awkward laugh that goes on for too long. His eyes light up. "Wait, *this* is your summer project? The one you mentioned?"

I stay quiet. I hate that Mac is actually a good listener. Most guys aren't. It'd be easier if Mac was more like most guys.

He climbs out of the car before I can stop him. I force open the door at last and follow him. He's way too tall, so his stride is faster than mine. Why does he have to be so tall? He walks right into the backyard and examines the mess. He spots my hand-drawn floor plan and takes it into his hands. “Camp Doom?” he reads aloud.

If a mass extinction event occurred right now, I wouldn’t be mad. An easy out would be nice. “It’s for an emergency.”

Understanding washes over him. “Your whole apocalypse thing . . .” He looks from the floor plan, to me, to the shed, then back to me. “I didn’t think you were building a fallout shelter.”

“Well, I am.”

He bursts out laughing.

There it is. Of course he’d laugh at me. Why wouldn’t he?

I barrel out of the yard. Mac springs forward and fumbles out a string of apologies, but it doesn’t matter. I don’t need this. I step inside and shut the door in his face.

NO COMMENT

NO COMMENT
NO COMMENT

MOM IS SITTING ALONE IN THE DARK LIVING room.

"Don't creep there in the shadows like a ghoul," I say. Never have I met a woman more addicted to sitting in the dark and scaring the hell out of people.

"Who was that?" She points out the window.

"Color Outside group leader."

"Interesting."

"Nothing's interesting."

"Okay."

"Okay."

"Will you keep on going?"

"Absolutely not."

SURVIVAL TIP #7: KEEP QUIET

The first rule of Prep Club is: Don't talk about Prep Club.

Avoid the unwanted commentary and side-eye from others by keeping prepping secretive.

Trust no one.

SO, YOU'VE BEEN ADDED TO A GROUPCHAT

SO, YOU'VE BEEN ADDED TO A GROUPCHAT

SO, YOU'VE BEEN ADDED TO A GROUPCHAT

< Andrew, Mac, Sage, and Me >

Andrew: mac gave us ur number. great meeting u yesterday! hang w/us soon pls

Sage: 👍

< Mac and Me >

Mac: im sorry again. are u free today?

TO BE ALONE

TO BE ALONE
TO BE ALONE

BY 11 P.M., I AM IN MY PAJAMAS BUT MY NIGHT is just beginning. For the next four to five hours, my mind will spin as I consume way too much media way too loudly and think about what my classmates are up to. Probably either at the movies or someone's parents' house or maybe a party. Everyone will be dressed cool and everyone will have something interesting to contribute to the conversation. Am I missing out? Will I regret spending all this time alone when I'm older? If I get older. But then again, I don't like big groups or even medium-size ones. I prefer my own company and when I do want social interaction, I can only handle two or three people max. I like other things, though. Like movies. Mostly horror, but action-adventure, too. Anything about a heist. I also like puzzles so long as they're at least five hundred pieces because the easy ones are boring. I like chess, too, but I like watching it more than playing. I like listening to math rock, 2000s metal, and experimental alternative like Björk. I like to make playlists. I like that when I make a playlist public, strangers on the internet add it to their collections and say that it's good. I like functional footwear, oversize sweatshirts that have been washed so many times that their insides are worn out like an old teddy bear, garlic bread, Friday the Thirteenth, the smell of the rum that my mom uses in her Christmas cake every year, orcas, and crew socks. I wish I could sing, but I can't hold a note to save my life. Plus, even if I could, I doubt I'd ever sing out loud. I don't like to call that type of attention to myself.

I'm settling into my nighttime routine when my phone vibrates with a text.

My stomach drops.

GHOSTS

GHOSTS
GHOSTS

< Unknown Number and me >

Unknown number: Niarah. Again. I'm sorry. Please call me back. We need to talk. Love, Dad

NOPE

NOPE

NOPE

EVERYONE'S OH SO SORRY. BOO-HOO. TOO BAD that I don't have a father anymore. No text message is going to change that. I blocked his number forever ago, so he must've gotten a new one or used someone else's phone. He's selfish like that—always trying to circumvent the boundaries that I've created.

Generally, I consider my mental state fine. Three stars. A solid 70 percent. Unlike Mx. Ferrante, I'd actually give myself a passing grade. I have my outlets (prepping, gaming, worrying) and most days, I feel okay. Perhaps I could have "healthier" coping mechanisms, but I've never claimed to be a saint. Over the years, I've learned that certain events can snap the thread that I so desperately cling on to in order to remain mildly functional. Anything related to my father is one of such triggers. Luckily, though, I have my solutions.

Delete message

Out of sight, out of mind.
I move on as if I never received the text at all.

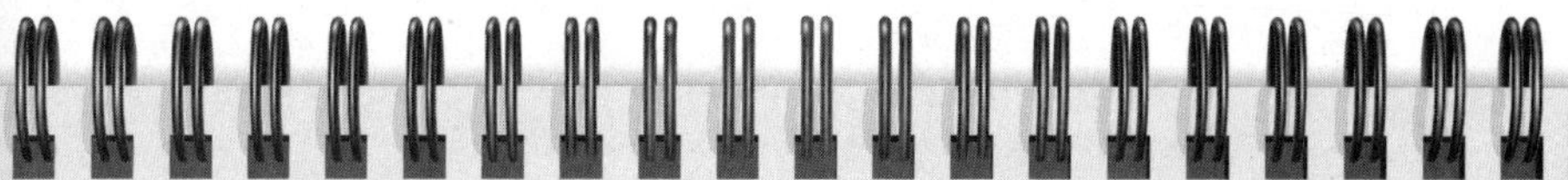

HOW TO BUILD AN EMERGENCY SHELTER, PART 2

Create a shelter with maximum protection against natural and man-made disasters.

Strengthen windows with security film: It keeps glass from shattering completely and will require an intruder to break the entire window to enter, which—despite what every action movie you've ever seen suggests—is much harder than you think.

Plant natural defenses: Spiky plants like cacti or blackberry bushes beneath windows make an impenetrable barrier. Watch your enemies get pricked, then enjoy a sweet berry snack.

Befriend sand: Sandbags are an inexpensive yet effective way to secure entrances and to provide flood protection. In a pinch, these can also be used to construct a makeshift dog bed in case you happen to own a creature who, despite their ferocious personality, simply would not survive three minutes in the apocalypse alone.

Fortify the perimeter: Reinforce the walls of your shelter with sheets of sturdy and weather-resistant scrap metal. Aesthetically, it will look awful, but who cares?

PROPOSITION

PROPOSITION
PROPOSITION

IT TAKES ME A HALF HOUR TO SUCCESSFULLY drive my first nail through the metal sheeting. This stuff is strong. No joke. I manage to drive two more nails through before I hear footsteps.

His voice comes out warm, feeling far more familiar than it should from a near stranger's lips. "Do you want any help with that?"

I should've known that Mac would show up. I ignored all eleven of his apology texts. Plus, there was a glint in his eyes, a gentle timbre of nervousness in his voice when he asked for my number, that made him seem like the type who'd drop by and say he was "in the neighborhood." So, when I open the gate and see him standing there—dirt-stained jeans, loose T-shirt, greasy bag of takeout in hand—I have no choice but to let him in.

"I was in the neighborhood," he says.

"No, you weren't," I retort.

"You're right. I wasn't." He holds up the paper bag, its corners turning slightly translucent from the oil. "But there's a solid breakfast burrito spot two blocks away, and I woke up with a craving, so in that sense, I was sort of in the neighborhood."

A craving. Even at nine a.m., the way that certain words sound coming from his mouth sends me into an unnatural stillness. I almost forget that I'm mad at him. Almost.

"You should go," I say.

"Niarah, I'm so sorry for yesterday." His foot rolls a rock in small circles beneath his sneaker. "I didn't mean to laugh. I was surprised and nervous, so I made things weird."

"Why were you nervous?"

"I had a cute girl in my car and was desperately trying to find a way to keep the conversation going. Why wouldn't I be nervous?"

Cute girl? The fuck?

I point to myself and raise my eyebrows. *Me?*

Mac laughs, pointing right back at me, and nods. *Yes, you.*

"You don't mean that," I say.

"Sure I do." He tosses me the breakfast burritos.

I open the bag. The scent of refried beans and tater tots floods my senses. I shut it before all the mouthwatering fatty smells hack my brain. "I'm dropping Color Outside. It's not the right fit. The activities take up too much time—they're practically all-day events. And if I go on the hikes, I'll be too tired at the end of the day to work on Camp Doom." I was already so sore this morning. I can't handle an entire summer of thigh pain.

He stares at the dirt. "You'd really rather do summer school?"

"At least with summer school, it's only ninety minutes a day, twice a week, and I can skate by there." *This is true.* "It's nothing personal." *This is less true.*

At summer school, I'm sure I can find an empty classroom where I can hide from everyone. It might take a second, but I can figure it out. Do the bare minimum and avoid who I need to avoid. I unwrap one of the burritos.

"Wait," he says.

When I look back at Mac, his eyes are wide. "What? You see your favorite bird again or something?" I try to open one of the hot sauce packets, but it's slippery from the oil. My fingers can't get a good grip.

"Can I help you?" Mac asks.

I use my teeth to rip open the packet at last. "No, I'm good." I slather the burrito.

"No, I mean help with the bunker."

I take a big bite. "When shit hits the fan, it will be everyone for themself, which is precisely why I plan to support myself. I don't need your 'help.'"

"But what if I count this? For your PE hours?"

"Count what?"

"Helping you with Camp Doom."

This gets a laugh out of me. A real laugh. "I don't know if working on my bunker counts."

"Why not? We're outdoors. We're physically moving things from one place to another. It's educational." Tempting. I don't say no fast enough, so he keeps talking. "My dad works in construction. I can be a real asset."

I look over at the pile of rusty garbage on the floor. It wouldn't hurt to have some help holding up the metal while I hammer it together, but still.

"You don't have any concerns working with the Doomsday Girl? Doesn't this conflict with your whole life philosophy on living in the moment, blah, blah?"

"Choosing to spend time with interesting people, even if they are doomsday preppers, is 'living in the moment, blah, blah.'"

We engage in a classic anime pre-showdown stare-down. Arms crossed, brows furrowed.

"Think about it," he continues. "If you let me help you, I'll count these hours. You'll barely have to go to Color Outside meet-ups and you don't have to go to summer school at all."

Pro: I'd have an extra pair of hands to help out.

Con: The extra pair of hands are leaving town soon.

"This feels like corruption," I note.

"Oh, it's totally corruption," he says, smiling.

"What do you get in return?" Nothing in the world comes for free.

"At the end of the summer, me, Andrew, and Sage are going on a three-night-long backpacking trip in the Sequoia National Forest. August seventeenth to twentieth. I want you to come with us."

Wow. He really had that idea locked and loaded. Maybe he's already thought about this before? Which, if true, would be . . . interesting. I repress the fluttery feeling in my stomach. "No way."

"Yup."

"Why? Do you actively want someone to slow you down?"

"I told you, I don't mind going slow." He casts me an enigmatic look that makes me wonder if his words hold multiple meanings.

"Mac. I hated hiking. It was not fun. The sun was very hot. I was so sweaty. *And* I got a blister. The idea of hiking for several days in a row, nonstop? Literal nightmare." Honestly, I'd rather repeat sophomore year.

"It gets better the more you do it," Mac says.

I hate this logic. It's like when people try to force you to watch their favorite TV show. The TV Pushers will insist that you "just need to make it to season three" but if I don't like something, I don't need to watch twenty more hours of it to get to the alleged good part.

"I tried hiking and it wasn't for me. End of story." The good thing about being a loner is that I'm immune to peer pressure, given my relative nonexposure to peers. I can see Mac is still trying to formulate a pitch in his head, so I keep listing more reasons for why this trip would be a disaster. "I don't have any gear. Your friends probably wouldn't want me to come—"

"They'll be fine."

I give Mac a silent you-can't-be-that-naive look. It's no mystery that Sage and I didn't necessarily hit it off, and Andrew's only humoring me because Mac is trying to be nice.

"We've been looking for a fourth person all week, but it's been tough. Pretty much all our friends from school will be traveling or spending time with their families before college starts. I planned the backpacking trip months ago originally thinking that my brother was going to join, but now he, uhm . . ." He trails off, a frown fixing where a smile was moments ago. "Anyway, he can't come. So, we need a fourth person."

I'm still not buying it. "But why do you 'need' four people?"

"I like even numbers. But more importantly, we've never gone on a multi-night backpacking trip without my parents, so our families made us promise that we'll be extra careful. They're obsessed with this scenario that an emergency will happen and we'll have to split up to find help, leaving one person alone. I guess in their nightmare, we separate, then we all die or whatever. They won't let us go if there's only three people."

"The buddy system," I say.

"Exactly. Plus, we have two tents that hold two people each, so four is better so nobody has to sleep alone." I raise an eyebrow and he panics. "You can stay in the tent with whoever, though. I'm not suggesting—"

I look at Mac and his stupid smile and his stupid hair. Backpacking could theoretically be a useful skill to master for prepping. "I'll think about it."

He beams. "So do we have a deal?"

"We have a rough draft of a potential deal."

"Yes. Okay. I'll take that." He claps his hands, then rolls up the sleeves of his shirt. He approaches the pile of scrap metal and grabs the hammer.

"What are you doing?" I ask.

"You said you'll think about the trip. So, in the meantime, I'll hold up my end of the bargain and help with your project." He grabs a piece of metal, holds it against the shed, and slams a nail through it, securing it in place in one swift motion. "Just in case."

NOTIFICATIONS

NOTIFICATIONS
NOTIFICATIONS

< Mac and Me >

Mac: here's that video I mentioned on orcas

Me: a sus late night text

Mac: I wanted to txt u and this felt less awkward than just "hi"

Mac: . . . I now realize this may have been even more awkward?

Me: we spent all day together and you still wanna talk?

Mac: ofc

Me: thanks for your help this afternoon. u didn't have to stay that long

Mac: ya I did. didn't want to blow my audition for the role of your helper this summer

Mac: how'd I do btw? on my audition?

Me: the casting committee is still in deliberations. you will receive a notification when the status of your application has changed.

Mac: well I am eagerly awaiting the decision

Mac: can I come help with camp doom again soon?

Me: I'll think about it

Mac: you say that a lot

Me: I think a lot

Mac: an intellectual. hot.

Me: easy, tiger.

Mac: *waits respectfully* 😇

DECISIONS DECISIONS DECISIONS

OX IS AN ENTHUSIASTIC EATER. HE CLOSES HIS eyes and moans with each bite, murmuring about how good the food is. Theoretically, this behavior isn't that suspicious. However, my mom is a terrible cook. I've considered sponsoring her to go on one of those *Worst Chefs in America* shows on the Food Network. Therefore, Ox's overwhelming glee at eating her muddled attempt at vegetarian curry smells like Grade A Bullshit.

I glance at the clock. Is seven minutes at the table long enough to count as "participation" in this "family dinner"? I place my fork down. "Can I please be excused?"

"Nope," Mom says.

Worth a shot.

"I got another email from Mr. Gutierrez. He says that the summer school registration window closes at midnight. Did you sign up?"

I smash a chickpea with my spoon. "Not yet."

"And your project for Mx. Ferrante? Have you started it?"

"Eh."

"I'm only letting you work on Camp Chicken Little—"

"Camp Doom."

"I'm only letting you work on Camp Doom despite your grades because I don't want you to be miserable this summer. You get that, right?"

"Yeup."

"So, you're going to take the assignment seriously? Turn in a capstone project that you're actually proud of?"

Bad curry and an interrogation. And she wonders why I don't like family dinners. "Yes." Mom nods, and the Stern Parenting portion of the evening program is concluded.

"When do summer classes end, Niarah?" Ox asks with a mouthful of undercooked carrots. Mom didn't cut all the vegetables the same size, so the potatoes are drastically overcooked and mushy, while the root veggies are practically raw.

I give him a side-eye. "Mid-August, I think. The fifteenth or something."

"Excellent." He claps his hands and his hair, pulled into a loose pineapple bun on the top of his head, bobs back and forth. "You can come with us, then."

"Ox, I wanted to be the one to tell her. I had a whole skit planned," my mom scolds, though she's smiling real big.

I grimace. "Come where?"

"VACATION," they say in rehearsed unison. I'm surprised they don't break out into song and dance.

"But we never go on vacation," I say. The last time we did, I was eight years old. Before my grandparents died, we went to New Orleans for a jazz festival. My grandpa carried me around on his shoulders and I made myself sick eating too many beignets. It was perfect. It was so long ago.

"Exactly. I want to change that. So, we're going to Palm Beach in Florida," Mom says.

"My homie has a timeshare out there and gifted us a few days in August to relax," Ox adds excitedly.

I scrunch my eyebrows. "Who is this *we* that you refer to?" They cannot possibly think I'm going with them.

My mom uses her gel-manicured finger to draw a zealous circle around the three of us.

This woman wants me to accompany her and her man to hurricane-prone Florida, aka the armpit of the South, in the dead heat of the summer to stand around a tacky timeshare where everyone is old and alligators lurk in the ponds on the golf course? Nah. I get swamp ass just thinking about the humidity out there. "Yeah, I definitely can't go. Sorry."

"What do you mean you *can't go*? Summer school will be over. You got some other big plans that I don't know about?"

In a split second, I weigh my options: (1) suffer through summer school, spending ten weeks avoiding my literal enemies Corey and Xander, then suffer heatstroke while accompanying my mother and her second chance at love on vacation in August, or (2) endure a summer of outdoor recreation, led by an overenthusiastic hippie, and avoid said vacation by trying not to die on what would be my first-ever camping trip.

It's not ideal, but my choice is clear.

UPDATE

UPDATE

UPDATE

< Mac and Me >

Me: the status of your application has changed.

Mac: !!!

Mac: !!!!!!!

THE TEAM

THE TEAM

THE TEAM

< Andrew, Mac, Sage, and Me >

Andrew: welcome to the official august backpacking crew niarah!!!!!!!!!

Mac: letsgooooooo

Sage: 👍

Mac: i'm so excited for you. clear, glacial lakes. bigger trees than you've ever seen. it's the prettiest place I've ever been in my life

Mac: you're gonna love it

Me: might be nice to see some of these places before they're extinct

Andrew: well that's bleak

Sage: 👎

SUMMER TO-DO

SUMMER TO-DO
SUMMER TO-DO

- Build Camp Doom
- Write the survival guide for my capstone
- Attend the bare minimum of Color Outside meetups necessary to obtain PE credit
- Avoid Mom + Ox
- "Train" for the August backpacking trip
- Survive said backpacking trip
- Don't let the boy leaving at the end of the summer get too close

SURVIVAL TIP #14: PRACTICE MAKES PERFECT

One of the best ways to test your survival skills is to spend time outdoors, without electricity, running water, and flushable toilets. Not every disruptive doomsday event will require you to live outdoors, but if one does, then you will be required to cope without modern conveniences. Ideally, such an event would be short-term in nature, but as the saying goes, "Hope for the best and prepare for the worst."

This means that if you happen to receive an invitation from a group of weird kids to go on a four-day hiking trip to god-knows-where California, it might be in your best interest to accept. At the very least, it will be a learning experience that will make you a better prepper.

It will suck, but so will the apocalypse, so at least you'll be staying on theme.

CONSTRUCTION DAY 1

CONSTRUCTION DAY 1
CONSTRUCTION DAY 1

"LIFT WITH YOUR KNEES," I COACH MAC AS HE wobbles from the mound of dirt in the middle of the yard to the walls of Camp Doom. I should've dumped the sand for the sandbags closer to the actual shelter, but when Mac showed up today in a thin ribbed tank top that clings to his chest, unlike his usual array of oversize tees, I dropped the wheelbarrow. It takes us a few tries to figure out the optimum weight of the sandbags. The trick is to fill them as much as possible without making them too heavy to move. Once we figure out that around two-thirds full is ideal, I pull out the survival guide to write it down.

"What's that?" Mac asks. A rogue strand of hair falls free from behind his ear as he peers over my shoulder.

I plant my hands over the pages. "It's for school. My makeup capstone for Mx. Ferrante."

"You're writing it about this?" he asks, gesturing at the pile of sandbags.

"Sort of. It's kind of . . . I don't know. My vision for the future, I guess."

"Can I read it?"

"No. Of course not." I furrow my brow. "You're very curious."

"Is that a bad thing?"

"Yes." I cut my eyes at him, but he just laughs.

"Damn, so you're stuck with me for the summer because you ditched PE, *and* you have to make up Ferrante's assignment, too? Mr. G's getting more strict. He didn't make even me do all that."

"How did you end up joining Color Outside anyway, Nature Boy?"

He stiffens up. "Behavioral issues."

"What kind?"

He doesn't respond right away, opting to instead fiddle with his rings and stare at the grass. He almost starts to stammer through a variety of *Um*s but is saved. Bruce sprints out into the yard from his doggy door, barking loudly as he tries to nip Mac's ankles. Mac melts to his knees to shower Bruce with scratches behind the ears. He spots Bruce's tiny cape. "Mr. Bruce Wayne. It's an honor to meet you, Batman."

Bruce barks back. *The honor is yours, peasant.*

Mac laughs. "Big personality in a tiny package."

"He maintains a well-justified suspicion of new people," I explain.

"Like mother, like son."

"Ha-ha."

"Where is your mom, anyway? Is she home?"

"Nope. At work. She works in guest relations at a museum downtown, so she's there all the time."

"Can I meet her?"

"Who?"

"Your mom."

"What? Ew. No." I can just imagine my mom with this look on her face like, *Wow! Niarah finally found a friend!* That'd piss me off beyond belief. She'd be right, but still. No thanks.

"Why not?"

"No meeting my mom. That's rule number one if you're going to help with Camp Doom."

"What's rule number two?"

"Wouldn't you like to know." I toss Mac another empty sandbag.

"So very mysterious." He looks at me with his head cocked to the side. I pull an empty sandbag over my head. I can hear him laugh.

His word choice is interesting. Is there a difference between being mysterious and guarded?

We get back to working and talking about school. All the teachers he had who were cool, all the ones I had who weren't, and which ones dress like Trader Joe's employees. And then, in between wiping down the exterior of Camp Doom and filling sandbags, we're talking about movies. He likes horror, too. *The Conjuring*. *The Shining*. The opening sequence of *M3GAN*. *Get Out* versus *Nope*. I start talking shit about how LA's food scene isn't all that, and Mac gets deeply offended. He orders Thai food from a local spot to prove a point. Unfortunately, he is right. The food is delicious. It's spicy, though, so I dare him to eat a spoonful of chilies, which he does without hesitation, only to end up red-faced, coughing, and chugging his entire Thai tea and half of mine. When I finally catch my breath between laughs, I look up. The sky has turned a hazy pink and purple.

“It’s sunset already,” I say. I’m surprised. The exterior of the shed has officially been cleaned, tested, and fortified. We’ve been together for nearly six hours.

Mac loads the tools back into the shed. “Time flies when you’re prepping for the end of time.”

PASSED A NOTE

PASSED A NOTE
PASSED A NOTE

ON HIS WAY OUT, MAC SLIPS A HALF-CRUMPLED piece of notebook paper into my hand.

"What is this?" I hold it up, frowning.

"It's for the survival guide."

"I don't take requests."

"It's not a request. It's a tip."

I use my thumbs to smooth out the paper. I sigh.

"Mac, this isn't a tip. It's a . . ." What is this?

"A quote."

I cross my arms. "There's no room in the guide for quotes."

"There's always room for quotes," Mac says.

"But—"

"Consider it an intermission." He jogs away. "I'll see you tomorrow."

I roll my eyes. I open the guide to a blank page and smush the loose page between the sheets.

MAC'S TIP FOR BEING ALIVE #1

Dear Doomsday Girl,

Please consider the following as an offering to your esteemed encyclopedia of survival tips.

On our first hike, you said something about progress. . . . How it's fake, or something? Anyway, I didn't have a good reply then, but I read this last night and it made me think of you.

"I'm not telling you to make the world better, because I don't think that progress is necessarily part of the package. I'm just telling you to live in it. Not just to endure, not just to suffer in it, not just to pass through it, but to live in it. To look at it. To try and get the picture. To live recklessly. To take chances. To make your own work and take pride in it. To seize the moment." —Joan Didion

Sincerely,

Nature Boy

NIARAH'S ADDENDUM TO MAC'S TIP FOR BEING ALIVE #1

NIARAH'S ADDENDUM TO MAC'S TIP FOR BEING ALIVE #1

NIARAH'S ADDENDUM TO MAC'S TIP FOR BEING ALIVE #1

MAC'S NOTE SOUNDS LIKE THE TYPE OF Pinterest philosophy that middle-aged moms screenprint onto discount mugs in the checkout aisle at T.J. Maxx. I'm not one for the whole live-laugh-love cult(ure).

Beneath it, I add my own take on the issue:

"The world is going to shit." —Niarah

NEVER MIND

NEVER MIND
NEVER MIND

IT'S NOT THAT I DON'T LIKE MY MOM, IT'S THAT I don't trust her anymore. She never sees anything coming until it hits her right in the face.

Exhibit A: the monthly blackout.

Every single month for the past year, the power goes out. Why? Because she forgets to pay the bill. Mind you, she has the *ability* to pay the bill. She simply forgets. Every month. And even more frustrating: She refuses to set up auto-pay. She convinces herself, *This time, I'll remember.*

But she never does.

So, every single month, when I'm in the middle of doing homework, or showering, or nearing an all-time high kill streak in my game, the power will shut off, then all I'll hear from down the hall is "Oops, sorry!" The lights always come back on within an hour after she calls the company, but that's not the point.

I have a strained relationship with "Oops, sorry."

When we're forty-five minutes late to a doctor's appointment because she neglected to write down the address and can't find the confirmation email: *"Oops, sorry."*

Back on the East Coast, when we got trapped in the car for hours during a winter storm because she forgot to put the chain on her tires: *"Oops, sorry."*

When I remind her four different times to remember to buy tampons because I'm all out and she tells me to stop nagging her because she won't forget plus she keeps extras in the house in case of emergency anyway, but then comes back from the store with only an armful of vanilla-coconut-scented body scrubs for herself and opens her alleged backup stash to find that she actually used them all last month: *"Oops, sorry."*

Before we left Syracuse, my father would take care of paying the bills. Not on some patriarchy trip, but that was simply one of the few things that he was good at. He was, I mean *is*, a lot of things (including being someone who is easier to talk about in past tense than present), but he is also timely.

You'd think that my mom would've been more prepared for the world when she left him.

But then again, like the monthly blackout, she was the last person to realize that we had to leave. There was no "Oops, sorry" the night that we left, but I could feel the words vibrating in the back of her throat. If we didn't have to be so quiet, I'm sure she would've said it, and I'm sure that in response, I would have screamed.

The adults in our lives are supposed to take care of us, and I guess they try, but not hard enough, and certainly not soon enough.

Maybe I'm too hard on her. The electricity bill was due on the first of the month. It's been a few days, and still no blackout. Maybe this will be the month that she changes. Maybe this time—

Never mind.

TAP OUT

TAP OUT
TAP OUT

"THIS TRAIL CAN KISS MY ASS."

Everyone else is a few steps ahead, so nobody can hear me, but I have to say it. Mac and Color Outside got me trudging up a literal mountain in the Angeles National Forest. Prior to this morning, I did not even know that Los Angeles had a national forest. There's no shade out here. The sweat soaking my cotton tank top causes my skin to grate against the straps of my backpack. My thighs chafe beneath my shorts. Chafing: the devil's work, indeed.

I don't know how early humans walked around the entire damn planet. I would've tapped out of the whole migration thing. Leave me with the wooly mammoths and let me die in peace. I'd wave goodbye to my clan: *So long, homies! It's been real.*

"How ya feeling?" Mac asks.

"Do not ask me that right now," I wheeze. This is no time for talking. There is not enough air to breathe in this hell.

He laughs before calling out to Sage, Andrew, and the others up ahead: "Water break."

If I sit down, what if I'll be too weak to stand back up? Whatever. I cave anyway. I plop onto the ground and down half a bottle of water in eight seconds. We're surrounded by a landscape of beige and pale green. Cacti and eucalyptus trees bake as lizards scurry across a trail that's more dust than dirt. California's perennial drought has left the area dry as the fried chicken from that white restaurant in Silverlake. We've been walking forever and I see no end in sight. Pure torture. "Where are we?" I ask Mac.

"On the unceded territorial land of the Gabrielino/Tongva people."

"No, I mean like, are we in the middle of the hike or the end? Please tell me it's the end."

Mac looks apologetic as he checks the route map on the AllTrails app on his phone. "Want me to lie to you?"

I groan.

Mac points at a canyon in the distance, trying to distract me from my obvious spiral. "There used to be a waterfall there," he says.

"The one with all the moss!" Andrew chimes in. "Can't believe this park can change so fast."

"Well, if it's any consolation, someday soon, most things will be gone." I say it as a joke, but it's another swing and a miss. Only Mac laughs. Technically, Andrew gives me a half laugh, but it's dripping with pity, so it doesn't count. Meanwhile, Sage lets out the single most judgmental sigh I've ever heard in my life. You'd think that existential dread was contagious by the way that Sage makes a show of scooting away from me.

"I think we've earned a snack," Andrew says. He pulls a Tupperware container from his bag and pops off the lid. "Salted dulce de leche blondies." The smell of caramel, warm from the heat of his bag, fills the air between us.

I nervously shove a pastry into my mouth. It's incredible. I decide that Andrew is my favorite. "You should audition for *Top Chef* or something."

"I would *thrive* on a competitive reality cooking television show."

"You'd be the person starting the drama and getting too drunk at the after-parties," Mac says.

"Yes. Like I said, I would thrive."

I take another bite, and it's sublime. "First the guava things, now this? You're gonna give me diabetes," I joke.

Silence whips between us.

Sage frowns and whips out their phone. This time, they turn the screen to me.

Andrew is diabetic.

I deserve an award for the absolute worst timing on the planet. "Yo, I am so sorry, I didn't mean it," I stammer. *Send me back to quarantine, please, so I can't offend anyone else*, I beg the universe.

Andrew holds up his hands. "It's fine. Truly." He takes a drink from his water bottle. "Being Type One and learning how to be in tune with my body, how to nourish it, is a big part of my chef journey. It's no big secret."

Andrew smiles at me and I grimace back. Mac steps in, steering the conversation in a new direction to distract everyone from my ignorance. They get to talking about the political themes of some Black lady sci-fi trilogy about geology and the intersection of systemic racism and climate change, but I'm lost. Every time that I almost think of something to say, it's too late—their chatter speeds onto the next topic that I also know nothing about. I'm honestly grateful when Sage stands, signaling that we keep hiking. At least while walking, my silence is less noticeable. The first footsteps after the break are brutal. I want to go wait in the car. Mac flashes me a thumbs-up and mouths to me, *Don't worry*. But I am worrying. Andrew seems okay after my faux pas, but Sage is still giving me the evil eye.

There are few things more embarrassing than being revealed as the least politically aware person in a group of your peers. Everyone my age is supposed to be better with this stuff—to know how to say the right thing. But I haven't had enough practice hanging out with people to get it right. Even with Sage, I've almost slipped up on their pronouns three times today, and I swear they've noticed. I'm not cool enough to be friends with these people. I can't keep up. With the hike. With the conversation. With the vibe.

I can't keep up.

AMENDS

AMENDS
AMENDS

LATE AT NIGHT, I COME DOWNSTAIRS INTO THE kitchen. There's a black box on the counter with my name written on it. Beneath the lone overhead light, it looks ominous. I am intrigued.

I creep forward. It's not a box, but a safe. There's a dial and number pad on the front and everything. I open the door and peek inside. Three boxes of energy bars, a jug of protein powder, a gallon-size bag of freeze-dried fruit, several sticks of turkey jerky, and powdered eggs stack together in neat lines. On top of the can of tuna, there's a note.

For Camp Doom.

Passcode protected to prevent hungry idiots from consuming the snacks.

—Ox

ROBIN

ROBIN

ROBIN

IT'S INCREDIBLE HOW MUCH JUNK HUMANS accumulate over the course of a life. Like with many homes in the neighborhood, the garage hasn't been used in centuries. Angelenos are spoiled in that they don't have to deal with weather besides heat waves, so most people don't bother putting their cars up at night. Thus, their garages devolve into glorified storage rooms. Ours is covered in cobwebs and filled with rusted garden items, broken glasses, and all the things that the previous owners were too lazy to throw away. With Camp Doom's exterior now done, it's time to tackle the inside. Today is Operation Clear Out.

Mac arrives with construction gloves in one hand and a pink box of panda-shaped Oreo doughnuts in the other. His hair is pulled back into a small bun that sits below a black backward baseball cap. I'm momentarily taken aback by the sight of him without the wild wisps of hair hanging freely around his face. With the hair tucked away, he looks a little neater, a little older. A plain terra-cotta flannel, dark jeans, and Converse round out the look.

With each pile of junk removed, I feel the space opening up. We find a box full of old, water-stained *National Geographic* magazines, which Mac immediately latches onto. He gets distracted, flipping through the pages excitedly, telling me random facts about the natural places on the covers. I don't really care, but I listen anyway. Once I finally get him to toss the magazines, he dusts off the old wooden crate in the corner and carries it to the center of the room.

"What are you doing?" I ask. He reaches up above his head, humming as he gently pulls on a matted sheet of cardboard taped to the ceiling. "Mac, I don't know if you should—"

He continues to tug at the cardboard until it gives away to reveal a glass skylight. Warm sunlight floods the room.

"Knew it. The garage at my house has one of these, too."

Huh. I assumed that the cardboard was there to cover a hole for a leak, not to hide a secret window. Mac pulls the gloves from his back pocket to clean off the thick layer of grime from the glass. As he wipes at the dirt above his head, his shirt rides up to reveal a thin strip of skin above the waistband of his jeans. I can see the faint outline of the bottom of his abs as he strains to reach the far corner of the skylight.

"Can you, uh, pass me a paper towel, please?" Mac asks. By the way he says it, I can tell that he's repeating himself. Apparently, I didn't hear him the first time. Too busy checking him out. When did I become such a creep? When we lock eyes, the faint blush on his cheeks confirms my suspicion that he caught me staring. I practically throw the paper towel at him.

"Thanks," he mumbles.

I nod, too embarrassed to say anything at all.

"The skylight will be nice at nighttime. You could probably even see the moon from here on some nights. Maybe we—"

SCREECH.

In front of the house, tires wail against pavement. A tiny, high-pitched yelp follows.

Bruce.

My heart drops. I sprint out into the street. There's a car turned at an awkward angle, driver clutching her steering wheel. She looks on the verge of a meltdown herself. My eyes prickle as I scan the concrete surrounding the car. Thankfully, Bruce is not here.

"That way." The driver points down the street once she catches her breath. "There's a coyote. It's chasing the dog."

Coyotes in LA are like raccoons in other places—often drifting around, largely minding their own business, until they're not. They're harmless . . . toward humans, at least. The first time that I saw a coyote, I swore it was a dog. Its skinny, shaggy body trotted down our street as if he belonged there. I didn't realize it was a coyote until I watched a woman swiftly pull her terrier up into her arms and cross the street. Her dog was wearing a sweater covered in spikes for this very reason. When I told mom about it later, she suggested that we get one for Bruce, too, but I refused. I figured he'd be furious if I swapped his majestic cape for a costume that made him look like a piñata. I regret everything.

The thing is, when your therapist prescribes you a dog after you tell her that you sometimes struggle with thoughts of not necessarily wanting to be alive, and you find the right dog that actually makes you feel halfway decent about existing, it's a fierce bond. On the days when I don't necessarily feel enthusiastic about being alive, Bruce is a consistent reminder that waking up is worth it.

I'm frozen in place until I see Mac whip down the street, running so fast that his unbuttoned flannel flaps behind him in the wind. His Converse slam against the pavement with each step, arms pumping. I snap out of it. I run as fast as I can.

I wish I actually went to PE. The dry heat singes my lungs. I hear another yelp in the distance—relief at the sound of his bark, terror at the obvious fear behind it. Mac leads a few steps ahead and suddenly bears left, diving out of the street and into a vacant lot. He plunges into a wall of overgrown bushes. I follow, wincing as the thorns cut my skin. My T-shirt catches against a spike, halting my momentum. I try to free myself, hearing another bark in the distance followed by a howl. My palms are sweating, tears prickling at the corners of my eyes. A frustrated gurgle leaks from my throat. I tear the shirt, plunging forward onto my hands and knees. Scrambling forward into the clearing, I spin around to look for where Mac went. When I spot the far corner of the lot in front of a wooden fence, I can finally breathe again.

With one arm, Mac cradles a shivering Bruce beneath his elbow. With the other, he wields his left shoe, shaking it disapprovingly at the coyote hunched four feet away.

"Bad coyote," he scolds. He throws the shoe, careful to not hit the animal but tossing it close enough to back him off. "Dogs are friends. Not food."

Mac's standing in his socks. He must've thrown the first shoe before I got here. Bruce barks in Mac's arms, presumably talking shit to the coyote, but Mac shushes him. "Not now, Batman. Let me handle this." Surprisingly, Bruce obeys. He quiets immediately.

Mac furrows his brow at the coyote. "We're walking away now. You're not going to follow us. You're gonna do your thing, we're gonna do ours. Understood?"

The coyote stares at Mac blankly. Poker face. Mac backs out toward me. We watch the coyote anxiously, moving as slowly as possible, until we find a gap in the bushes. When we finally hit the pavement, all three of us—me, Mac, and Bruce, too—exhale.

Bruce squirms from Mac's arms into mine. I burrow my face into his fur. If depression is a cartoon tornado, Bruce is the string keeping me from flying away. I clutch on to him for dear life, grateful that he's still here. My little anchor.

"What type of bullshit city has coyotes?" I ask.

"The trials of coexistence," Mac says with a sigh. "They live here, we live here. We all try our best." Bruce wiggles in my arms, now jumping back to Mac, panting as he licks Mac's smiling face. "You're welcome, lil man."

"Yeah, uh . . . thank you. If I couldn't find Bruce—" My voice catches in my throat. What are the right words to convey how much this little psychological support fur-demon means to me? I try again, gripping Bruce's fur for comfort. "I know he's a dog, but I . . . He . . . Sometimes, I can't, or at least don't want to . . . So, Bruce helps by . . ."

"Hey," Mac says, meeting my eyes with staggering softness. "I'm happy we found him."

"Me too." I appreciate the space to leave some things unsaid between us. I look down at Mac's feet, his black socks now covered in those tiny brown spiky things that litter grass lawns in the summer. "Wanna go get your shoes?"

"Eh. I'll come back for them later. Let's get Bruce home first."

The walk back to Camp Doom is quiet. I lock Bruce inside and he doesn't argue, probably exhausted from his run earlier. When I come back outside, Mac's standing there awkwardly. He could go home. It's pretty much about the time he usually goes home. But he lingers.

I wait for him to announce that he's heading out, but he

doesn't. After a beat, I re-collect his work gloves from the floor and hand them to him. Our fingers brush in the exchange. I watch a tiny bolt of surprise race across his face. He clears his throat and steps backward, gripping the back of his neck. He offers me a small half smile before opening the door to Camp Doom to keep cleaning, still sans shoes.

The silence is charged until Mac clears his throat. "Niarah. I, uh, have a serious question for you."

For the second time this afternoon, my heart drops. What could he want?

"Sure," I mumble. "What's up?"

He looks at me, brows knit together. "If I . . ." He stops himself. Anticipation runs through my core. He takes a deep breath and tries again. "If I saved Batman, does that make me Robin?"

A grin tugs at the corner of his mouth. We break out in laughter.

"You're actually proud of that one, aren't you?" I ask.

"Unfortunately, I am."

"I secretly love *Teen Titans*. Robin's too intense, though. I prefer Beast Boy." The words jump out on their own. I don't know why I'm telling him this.

"Well, then. I change my choice. I wanna be Beast Boy." He wags an eyebrow at me, and I roll my eyes.

"No changes allowed." I toss him the broom to sweep the goofy look off his face. "Also, if you're anybody, you're Starfire."

"Hey!" he yells. Then we're both fighting back fits of laughter again. We work quietly for another twenty minutes, but the silence is dotted with knowing smirks. In between clearing out the junk and sweeping spiderwebs, I feel him look at me. I try to catch him staring. Sometimes he pulls his eyes away right on time. Sometimes he stares right back, so that I'm the one to dodge. It becomes a game—taking each other in, while the other pretends not to notice.

When it's my turn, I see new details about Mac. A sickle-shaped scar right above his left elbow. A vein that's slightly more prominent than the others on his right hand. A birthmark on his clavicle.

I wonder what he sees when he looks at me.

LET ME TELL YOU ABOUT MAC

LET ME TELL YOU ABOUT MAC

LET ME TELL YOU ABOUT MAC

LET ME TELL YOU ABOUT MAC. WHAT I'VE learned about him over the past couple of weeks.

Mac is too much of a morning person. He often begins the workday with some long, rambling story, punctuated with excessive sound effects.

Mac is highly distractible. Every time that a bird lands in the yard, he launches into a spiel about the species and its migratory pattern, despite my repeated insistence that I do not care.

Mac appears to have a slight phobia of spiders, despite his repeated insistence that he does not care.

Occasionally, Mac will receive text messages that darken his expression, leaving him standing with hunched shoulders. He'll type furiously until he notices me watching, before slipping the phone back into his pocket and pretending it didn't happen.

Mac is good at pretending his moments of frustration never happened.

Mac possesses a seemingly bottomless reserve of fun facts

about mushrooms. He is obsessed with how mushrooms can communicate with one another via electrical signals. He has repeated this specific fact to me three times.

Mac is irritable when hungry.

Mac likes to hum old bolero songs while he works.

Whenever I join a hike, Mac lingers with me in the back, often stopping to wordlessly collect random plants, crumbling them into his palm, then handing them to me to smell. He's skilled at identifying wild lavender, fennel, and eucalyptus. Sometimes, the faint earthy scent of foraging lingers on his shirt and I can still smell it on the drive home.

Mac is leaving Los Angeles in fifty-four days.

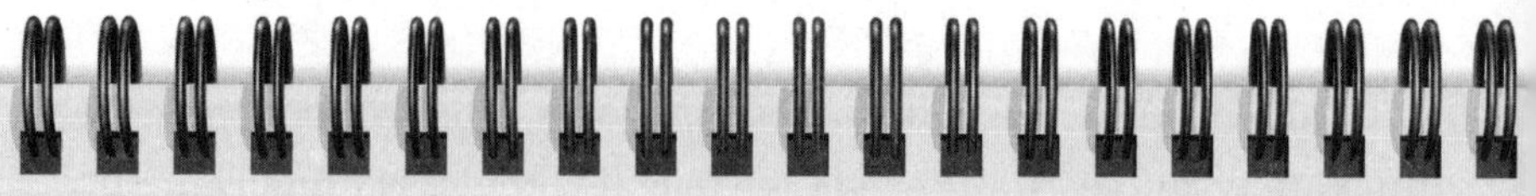

SURVIVAL TIP #23: NONPERISHABLES

Nonperishable food items have long shelf lives and, if taken care of properly, stand a solid chance of never spoiling within your lifetime.

The best place to keep a survival food stockpile is in a dark, cool, and dry spot, free of humidity, moisture, and direct sunlight. Keeping consumables in an air-tight container, or better yet, vacuum packed, is key to increasing shelf life. Consider adding the following to your supply:

- Rice: white, wild, jasmine, and basmati (brown rice does not keep forever)
- Hardtack crackers/biscuits
- Dried cranberries
- Maple syrup
- Dried lentils
- Dried beans

A diet of bland biscuits and unseasoned beans might not seem enjoyable, but nonperishable items are underrated. If they never expire, you can count on them for the long haul, which is rare in a world where it's often hard to count on anything at all. You should appreciate things that you can trust will be there for you down the line when you need them. A nice bowl of fruit might be nice in the moment, but it spoils quickly.

And nobody likes an expiration date.

INVITATION

INVITATION
INVITATION

< Mac and Me >

Mac: color outside beach bonfire. tn. come? please?

Me: no.

Mac: why not

Me: beach at night = prime horror movie setting

Mac: we both know that you're way too resourceful to die in a horror movie

Me: yes obviously but i still don't want to watch you get killed

Mac: awwwww

Me: 😣😣😣

Mac: comeeeeeeeeeeeee

SKYLINE TO

SKYLINE TO
SKYLINE TO

FOOT-SHAPED DIVOTS CUT A PATH FROM THE cars to the sand. The air is dense with sunset mist and smoke from the corn grilling two firepits over. Families and crews of twentysomethings in hoodies gather around miniature campfires, stoking flames with sticks and competing over who's got next in spike ball. Up the coast, ocean-view homes glitter like daydreams. The Pacific Ocean roars, dark and elegant. It's the type of West Coast scene I've never imagined myself in before.

Mom is working tonight, so Ox offered to drop me off at the bonfire, which was nice, I guess. Except that he kept trying to talk to me. I held out for as long as I could, but when we hit traffic, I caved and responded to a question or two. He's a good listener. And he has good taste in post-punk music. Two things that I didn't expect.

Andrew got to the bonfire early to set up his cooking spread, while Sage and the others are setting up the foldout table and beach chairs. I don't see Mac anywhere. I try not to appear disappointed.

I must look pitiful standing awkwardly by myself, though, because Sage of all people passes me a lighter and motions toward the firepit. They don't stick around to help or anything—just give me yet another cold, bored expression, then keep walking. I guess that means it's my job to start the bonfire.

I'm not thrilled. Sure, I've watched a bunch of videos about how to build a fire, but I've never actually tried it before. I'm always afraid of screwing up and ending up like that asshole who accidentally burned down half a national forest. Plus, do you know how hard it is to start a fire at the beach when everything is slightly damp? I'll tell you: *hard.* Every time I put a piece of wood into the firepit and light it with a match, it doesn't catch, but instead, just smokes. I feel bad for the people sitting downwind from me because I'm pretty sure that I've made the air completely unbreathable from all my failed attempts. I have one job—start the fire—and I can't do it. I only know three people here, and two are busy, and the other is nowhere to be found. This is exactly why I don't leave my house.

I give up and go stand next to Andrew by the food. He's tearing Tupperware from coolers and sprinkling little sprigs of cilantro onto a spread of very tiny appetizers. And by tiny, I mean *microscopic*—like the most ornate snacks I've ever seen balanced on crackers the size of quarters. The man is literally using tweezers to place garnishes. I've never met someone so attentive to detail before.

"Please let me help you," I beg him.

"I say this with love and respect, but I do not trust you to not mess up my plating," Andrew says.

"Fair," I say. "You have stellar instincts." I settle into watching Andrew work, but after a few minutes, I can't help but ask, "Is Mac still coming tonight?"

Andrew glances at his phone. "It's not Monday, so he should be here."

"Why does it matter that it's not Monday?"

He squirms and passes me a small bowl of peanuts. "Just sprinkle a few on the top of that bowl over there, okay?"

I grab the bowl, psyched to have something to do to feel less useless, but then I hear it. The sound of my name over the crash of a wave.

When I finally see him, it's like my brain is full of soda and everything is fizzing. Mac jogs toward me, wet suit dripping a line of water onto the sand behind him. He's backlit by the dwindling sun. A tall shadow moving closer and closer.

Andrew elbows me in the small of my back. I stumble forward, nearly knocking into Mac. "Oops," Andrew says innocently, eyes full of mischief as I glare back at him.

I get my footing and stand up straight to face Mac. "Sorry. Hi."

"What about your horror movie concern?" he asks.

"I brought Mace, so I'll be fine," I say.

His hair is messy, sweeping down over his forehead as he laughs. When he reaches out for a hug, I don't mind that his touch leaves giant water marks all over my sweater.

"Sage says you're Fire Master for the night. How's it coming along?" he asks.

I point over my shoulder at the pile of ash and broken matches behind us. He chuckles. "I'll come help in a minute." He walks toward the parking lot, but stops before he gets too far. He takes two steps back. He calls my name in the tone of a question. I look up from the firepit. "You, uh, look pretty. With your hair like that."

I'm trying a new hairstyle: half-up, half-down. I wasn't sure if it made me look good or just highlights my massive forehead.

I short-circuit. "Th-thanks."

His shoulders pitch up toward his ears and he sort of grimaces, coughing out an awkward half laugh, before walking away. I don't know why but I immediately retrieve the scrunchie from my pocket and pull my hair into a bun. Andrew drops his tongs and rips the scrunchie right back out.

"Ouch?" I rub my scalp.

"Bad Niarah," Andrew scolds. "Let the boy be nice to you."

"Shut up. Your food is burning," I say.

Andrew gasps and turns his attention back to the grill.

I watch Mac as he loads his board onto a rack of an all-black F-150. Two surfer girls stand by the truck and Mac says something that makes them laugh hard. Little water droplets shake from their heads onto the car windows. An odd feeling tugs at my chest. I turn back to the firepit, poking the sandy perimeter more aggressively than before.

A sharp whistle catches my attention. Sage is facing me a few feet away. They toss me a small brick-shaped item. I reach out my hands, but the package hits the sand with an awkward thump. Somebody nearby laughs. Why do cool kids always throw everything to one another? What's so terrible about a civilized handoff? We're not in the MLB. I shake it off and read the label. It's a fire starter, thank god. I place the brick into the pit and the fire catches immediately. Andrew rallies everyone to applaud, even though using a starter feels like cheating. I smile anyway.

Mac returns wearing baggy sweatpants, an even baggier sweatshirt, and a denim jacket thrown over the top. He looks good in the way that hot people always look good in loungewear. The comfy aesthetic makes their hotness seem more accessible for us non-hot people. There are tons of open spaces around the fire, but he sits next to me. I try to not think too much of it.

"Food is served." Andrew carries several trays of his precious creations right up to the bonfire. "Eat up and tell me how talented I am."

ANDREW'S BONFIRE MENU
ANDREW'S BONFIRE MENU
ANDREW'S BONFIRE MENU

- Rijah buah: mango, papaya, pineapple, and cucumber coated in a thick and gooey rojak dressing, served on crispy crackers and topped with chopped peanuts
- Egg tarts: flaky on the outside, soft on the inside
- Karipap: small, deep-fried curry pastries
- Popiah: pandan-flavored crepes stuffed with cucumber, carrots, eggs, ground peanuts, and cooked jicama, served with a sweet chili sauce
- Pau: soft steamed buns stuffed with lotus paste
- Red bean ice pops: extra sweet

LIMINAL

LIMINAL
LIMINAL

EVERYONE STARTS TO EAT AND THEN SOMEONE passes around a flask. The night gets colder, and everyone huddles closer. I have one drink, then another. Am I overdoing it? Do I care? A gust of wind blows in from the ocean, and Mac leans into my side. "For warmth," he says with a smile. The fire lights up his face, showcasing the bold lines of his cheekbones. Has anyone ever asked to draw him before? If I had even a single artistic bone in my body, I know that I would.

The rational part of my brain understands that I shouldn't lean into Mac, "for warmth" or for anything, but the other rational part of my brain is telling me, *Bitch, you're cold, don't be weird.* So, I let his leg rest against my leg, my arm against his arm.

Sage changes the music to a playlist called Electronica Romantica, as if that's a real genre. Andrew empties an entire flask into a cup, adding a shallow splash of mixer. Mac reminds him to take it easy. In response, Andrew downs two more shots, then sticks his tongue out.

It's hard not to feel nervous looking around the circle of Mac's friends. They're all cumulatively, collectively, intimidatingly cool. And tan. Exceptionally tan. They're the type of teenagers that VICE would make a documentary on. Edgy and interesting with defined points of view. Meanwhile, I'm a nihilism mug of vitamin-D-deficient goop.

"You doin' all right?" Mac asks.

"I'm good." A little overwhelmed socially, but nothing new. I've managed to go all night without offending anyone, though, and the competitive gamer in me wants to keep up my streak.

Andrew saunters back to the bonfire with a hardcover book, a tiny black-and-red speckled tin, and a flat cardboard container the size of a credit card. He lays out all the components like a feast. "Anyone tryna smoke?"

A tiny spark of curiosity ignites in my chest. I've never smoked weed before. Never been motivated, but also never been given the chance.

Beside me, Mac lets out a worried sigh.

"Hey, you're the one that first put me on, Mac," Andrew says. "Don't get all self-righteous now that you're on your my-body-is-a-temple bullshit."

"Your body is a temple, though," Mac says, painfully sincere.

"No, babe. In the words of my hero Anthony Bourdain, my body is not a temple—it's an amusement park. And I'm here to enjoy the ride." At this, everyone breaks out into cheers. Mac forces a smile as he nods in concession, but a hint of concern still lingers in his eyes.

"What happened to the whole 'I don't judge' thing?" I ask Mac, teasing.

"With Andrew, it's complicated," he whispers to me. "Don't overdo it, man," he shouts to Andrew.

“I always do, and that’s why you love me,” Andrew says with a wink. He rolls the joint with staggering precision despite the darkness and wind, which I can’t imagine are optimal conditions for such a precise task. He creates a little shield with his hands to light the joint, inhaling a long, exaggerated pull. Once the end is burning bright, he holds it out to me. “You in?”

I always assumed that the first and last time I’d try weed would be in some frat boy’s dorm room during a miserable party that I’d get dragged to as a pity invite from my overbearing future freshman-year roommate. The prospect of trying it surrounded by people that I don’t hate never occurred to me.

I grasp the joint with sandy fingers. Andrew explodes with excitement as he coaches me on how to smoke. Even Sage reluctantly gets pulled in, demonstrating how to hold it and not look dumb. I didn’t even know smoking is something that you need to be taught. I try the first time, and nothing happens. Then a second time, and again, nothing. But then the third time . . .

I cough so hard that my ribs nearly shatter.

“Attagirl,” Andrew cheers. “How do you feel?”

I take a deep breath of ocean air. Everything inside of me, every part of my body, every emotion, begins to take on an amber glow, slowly at first, then all at once.

“Like a temple and an amusement park.”

5 MINUTES LATER

5 MINUTES LATER
5 MINUTES LATER

MY MIND SLOWS AS THE BASS FROM THE speaker slips into my body through my fingertips, plunged deep into the cold sand. My heart pounds in rhythm with the song, generating an inner warmth that radiates up toward my brain and culminates in a visceral experience of all-out bliss. It feels like someone took an invisible string between my eyebrows and pulled the top of my face upward, then let the bottom half sink into my chest. How long have I been lying on my back for? I crack my toes and it feels good. I touch the sand and it feels good. I look at Mac and he looks at me and I laugh and he laughs and it feels good.

"I think I love weed," I announce.

"Willkommen, bienvenueeeee," Andrew breaks into a syrupy dance routine from the musical *Cabaret*. Sage joins Andrew, performing a burlesque sequence, seductively removing their Crocs in the smoky light of the campfire. I guess *quiet* isn't synonymous with *shy*. Andrew stiffens as he watches Sage, fully entranced, eyes charged. Mac notices, too, and sort of chuckles and rolls his eyes. I don't realize I'm laughing so hard until a viscous cramp seizes my left side, twisting with each exhale. I curl into fetal position, writhing.

"We good here?" Mac asks, eyes dancing with amusement. He joins me on the sand, sitting close, but not close enough.

"I feel like a hot air balloon." I turn toward him. "The bonfire is the fuel thingy. I think I'm going to float away."

He inches the tip of his shoe over ever so slightly so that it taps against mine. Suddenly, I'm no longer afraid of drifting away.

"Better?" he asks.

I've never seen anyone so beautiful so close. If my arms didn't feel like empty paper towel rolls stuffed with Jell-O right now, I'd reach up and touch his face.

I sigh. "Better."

20 MINUTES HIGH AF

20 MINUTES HIGH AF
20 MINUTES HIGH AF

EVERYONE STARTS TALKING ABOUT COLLEGE and relationships and art and other important stuff. I feel the overwhelming urge to say something Big. Something Important. Really add to the moment. But the only sentence my brain can form is: "My mouth is dry."

Mac bursts out laughing. "Let's get you some water." He stands, offering to help me up. I let him. His hand is warm.

"My legs don't remember how to be legs," I admit once on my feet. "Actually, I think my legs are hot dogs." I poke my thigh and feel the weight of walking around Earth in this meat sack. "Yup. Definitely hot dogs."

"You'll get used to it." Mac passes me a cup, and I wordlessly down five Solo cups of water within one minute. I love water. A Top-Tier Invention of Mother Earth.

He's watching me with a smile. He bites his lip.

"What?" I ask.

"Do you want to see the tide pools?" He rushes his hands nervously through his hair. "With me?"

"Mac. Let me tell you something." I grab his shoulders. "I have literally never wanted to do anything more in my life than see the tide pools right now."

He beams and offers an arm as we walk toward the massive rock formation to the right of the bonfire setup. It's quieter over here. Low tide at this hour means that the ocean has pulled itself far back enough to reveal dozens of mini aquariums nestled between gaps in the oceanic rock. I climb onto the main strip of coral, still slick from the water, and try not to step on anyone or anything. Mac leads the way out to a larger rock close to where the waves are breaking. He takes out his phone's flashlight and kneels down, shining the light at something below his feet. "Yo, you have to see this." He looks at me with an expression that can only be described as glee. Pure, childlike joy.

I wobble over and crouch down beside him. "What am I looking at?"

"We found a lil starfish." He points down and—lo and behold—an actual, living Patrick Star has plastered itself against a wall of coral. It's too dark to see much else, but the pink star shimmers beneath the water.

"I wish I was a starfish," I find myself saying. Never in my life have I had such a thought before, but tonight, it feels true.

"You can totally be a starfish. All you have to do is tap into your cosmic connection." He presses his fingers against his temples.

"You're nuts."

"Nah, hear me out." He shifts on the rock, and I inch a little closer. The smell of the bonfire and ocean lingers in his hair. "Humans are obsessed with seeing everything as separate from one another—you versus me, the sand versus the sky, the ocean versus the air. But it's not that simple. It's easier to think of the world as made up of all these separate things because that helps us feel stable. Like if I can look in the mirror and say, 'I am Mac. This is me. I am my own thing, and I'm definitely not connected to anything else,' that makes me feel grounded. But the truth is that we're all entangled. The same cosmic dust that created our planet made our cells and the ocean and these starfish. So, if we take seriously this idea that we're all entangled, then the idea that everything is separate from one another becomes less and less possible. It's crazy to believe that we're not all connected."

I stare at Mac, dumbfounded. "You're high."

He shoots me a goofy grin. "I am." We crumble into each other, laughing harder than the force of the wave that crashes against the rock in front of us. "I mean it, though. We're all entangled, Niarah."

He gives me this hazy look that makes my skin vibrate.

"You've been laughing a lot tonight," he says, inching closer. "You must be warming up to me."

"Trust me, it's the weed. You're usually not this funny."

He feigns a wound to his chest before letting his movements become slow. His gaze drifts from my eyes to my mouth, then back up to my eyes. I become acutely aware of how chapped my lips are and almost reach into my pocket for ChapStick, but I'm too afraid to do it. Afraid to do anything to bring more attention to my lips. Not while all I can think about are his.

"Sooo . . ." Mac says, fiddling with the drawstrings of his hoodie. "Are you, uh, seeing anyone?"

"As in hallucinations?" I thought it was only weed, not like shrooms or anything. I wave my hand in front of my eyes to check. "No. I think I'm good."

Mac gently knocks his shoulder against mine. "No. Like . . . dating."

My head snaps up. Panic mode initiated. "Wh-why?"

"Uhm." He faces me, his eyes turning heavy. His body is loud in its closeness. "It's been fun. Hanging out at Camp Doom. So, I was wondering—"

Is he leaning in? Oh god, he's leaning in. This was not supposed to happen in real life. In my head, sure, but out here, in the wild? Unprecedented. All my plans to keep him at a distance start sounding real stupid when he puts his hand on my knee. What does he see in me? I have no clue what I have to offer him. Maybe he's bored. Maybe I'm bored. Could that be it? My pulse thrums in my ears. My throat goes bone dry. No, I don't think that I'm bored. I don't know what I'm feeling right now. But I do think that I want this. No—not think. I want this. Just once.

A foreign impulse takes over me. I cut him off by rushing toward him, but without any smoothness, it comes out like a jack-in-the-box. The movement is erratic and it startles him. And even worse, I miss.

I sort of almost kiss the side of his mouth. Sloppily, awkwardly. When he touches my arm lightly to politely steer me back in the right direction so that our lips can actually touch, I cough in his face. Like a toddler. I wince. "Sorry. It's the weed."

He smiles patiently. "It's okay."

Mac recovers, placing his hand back on my knee as he inches closer. He guides my hand up to his shoulder. My fingers wander into his hair, and it's even softer than I imagined. He looks good. Really good. And the wind's tossing his waves just right. And the moonlight's hitting his chain, making it twinkle. And his voice is low. Our eyes flutter shut and he inches closer and I'm totally focused and not freaking out at all until something cold stirs in the back of my mind.

All good things come to an end.

My eyes shoot open. Mac senses the change and pulls back.

"You okay?" he asks, a crease forming in his brow.

"Sorry, I'm fine," I wheeze, removing my hands from his hair. I sit up straight and press a couple of curls back over my shoulders.

Mac watches me warily. Confusion and worry flood his face with a sincerity that makes the corners of my eyes prickle. Spiders crawl across my brain. An all-too-bright spotlight zeroes in on my stage-fright lungs. I start to think about my breathing and, in doing so, forget how to do it right.

This is pointless.

I wake up every day depressed. There's no color in anything. And yet here I am, on the fringe of a different feeling. One that feels something like happiness. But the feeling is so new. Too new. I'm afraid it's not strong enough to stand up to the depression. What would happen to me and Mac if my fledgling happiness is too weak? What will happen when he leaves? Will it have been worth risking this friendship—the very thing that brought me this happiness in the first place?

My breath becomes unsteady, shallow in my throat. My palms sweat. Mac looks at me with nothing but kindness and patience. That's when it dawns on me.

I don't know what the fuck I'm doing.

I swerve, stumbling back away from Mac and onto the rocks below.

"I'm sorry. Sorry. Are you okay?" He jumps up and keeps

apologizing profusely. I wave my hands in his face, begging him to shut up.

"I'm fine. Sorry. I'm just high. Wow. I . . . This is . . ." Hell? Literal, actual hell? I start to walk fast, but I slip on a slick rock. My left foot falls ankle deep into a tide pool. I try to pull it free, but it's stuck.

Mac launches over. "Shit. Let me help you."

"No, I'm okay." I brush him away, but he tries anyway.

"Please let me help you."

"I said I'm fi—"

A wave comes up tall and dark, crashing closer than the previous ones. Mac flinches, covering his head with his arms, but I'm still tugging at my leg, so the wave hits me entirely. I am soaked. I pull my leg free and sprint away.

35 MINUTES HIGH AF

35 MINUTES HIGH AF
35 MINUTES HIGH AF

AS I SPEED-WALK BACK TO THE FIREPIT, I TEXT Ox, asking him to pick me up *now.* He responds immediately, saying he'll be here in ten minutes. We live way more than ten minutes away from the beach, so he must've decided to hang out in the area for some reason. I'm grateful.

I find Andrew and Sage back at the firepit. "Late-night swim?" Andrew asks when he sees that I'm completely drenched.

Mac looks like he's about to come over and ask to talk. Panic seizes my chest. "Andrew, do you have more weed?"

He grins mischievously. "Darling, I always have more weed."

Sage pulls a half-burned joint out from their pocket and passes it to Andrew. He cups the end, shielding it from the wind as he tries to light it for me, but the flame keeps extinguishing. I glance at Mac as he sulks over by the boulders. I feel worse and worse by the second. I shouldn't have come tonight.

"Let me try," I say to Andrew, swiping the lighter from his hand. I need this. ASAP. I try to spark the thing once, twice, without luck. It's tricky because my movements are still syrupy from earlier, but I want to be higher. Further away from the humiliation of the past ten minutes. On the third try, the lighter's flame finally holds. I rush it toward the joint before it re-extinguishes, copying what Andrew did earlier. I light the end at last, but it smells weird.

"Holyshitniarah," Andrew shouts. Sage's hand flies to cover their mouth.

I don't know why they're freaking out. But the smell is stronger now. My face gets warm, and I realize what is happening.

I cross my eyes to glance up at my bangs, burning alongside the end of the joint. Everyone gapes.

This is fine.

This. Is. Fine.

THE COME-DOWN

THE COME-DOWN
THE COME-DOWN

SAND INFILTRATES MY SHOES AS I RUN TOWARD the parking lot. Ox is waiting in his truck. I rip open the door, slide inside, and tell him to drive. He gives me a concerned look, like he knew all along that I'd ask him to pick me up early. Thankfully, though, he doesn't say anything about that, or about the fact that my barbecued bangs are stinking up the car. Instead, he passes me a paper bag. It's warm, borderline too hot, as it sears the tops of my thighs. The smell cuts through my adrenaline. It's french fries. I shove a handful in my mouth. If I focus on the taste of salt on my tongue, maybe I can suppress the urge to cry. The munchies kick in and I start eating like there's no tomorrow. I don't feel better, but at least I'm distracted. Ox really knows how to stage a rescue. He puts on some music—early Radiohead. Melancholy as hell. Devastatingly on point. We drive home in silence.

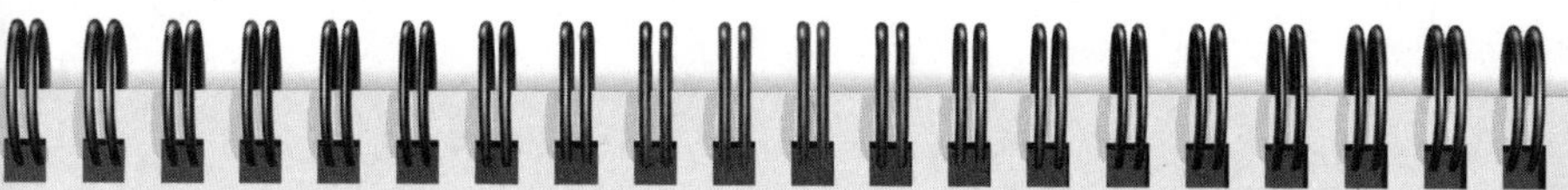

SURVIVAL TIP #29: KNOTS

~~You may think of yourself as an individual, separate from others, but we're all entangled, so learning to tie~~

The bowline is arguably the most useful knot in the prepper world. Its sturdy design can hold heavy weight without the threat of untying, with the knot increasing in tightness the more pressure that is added.

When to use it:

- Hanging objects and food from trees
- Constructing an emergency shelter
- Securing gear to a trailer
- Constructing a loop style handle to carry heavy objects
- Tying an anchor to a post so you can lower yourself out of a burning building

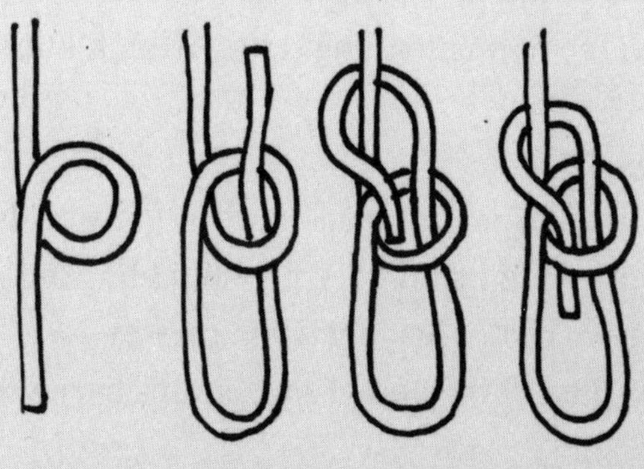

DISTANCE

DISTANCE
DISTANCE

WHEN MAC WALKS INTO THE BACKYARD FOR Camp Doom prep, I don't know what's worse: the fallen look on his face or the fact that he gets right to the point.

"What happened the other night?" He asks it in a way that feels a little rehearsed, as if he said it to himself a few times to hype himself up.

"Do we have to talk about this?" My tone is biting.

"We don't *have* to do anything. I just wanna know."

"Why?"

Mac frowns. "Because."

After burning off my bangs, I had to get braids to hide the damage. I flip a rogue braid over my shoulder and roll my eyes. "It doesn't matter. You're leaving soon anyway."

"I'm not leaving 'til the end of August. It's barely July. I'm here all summer."

He says *all summer* like it actually means something. "Yeah, okay. 'All summer.' Got it." I put it in air quotes, dripping with sarcasm.

"The world's not ending tomorrow," Mac mumbles. I glare back at him. For a second, I think he's about to make fun of me, but he takes a deep breath and chooses a different path. "So, what, then? Since I'm leaving for school, I can't meet anyone new?"

"Maybe you should spend break with your friends." The urge to push him further snarls at the fringe of my consciousness. "Or another girl. I'm sure you'd like that."

Mac staggers backward. I keep my eyes glued to the floor. A metallic taste spills across my tongue as I bite the inside of my cheek so hard that it draws blood. There's the sound of him gathering his things, then the sound of him stomping away. "Maybe I will."

I hammer the wall with all my strength. "Good."

TOUGH CROWD

TOUGH CROWD
TOUGH CROWD

I'M SURPRISED BY HOW HARD IT FEELS WORK-ing on Camp Doom without Mac to help carry things around. I got used to him too fast. Surprise morphs into frustration. This is why teamwork, contrary to popular belief, does not "make the dream work." It makes you weaker. I decide to do push-ups. I should get stronger. If everything goes south, people might try to mess with me because I'm young and sort of frail or whatever, but imagine how shocked they'd be if I rolled up my sleeves and was actually ripped. Like action-hero, Marvel ripped. That'd be fun. I hit nine push-ups before my arms start quaking. The kitchen door swings open behind me.

"Want to come to lunch with us?" Mom asks.

My arms give out from under me, and I fall on my face. I catch my breath on my stomach before rolling onto my back. "Depends," I say. I use my hand to shield the sun above me to get a better look at her. "Where are you going?" If it's pupusas or dumplings, I'm in, but if it's salad again, I'd rather scavenge for frozen food in the back of the freezer.

"I was thinking of—" she begins, but then her energy shifts. She blinks rapidly. "Where did you get that shirt?"

I don't pay attention to what I wear each day, so I have to look down to know what she's talking about. I dust away the dirt from my failed push-ups. "Yard sale."

Mom crosses her arms. "Go inside and take it off."

"What? No." I instinctively clutch the fabric. "C'mon, it's funny."

The shirt on trial is black with a giant thumbs-up on it below the words *Not Actively Suicidal.*

She lets out a slow exhale that sounds more like a hiss. "It is *not* funny."

I look at the shirt again and—I promise I'm not trying to be an asshole—laugh a little. This sets her off.

"Why would you wear something like that?"

"Because I'm . . . not actively suicidal?" The shirt feels pretty self-explanatory to me.

"When you wear stuff like that, it sends the wrong message." Mom's tone and volume register a hair below a full-blown shout.

I couldn't disagree more. I've never seen an item of clothing that sends a more accurate message.

This isn't breaking news; she knows the deal. I don't always feel strongly about being alive. Nine times out of ten, it's a mundane thought, not backed by any plans or harm or anything active. But I don't always want to exist. It sucks to admit, but it's true. Yeah, it's serious, but also, it's not as serious as it sounds. I have a phone number for a therapist I talk to every now and then. I know all the calming breath techniques. I'm safe and there's nothing to worry about, but yeah, I mean it.

"Everything okay out here?" Ox says, opening the door to peek his head out. Our argument must've disrupted his snack session because he's discreetly wiping potato chip dust off his fingertips.

"Niarah thinks that her ending her life is something to joke about," my mom snaps.

"The joke isn't about ending my life, it's about *not* ending it," I explain. "The fact that humans are even alive is the biggest joke, actually. The big bang happened and now we're all here, composed of star dust, arguing about novelty T-shirts." I gesture between us. "Like, life is kind of a joke, if you really think about it."

My mom's eyebrows shoot up her forehead. "Are you high?"

"What? No." I suck my teeth. "You don't get it."

"You're right. I don't. So, take that shirt off." She turns to walk back into the house, where Ox is still hovering awkwardly by the door.

"The fact that it says I'm *not* actively suicidal should be good news considering—"

"I SAID TAKE IT OFF." When her eyes meet mine, they're glossy and full of rage. It sends a spear through my chest.

I get up quickly, brushing past her into the house. "*This* is why I don't talk to you," I mumble just loud enough for her to hear. I storm down the hall and shut my bedroom door behind me. I assess my reflection in the mirror.

Okay, maybe it's not funny. But at least it's honest.

I stuff my mouth with the T-shirt and scream until my throat spasms.

FITTER HAPPIER

FITTER HAPPIER
FITTER HAPPIER

IT'S SO DISORIENTING BEING ALIVE. ONE SEC-ond, you're reading the news, and it's the most heinous shit, and then *boom*—you're back in school. Business as usual. A headline will say that some horrible politicians got caught embezzling millions of welfare dollars to build a private golf course. Then you go to class and your teachers are like, "Hey, it's time to learn about sine and cosine." Then you check again and it says that the politicians didn't just steal the money, but also struck a deal with foreign leaders in another country to authorize an air strike against innocent people in exchange for tax breaks on the cost of their private jets. Then in class, someone's flexing about their SAT score and there's a pop quiz on tangents and you have no idea what a tangent has to do with calculus. Back online, there's a full-blown war happening and apparently the private jets leaked their fuel into the sea and now the Pacific Ocean is on fire and all the coral reefs are dead. Then in class, they're like, "Actually, if you don't pass this quiz on sine, cosine, and tangent, you will fail and be stuck in high school forever and won't get into college and will never have a job, good luck!" And that's it. That's the boiling cauldron of terror we live in.

And somehow, despite it all, I'm still expected to write this stupid capstone project.

What a scam.

AIRWAY

AIRWAY
AIRWAY

I DON'T FEEL LIKE GOING TO COLOR OUTSIDE today. I want to sleep in. But Mac hasn't shown up at Camp Doom since our fight, so I have no choice if I want to rake in any PE hours this week.

Everything is tolerable. Whenever my pace aligns with Mac's, he either hangs back or speeds up. I pretend like I am suddenly very into trees and keep my eyes anywhere but on him. Mac is doing the annoying thing where he's acting like everything's fine. I am doing the reasonable thing of acting like I don't care. Sage is watching us silently. Andrew is insisting that it's just a few more meters to go.

There's a secret waterfall—a mini one, much less majestic than the big one that we're all on our way to see with the group—but the water's supposed to be turquoise. I'll admit that it sounds kind of cool. So, while everyone else is sitting down for lunch, we're wandering off, promising to not stray too far.

"That doesn't count as a hobby," Mac complains to Andrew. Sage nods in agreement, but their eyes are mischievous, clearly enjoying taking Mac's side just to piss Andrew off.

Andrew scoffs. "If it were up to me, all I'd do is cook, eat, take hot baths with that honey lavender bath bomb . . . drink, smoke . . . watch British competitive baking shows after smoking, and yeah, make out with people."

There's silence for a beat, until—

"Andrew, that literally is all that you do," Mac says.

"Oh, well, yay me, then. Life rocks and I win." Andrew flashes a peace sign and jumps over a troll-shaped rock. "You're quiet today," Andrew says to me. I hate being called out. I shrink a little. "Jeez, it was just an observation—don't look at me like you want to rip my eyes out."

"Sorry," I mumble.

Sage types on their phone and holds it up to the three of us:

I don't think you guys know where we're going.

"We have a general sense," Mac says.

I scoff, and he narrows his eyes at me. A *general sense* is boy-speak for *he's lost*. We're lost. So, I see this big boulder and suggest we climb it to get a better vantage point. It's all fine and normal, but kind of difficult, so we're out of breath when we reach the top, but the thing is, Mac never catches his breath. He starts wheezing. At first I think he's joking, but then I see tears gather at the corners of his eyes.

His breath strains like an engine that won't start. The sound is chilling.

"What do we do? Do we call someone? Fuck, fuck, fuck,

fuck—" Andrew's panic builds as Mac presses his chest harder and harder.

Eyes wide, Sage types furiously and shoves the screen at Mac:

INHALER?????

Mac frantically pats the back pocket of his faded jeans. "Shit," he croaks out. "I left it with the group." I conjure a quick image of Mac's backpack leaning against a rock back at the lunch spot with the others.

I pull my phone out to call for help. No service.

"I'll go get his inhaler," I volunteer, but I hesitate, disturbed by his erratic breath. Clumps of hair stick to his forehead where he's started to sweat.

"Hurry," Andrew insists.

Right. I slide down the boulder, landing roughly on my hands and knees. My knee stings where a rock scraped and broke skin. I sling my backpack over my shoulder and get ready to run, but then I remember. *My backpack.* My EDC.

I slouch the bag off and tear at the zipper. I rummage through the bag's contents until I find what I'm looking for. I'm not sure it will work, but it's better than nothing.

I retrieve a tiny glass vial and toss it at Mac's face. He catches it, coughing.

"Dab the oil on your hand and rub it on your chest." His brows knit together as he stares back at me. "Do it."

He follows instructions between coughs while I keep ransacking my bag. I retrieve the thermos of hot coffee that I packed this morning when I heard that we were meeting at the ungodly hour of 6:30 a.m. I throw it at Sage, who catches it with one hand. "Make him drink this."

Mac places his head between his knees. He rubs some more oil on his chest and takes tiny sips from the thermos with the help of Andrew.

I hold my breath until I know for sure that Mac finally catches his. He winces on the inhale, but after a few minutes, he gives us a shaky thumbs-up.

From the top of the boulder, Sage stares at me, dumbfounded. Andrew marvels at the thermos in one hand and the tiny glass vial in the other. "What is all this stuff?"

"Eucalyptus oil can ease tightness in the chest. Caffeine has similar properties to asthma medications and can help temporarily improve airway functions."

"Where'd you learn that?" Andrew asks.

"Online."

"Impressive," Sage says with a nod.

I freeze. I've never heard their voice before. Did they actually just talk to me?

Andrew's mouth falls open. He does a double take at Sage and raises an eyebrow. Sage gives him a soft smile and a shrug in response, which makes Andrew let out a booming howl. "All right, Niarah! You made the cut!" He tosses an arm over Sage's shoulder and points at me, cheering, "Ten points for Doomsday Girl."

At this, Mac chuckles slightly, but it looks like it hurts to do so. His head remains tucked between his knees as he sits as still as possible. Once it's clear that a full-blown asthma attack isn't coming, I scramble back up the boulder to join them.

I put my palm between Mac's shoulder blades, hoping that it will somehow help. He reaches for my hand and squeezes it, hard, but I don't dare say anything. We sit like this, Mac shaking slightly, until he brings his head back up.

"What does it feel like?" I ask, which is a stupid place to start, but I don't know what else to say. I never know what to say when other people are going through it.

Mac makes his hand into a fist and massages his chest. His other hand remains intertwined with mine. I pretend like I don't mind. I pretend like I don't notice Andrew and Sage noticing with matching smirks.

"It's like getting the wind knocked out of you, then trying to get it back by breathing through a rapidly disintegrating cardboard straw."

"Sounds horrible."

"Other people have it worse." Mac's face hardens into a deep-set frown. Andrew and Sage exchange a knowing, concerned glance. Am I missing something here? I want to press further, but I feel him squeeze my hand again. This is all the information I'll get from him on the topic. For now, at least.

When he finally sits up straight, Mac gives me a long up-down. My right knee is bleeding. Tiny bits of gravel have dug their way into my palms and my hair from my slide down the boulder. I must look feral. Andrew and Sage focus on me as well. When none of them say anything after a few more seconds, I smooth my hair back to try to salvage the situation. Is it that bad?

Sage breaks the silence by kicking a heavy pebble as they climb down the boulder. We follow, making our way down slowly. Sage and Andrew jog ahead to get Mac's inhaler, just in case. While we wait, Mac examines my knee again. "You got a first-aid kit in that backpack, Dora the Explorer?"

I pull it out because, duh. Of course I do.

He responds with a soft laugh, his eyes crinkling at the corners. "Sit."

I do. He cleans the wound on my knee and places the bandage carefully. His hand lingers on my knee. He traces the seam of the bandage with his finger before gently cupping the back of my leg. Goose bumps erupt across my skin, slick with sunscreen and sweat.

His voice is low. "Does it hurt?"

I shake my head.

"Good," he hums. He doesn't move his hand from my leg. What is he thinking? Is my skin too rough? Can he hear how heavily I'm breathing?

All thoughts stop when he drags his hand up from my calf onto my thigh—low enough to remain respectful, but high enough to feel important. That emotion from the bonfire rushes back. The one that rustles my breath and makes my skin buzz. What if this feeling is here to stay? What if I can't stop it?

Mac gathers himself, breaking the trance. Our eyes skirt away from each other as we stand. He starts down the trail again, but not before giving me one last look. "I'm very lucky to be friends with the girl who's prepared for anything."

A GIFT FROM MAC

A GIFT FROM MAC
A GIFT FROM MAC

MAC CARRIES A HEAVY CARDBOARD BOX OUT from the trunk.

"What's that?" I ask.

"It's a gift for saving my ass." He huffs as he plops the box onto the ground. "Open it," he says, trying but failing to conceal his excitement.

I get a little self-conscious, but I do it anyway. When I unfold the top and peek inside, laughter rips through my chest.

1.4
EXPLOSIVES
S
1

PERFECT FIT

PERFECT FIT
PERFECT FIT

"FOR PROTECTION," MAC SAYS AS I PICK UP one of the novelty ninja stars, spinning it in my hand.

"It looks like you cleaned out the entire surplus store," I say.

"I may or may not have forgotten to take my medicine this morning, so I may or may not have slipped into impulsive mode and bought every item that caught my attention." Behind me, he leans against his car. "Thrifting with ADHD isn't always productive, but it is always fun." Even with a gas mask covering his face, I can feel him smiling as he tips his head at me like a cowboy.

I put on my own gas mask and face him. "Thank you, Mac."

"No big deal." Behind the faded plastic lenses, Mac's eyes shy away, retreating to the floor. I feel a rush of affection tighten my chest. I let the feeling carry me into his arms. I hug him, and honestly, we're both surprised. I'm not an affectionate person—even my mom and I only have a triannual hug at Christmas, my birthday, and hers. So, when I wind my arms around Mac's torso, he tenses up for a second before settling in. He feels taller with my head against his chest. His cotton shirt is soft against my cheek. I wonder what body wash he uses because he smells comforting, like—

Mac pulls back a little to look down at me. His arms linger around my back, eyes partially obscured by the ridiculous gas mask. Still, I can see the silent question he's holding.

Right. This hug is too long. I tear away, nearly tripping over a sprinkler as I shake off the embarrassment of having not even hugged Mac, but *held* him. Embraced him. Like a character in an old black-and-white movie. Humiliating.

"I appreciate the, uhm, donations to Camp Doom," I say. "Warm regards."

Warm regards? Where do I think I am? Trapped in a postcard?

"I'm glad you like it," he says, absentmindedly rubbing the spot on his shirt where my head had been moments ago. "There's one more thing."

"Mac, this is already a lot of stuff—"

My words stop when he touches my shoulder. His hand is warm. Firm. "Last thing, I promise."

He opens the back seat of the car and retrieves a brown cardboard box, painted with flowers. I wait for him to pass it to me, intrigued by this last twist, but he hesitates. "If you don't like them, it's fine."

"Okay," I say, still waiting. He continues to clench the box, suddenly looking nervous. "Mac, I'm sure I'll love it."

He shakes his head. "Yeah, sorry, here." He hands me the box, skirting his eyes away as he does.

I open the last gift. It's perfect. A pair of old-school-looking hiking boots, brown leather with thick burgundy shoelaces.

"On the hike, you said that your sneakers weren't comfortable, and since you're going on the backpacking trip with us at the end of the summer, I figured you need a proper pair."

It's so thoughtful that I don't know what to say. The boots are cool. Really cool. I like that he went for something classic and rugged, no frills, no colors, just a pair that screams 1970s nostalgia. We haven't known each other long enough for him to know my taste, but somehow, he nailed it.

On the heel, there's a Post-it note that says *Reserved for Mac* with a timestamp of a date on it from three weeks ago. "Sorry," he says, frantically reaching for the note and crumbling it before shoving it into his back pocket.

If he reserved these for me that long ago, that meant that he picked these out before the asthma thing. He must've put them on hold not long after we went on that very first hike. He shoves his hands into his pockets, shoulders pitching upward as he tries to look chill.

"Can I try them on?" I say at last.

"Definitely." We sit on the curb and he talks me through how to see if the shoes are a good fit, then launches into a weirdly spirited conversation about the importance of choosing the right socks while backpacking (always wool, never cotton).

"I'm happy you're coming on the backpacking trip," he says.

"I'm only going because it's good research for the survival guide."

"Suuure." He smiles at me with a flash of something I've come to recognize as signature Mac mischief. "Ready to try them out?" He grabs his own hiking shoes from the car now and slips out of his Vans. "I know the perfect spot."

NOT-A-DATE

NOT-A-DATE
NOT-A-DATE

"FUCK THESE STAIRS, DUDE," I GROAN AS I attempt to pull myself up despite the oppressive heat encouraging me to roll back down the hill.

"You're doing great," Mac cheers, leading the way. It was a short five-minute drive down a quiet, windy street that I had never noticed before. Mac parked at the foot of this hill. He says this is his favorite secret hike in the neighborhood—a hidden staircase that leads to . . . Well, I have no idea where it leads, but right now, given how hard it is, I'm assuming hell?

"Break?" he suggests.

"Yes, please." I plop down in the middle of the stairs and rest my head between my knees. "I told you I'm out of shape."

"And I told you that's totally fine." He joins me on the sole step with even a sliver of shade. "When we get to the top, it'll be worth it, I swear."

We sit quietly as I catch my breath. At the bottom of the

staircase, a couple of skaters gather to shoot a video, attempting to land a trick after speeding down the steep hill.

"Do you skate, too?" I ask Mac.

"Not really," he says.

"Isn't it the same thing as surfing?"

"Eh, sort of. The skills transfer, but not my confidence." One of those tiny brown lizards that rule LA scurries past our feet. "If I die skating, I crack my head open and bleed out and that's it. But if I die surfing, the ocean will swallow me up."

"And then a shark eats you."

"Exactly. If I die prematurely, I would love to become part of the food chain." He pulls a water bottle from his backpack and passes it to me. He put ice in it. The water's perfectly cold.

"On our backpacking trip, if some crazy shit happens and we get stranded, would you eat me, Sage, and Andrew?" I ask.

"I'm a vegetarian."

"Don't be boring." I pass back the ice water.

"Eating all three of you feels like overkill," he replies between gulps.

"Would you eat at least one of us?"

He wipes his mouth. "Niarah, I would definitely not eat you."

"Well, that's stupid, because I would eat you."

"Brutal." He hands me a granola bar.

"After a week, respectfully. I'm not a monster."

"Promise you'd give me a funeral first?"

"No. Funerals are for the living, and in that case, I'd be the living, eating you, so I wouldn't want a funeral to ruin my meal." I point at his right boot. "Shoelaces."

He groans and begins his journey to tie it. "You're hard to negotiate with."

I lean back, settling into the break. “You give up easy.”

“No, I don’t. I just pick my battles wisely,” he says.

“What’s your next battle, then?”

There’s a moment where we lock eyes for a second longer than we’re supposed to. A thrill runs through my body. He inches closer, our foreheads nearly touching. “You really wanna know?”

“Yes.” I force myself to hold his gaze. The moment lingers. Things unsaid—feelings unsaid—swoop within reach. Any second now, one of us will say or do something that can’t be taken back.

The crack of the skateboard makes us both jump. Mac swears under his breath. I laugh nervously, shattering the charged silence. Words unsaid scatter into the wind.

“You never told me the story of how Mr. G roped you into Color Outside,” I say. The words spill out my mouth. I don’t even know why I’m bringing this up now. Maybe I’m just that desperate to stave off the charged silence between us?

“Long version or short version?” he asks.

“Honest version.”

He takes a deep breath. “Aight, so freshman year, I was on ‘a path,’ as Mr. G would say. The school resource officers were all over me. I was in the office a ton. Fighting constantly. Mad as hell.”

My ears perk up. One: I can’t imagine Mac mad. Two: I don’t like guys who fight. I have my reasons.

“But then, one time, the SRO threatened to call the cops. Luckily, a teacher stopped it, but she told my parents. And when my mom came to pick me up?” He lets out a hissing exhale. “One look and I was eviscerated. She was like, ‘Boy, if you don’t get your shit together, you’re about to find your behind in jail. These people won’t hesitate to throw your future away if you give them the chance.’ She told me how California has the highest incarceration rate per capita in America. And here, LA County, is the biggest incarcerator county, so—"

"So, we're living in the biggest incarcerator county in the biggest incarcerator state in the biggest incarcerator country in the entire world?" I finish his sentence. Not exactly the stats that usually come to mind when people think of California.

"Exactly," Mac says. "Anyway, she said that I needed to let go of whatever part of me made me want to . . . act up. She called Mr. G and told him that I needed to be in more extracurriculars. Something to calm me down."

"And that led to Color Outside?"

"That led to the environmental club, which led to a hike one Sunday, which led to an obsession of mine, which turned into cofounding Color Outside." There's a little swell of pride in his voice as he talks. It's sweet. "My mom told Mr. G that I needed to either pick trash, plant trees, or find God. I'm happy option two panned out for me."

His laugh is infectious. I join in.

"Anyway, I'm talking about myself too much," he says. I couldn't disagree more. I like his voice. A lot. He has one of the very few subtle LA accents that isn't too annoying. The long *a*'s and hard *i*'s hint at his bilingual abilities. The pacing of his sentences is calm.

"I want to know more about you," he says.

"Uhm . . ." An alarm goes off in my head. "Race to the top?" I jump up and sprint the final stretch of stairs. Dodging his personal questions is a cop-out and it's not fair. I know that. But still. I can't go there with him. Don't want to. So, instead, I steer us somewhere else.

The secret spot at the top of the hill is even cooler than I imagined. We can see everything: the white dome of Griffith

Observatory, the Hollywood sign in its bizarre yet iconic glory, the layers upon layers of rolling hills that surround Los Angeles, the colorful homes that occupy them. Sneakers hang from telephone wires that slash harsh lines across the backdrop of the downtown skyline in the distance. We stand in the shade as birds chirp around us. A tiny gopher runs from one hole to another as shiny-backed lizards chase one another around clusters of daisies. A breeze whisks through my braids.

When you look closely, Los Angeles has its charm.

We spend hours up here talking. About the crazy things we see online, dub versus sub, embarrassing memories from elementary school. I share with him my opinions but not my feelings. This is all I can give him. I hope it's enough. After a while, the sun dips behind the hills in the west. Warm amber light paints the succulents around us.

He was right. Despite the stairs, despite the heat, the view is worth it.

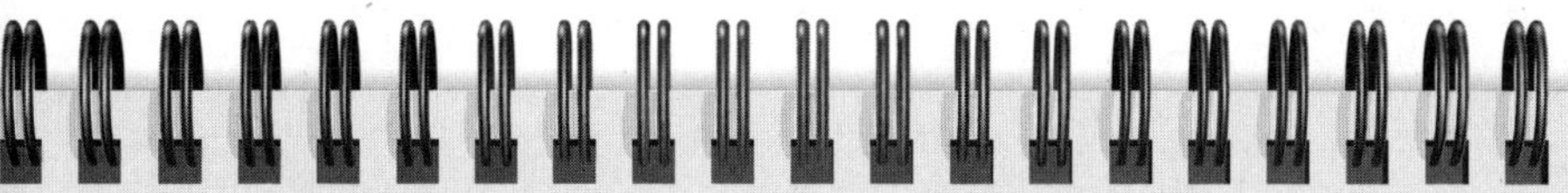

MAC'S TIP FOR BEING ALIVE #2

Once you said that nothing really matters and one day everything you are, everything you've been, everything you've ever done, will be forgotten. I don't agree.

The earth will remember you.

—Mac

NEW SKILLS

NEW SKILLS
NEW SKILLS

DYING LIGHT 2 **IS ON THE PLAYSTATION.** *Aggretsuko* is on my laptop. During commercials, I let the controller rest to check whatever's trending on my phone. I read the Urban Prepper Discord channel during the closing credits. Occasionally, I pause to google the stories behind various song lyrics that are stuck in my head. I am in my happy place.

"I don't know how you can function with all those screens flashing at you," my mom says as she appears in the doorway. Without knocking. Happy Place obliterated.

"I like to consume several different forms of media at the same time so that I can minimize the chances of a thought occurring."

She shakes her head. "Your generation."

"We're the worst, I get it."

"I'm, uhm, disappointed that you won't be able to come on vacation with us," Mom says. Her voice is sheepish. I feel bad that she has to speak so delicately with me.

"Yeah, I wish I could, but . . ."

"The backpacking trip, I know. I'm happy that you're doing that. Making friends."

My mom is standing right in front of me, yet suddenly, I miss her. The sensation hits like a football to the stomach. Before we moved to LA, I'd tell her everything. Every weird thing that happened at school, every bizarre dream, every theory about the inner workings of Bruce's mind. We spoke easily back then. We don't speak like that now. I don't know when exactly things changed.

"Well," Mom says gently, "I'll leave you to it."

Conversation over. I give her a polite, tight-lipped smile and return to my game. She retreats down the hall, her footsteps faint. I've always thought of my mom as loud. When did she get so quiet?

BAM-BAM-BAM.

There's a pounding on the door one room over, disrupting my flow. I pause my game to go investigate. It's Ox. Hammering at something in his new workspace.

"Perfect timing!" He beams. "Can you hold this for me?"

I relent for the sake of helping him finish this fast so that I can have some uninterrupted peace. "What are you building?" I ask.

"A bookshelf." He drives a nail through some wood. "Want me to make one for your project?"

"Uh . . ." A bookshelf could be nice. I don't want to bother, though. "I'm okay. Thanks."

"Well, it's easy to make one yourself, too. Want me to show you?"

I hesitate. The survival guide could use an entry about basic carpentry skills. Every good prepper should know how to build the essentials, right?

"Sure," I say.

Ox is clearly shocked but does his best to hide it. He puts on some solid music—Violent Femmes and X-Ray Spex—and shows me how to use the power saw.

It takes a couple of hours, but I make a miniature shelf. It's lopsided, but it works. I leave it by the door. I can't wait to take it to Camp Doom when the paint dries.

TONIGHT
TONIGHT
TONIGHT

< Andrew, Mac, Sage, and Me >

Andrew: it's my birthday. house party. be there.

Sage: no flaking allowed.

Mac: see you tonight, doomsday girl

FAMILY MATTERS

FAMILY MATTERS
FAMILY MATTERS

I HOLD THE COAT RACK NEXT TO THE FRONT door for balance as I slide on my shoes. “You’ve been going out a lot,” Mom says. I hate it when parents make obvious statements steeped with subtext that they’re refusing to be outright with. Just say what you mean, don’t do the whole I’ve-been-quietly-surveilling-you-and-waiting-for-you-to-confess-your-sins bit.

“You said that I should go out more,” I remind her. Mac should be here to pick me up any minute.

“Watch your tone,” she scolds.

I bite my lip and mumble an apology. She presses her nails, bright orange with a shine capable of blinding oncoming traffic, against her forehead.

“I should go.”   “I don’t want to argue.”

We speak at the same time. I stop and wait for her to try again.

“There’s something important that I have to talk to you about,” she says. “About your father.”

My stomach drops momentarily. I swallow and shake it off.

"Can we do this later?" Her track record for Serious Conversations isn't great, especially when it comes to my dad. They usually end in tears (hers, not mine). I give her a pleading look. *Just let me have a fun night, okay? Please?*

"Okay, later," she says, giving in.

I thank her and slip out the door. On the short walk to the curb, I shake at the mention of my dad. *Don't think about it, don't think about it, don't think about it.* I repeat the mantra until it sticks. By the time I reach Mac's car door, I've forced a grin back on my face. My smile is fake, but maybe if I wear it long enough, it will start to resemble something real.

SMELLS LIKE TEEN SPIRIT

SMELLS LIKE TEEN SPIRIT
SMELLS LIKE TEEN SPIRIT

SAGE IS SNEAKING UP BEHIND ME. EVER SINCE Mac's asthma attack in the park they've been reaching out—texting me about packing lists for the camping trip and offering to take me shopping for thermal underwear. Within seconds of stepping through the door of the house—a modern architecture masterpiece overlooking the hills of northeast Los Angeles—they pounce on my back, grinning. They smell like cedar and ginger, earthy with a kick of brightness. They pull me into the crowd. Nearly everyone stops to say hi to Sage or ask about the last song on their playlist or compliment their outfit—an all-black ensemble with a leather corset as the centerpiece. They give everyone a friendly wave or shoot off a quick text response and keep it pushing. The ease with which Sage weaves through the space gives me goose bumps as they tug me along, and I wonder if this is what it feels like to be liked.

Andrew is fixing me a drink. No, sorry, a *cocktail.* He demands that I call it as such out of respect. He pulls fresh mint from the windowsill herb garden and adds it to the drink, explaining the importance of incorporating fresh herbs into any beverage concoction. I laugh at first, but when I take a sip, it's incredible. Fruity with a hint of bitterness. I disclose that this is my first cocktail. Andrew laughs, saying that with him, it certainly won't be my last. A classmate walks by and requests a chef's choice beverage. A small crowd forms and soon Andrew's standing on a chair, shaking tumblers in the air, turning pours of cheap vodka stolen from older siblings into something memorable while the whole kitchen cheers. He tasks me with adding the garnish to each drink, and whenever someone compliments him, he points to me and calls me his sous chef. The alcohol, the flavors, the sound of Andrew's laughter as he throws his head back in glee at his own jokes start to warm me from the inside, and I wonder if this is what it feels like to unwind.

Mac is holding the patio door open as we step outside to get some air. A swoop of dark hair falls in front of his eyes as he leans against the balcony railing overlooking the city at night. He's wearing a crisp black tee with baggy, paint-splattered workpants and black-and-white Jordan 1s. From where we stand, we can peek into the homes of those who keep the lights on. In one house, we see a dog's face, pressed against the window and wearing a very out-of-season Santa hat. In another, we catch the bare back of a woman, climbing over a velvet couch. The accidental sighting of so much skin makes us blush, so we stop looking into windows. The porch light casts a sharp line across Mac's cheekbone. He tells me a story about the time he tried to hug a donkey when visiting family in Mexico and got fleas. We laugh so hard that I can hear the echo of our voices reverberate through the canyon. As soon as we manage to stop, our laughter bounces back to us and we start up all over again. He casts me a look that's destabilizing in its sincerity, and I wonder if I made a mistake fortifying the wall between us.

I am lying. I am telling myself that this party, all parties, are overrated. I'm convincing myself that this will be the last time I go out this summer. I'm thinking of an excuse to leave before I get too sucked in. I'm negotiating with myself how much longer I'll stay. A half hour, no, maybe an hour. It'd be rude to leave so soon, right? I'm resting against the wall, watching everyone else have fun. I'm fighting the feeling of disappointment that I've never really gone out before. I'm reminding myself to not get used to this. These people around me, this house with a view, the energy coursing through each room. None of these things will still be in my life come August. Everything is temporary. This is temporary. I am not going to get attached.

NOT SO ALONE

NOT SO ALONE
NOT SO ALONE

TIME STOPS WHEN I SPOT COREY THE CRETIN from school in the backyard. Why is he even here? Who does he know? My heart starts to race. Andrew, Mac, and Sage invited me—I have every right to be here. So why do I suddenly feel so exposed? Corey scrambles up from a lawn chair, so I speed into the kitchen. I reach into the fridge and grab a half-empty carton of eggs. I sneak out the front door. I know which car belongs to Corey.

I take myself on a little side quest. *Splat-splat-splat.*

No one has to know.

I feel both lighter and heavier when I slip back into Andrew's house. Stepping outside broke the spell and now I see everything with too much clarity. In one room, people take turns belting out karaoke. In another, competitors squeal in a game of Twister. I didn't even know people still played Twister. I grab another beer. I wander from room to room, the drinks hitting harder and harder as I cross each doorway. Is everyone actually having a good time or are they also just cosplaying the part of happy teenagers?

I slip into an empty room to take a break from it all. I can feel my Depression Brain warming up. Maybe if I sit by myself for a minute, I can prevent a full-blown spiral. But as soon as I lie down on the fluffy shag rug, someone tumbles in through the door, shutting it behind them.

"Thought I saw you running away."

My breath hitches until I see who it is. Andrew joins me on the rug that feels more like a stuffed animal than something designed to be stepped on.

"Is this your room?" I ask.

"For now. Though my brother Frankie is begging my parents to let him take it over once I leave for school." He reclines. "You like it?"

I take it in—the travel posters from around the world, the candles everywhere, the stacks of cookbooks. This is the room of someone who knows who they are, someone who cares about the nice things in life. It couldn't be more different from my own.

"It's amazing," I say.

I didn't mean for my voice to sound sad, but it must have because Andrew rolls over onto his stomach to examine me more closely. "Are you okay?"

"I'm fine." *Fine* doesn't sound very enthusiastic, so I try again. "I'm having fun. Really."

"But?" Andrew presses.

I close my eyes to try and quell the faint spinning sensation brought on by my last beer. I don't think I like alcohol. Maybe I should stop drinking.

"This summer is better than I thought it would be. But still. I'm . . . I don't know." Andrew's the one I spend the most time with besides Mac. He's the easiest to talk to. If I opened up to Andrew right now, I know he'd listen. But still, I hesitate. Would it even be worth it?

"You don't know what?" Andrew asks.

"Have you ever . . . Do you ever feel like you're not always that attached to the idea of being alive?"

My words hang in the air between us.

I don't know why I'm bringing this up to him. Maybe it's the drinks. Maybe it's the fact that I've always suspected that there's something shadowy lurking beneath Andrew's own chaos. I sit in silence, waiting for him to launch into the classic pep talk about beating depression or recommend that I turn to some online resources. But when he finally speaks, his voice is quiet. "Yeah."

I raise an eyebrow. "Really?"

"Not all the way, but like . . . I don't know. For the past few years, every birthday has been a surprise. Like I'm never entirely sure that I'm going to make it another year."

"I get it." I feel the same way. No plans, just this creeping feeling. Every holiday. Every last day of school. At the grocery store. At the mall. I'll be totally fine and then get this wave of shock, like, *Huh. How fascinating that I'm somehow still doing this.*

"I feel like an alien," I say. I roll over on the floor toward Andrew's leg. He's sitting up again, legs outstretched flat in front of him. I play with the fraying denim lining the hole in his jeans above his knee. "I wish I was an extrovert like you."

"Not an extrovert. Just afraid of being alone." Andrew places his hand on my head. It's sturdy and soothing. Maybe this is what having a brother would feel like. "Speaking of being alone, I suspect that there's somebody wandering around outside looking for you right about now."

I close my eyes. "I have no idea what you're talking about."

"C'mon." I can hear the mischievous smile in his voice as he says it. "You know Mac likes you." I stay quiet. "Oh, don't act like you don't know."

"It's not that I don't know, I just don't get it."

"Don't get what?"

Why he'd like a depressed girl. A prepper. A loner. A cynic. A nihilist. An insomniac. A pessimist. A me. I don't have to say the words aloud. Andrew can read it all in the wince that I can't contain when he presses further.

"Hey, no, don't do that," he says. "Don't do the thing where you let the demons win."

I smother my face with a pillow. "You have no idea how persistent the demons are. They're an elite squad. Highly trained. Top tier."

Andrew's laugh rings out between us. "Oh, ma'am, trust me, I know." He pulls the pillow off my face.

"Can we talk about you and Sage instead?" I beg.

The tips of Andrew's ears redden. "Nothing to talk about there."

"Sure. We all definitely believe that."

Andrew flicks my shoulder. "We are discussing *you and Mac.*"

I groan. "Okay, so, sure, Mac is . . ." He leans in eagerly. "Mac is great. He's nice, and goofy, and . . ."

"Hot," Andrew adds.

I sink my head onto my knees. "Yes, and hot."

Andrew lets out a feral scream and claps his hands in victory. "Wait, has he made a move yet? He won't tell me shit."

"But—" I cut him off before he gets too excited. "I can't do it. Can't get all involved. Even hanging out with you tonight, this is great but like . . . you're leaving so soon."

"Okay, first off, I'm *barely* leaving. I'm going to Irvine, which is less than two hours away, and I promised my mom I'd come home for dinner once a week. So, you and me?" He leans in. "This friendship doesn't have an expiration date." He kisses his palm, then places his hand on the crown of my head in a gesture of unexpected intimacy. "And don't be so dramatic. Mac is starting college, not dying."

"But we're friends and the minute that we cross that line, *if* we cross that line, everything will change. Different feelings will be at stake. It's way riskier."

"High risk, high reward," Andrew says.

"I don't want to get attached," I admit.

"Okay, then don't get attached, duh," Andrew says. "But you're clearly dying to kiss him, so . . . just kiss him."

CLOSER

CLOSER
CLOSER

WE ARE DANCING IN A CIRCLE. IT'S ME, Andrew, Sage, and Mac, plus three of their friends whose names I couldn't hear over the sound of the music. It's all of us, together. Until it's not.

Andrew swings his hips, roping Sage into a Macarena that turns into a conga line straight toward the drinks table. Two of the randos start whispering something into each other's ears while the last person splits off from the group. Suddenly, it's just me and Mac.

Mac raises an eyebrow, shrugging. He does a ridiculous shoulder wiggle paired with a goofy two-step. I laugh, both delighted that he's a horrible dancer and lightly mortified on his behalf. He offers me his hand, extending an invitation to join whatever barnyard jig he's putting on. I accept, mostly to put him out of his misery. We dance silly at first. Old school, '80s-style moves, face-to-face. There's at least two feet of space between us. More than enough room for Jesus and even a couple of Biblical plus ones, too. We frantically flap our arms up and down like chickens. But then the music changes.

A reggaeton hit comes on and the room erupts. Everyone who wasn't already dancing stampedes toward the center of the room.

I lean into Mac, shouting in his ear over the music, "Looks like this is for professionals only. Want to sit this one out?"

"Why would I want to sit this one out?" he asks.

"Dancing isn't your strong suit."

He looks at me aghast, feigning shock. I'm about to offer a half-assed *No offense* but the words never have the chance to form. Mac grasps the hand dangling by my left side and slowly guides it across my body to the beat of the music. I play along, smiling as I move in sync with a little whine in the hips. He draws his arm in an arc, prompting me to spin. I try to gain some momentum, but I'm met by resistance. I'm stopped at a half turn, standing right in front of him. He squeezes our joined hands and leans in to whisper in my ear, "Do you want to dance for real?"

I nod as the beat drops, and Mac pulls me closer.

This was another thing that I misunderstood about Mac: He is not a horrible dancer.

I grind on him jokingly at first. We're both laughing and I'm only touching him a little bit. But as more people fill the dance floor, the inches between us disappear. By the time the chorus hits, his head is bent against my neck, the chill metal of his chain pressed into my back. We are no longer laughing.

The silliness from before is gone, replaced with a steady grind. He grips my hips, lightly scratching at the denim of my jeans. The tiny vibration sends a shiver down my spine. I get caught up in the feeling of his hands somewhere new. His thumbs, miraculously cold despite the heat of the dance floor, find the stretch of skin where my crop top ends and my high-waisted shorts begin. His grip freezes, waiting to see what I want. I consider my options: stop things now before they escalate or see where this goes.

Right now, I choose this feeling.

My hands float on top of his. I intertwine our fingers and tighten his grip on my waist. I arch farther into him. By the end of the third song, we're against the wall. When I lean into his body, he pushes right back, letting gravity drive us closer and closer. I feel the muscles in his arms flex as he catches my whine. At one point, he gently gathers my hair all to one side so that he can find the space where my neck meets my shoulders. I feel his breath on my skin and lose the rhythm. I hear him say my name and—

"Sorry, it took forever to find cups." Andrew's voice shocks like an ice bath. In a split second, I jump away from Mac, snatch the drink from Andrew, down it in one gulp, and scramble as far away from Mac as possible given the density of the dance floor. I don't look at Mac's face. Instead, I slip back into the position where I was standing when we were all dancing in a circle, as friends. Back in the Safe Zone where some curly-haired boy who's about to leave at the end of the summer doesn't hook his thumbs centimeters under the seam of your shirt and you like it and want him to do it again and again and again and—

"Perfect timing," I say. "I was just leaving."

MAC'S TIP FOR BEING ALIVE #3

If we're not supposed
to dance,

Why all this music?

—Gregory Orr

SPEAKERS

SPEAKERS
SPEAKERS

"CHECK OUT THIS SPEAKER," I SAY. MAC AND I wander around the thrift store, scavenging for an old rug for Camp Doom now that the space is cleared out. As we move down the aisles, we keep bumping into each other like magnets. A brush of shoulders here, a lingering of eyes there. The past few days since Andrew's party have all been like this: laced with adrenaline that forms an edge around each interaction.

Mac strolls over to examine my surprise find. He stands closer than necessary. The speaker is giant—one of those vintage systems that has both a CD player and an aux cord in the central structure, bookended by two hefty black speakers. "Does it work?"

The weird sales guy with a mullet across the counter gives us a silent thumbs-up.

"Awesome. Let's get it," Mac says, crouching down to pull it into the cart.

"No, no." I reach out to stop him. "It caught my eye because it looks cool, that's all. We don't need it."

"Why not? If shit hits the fan, do you want to be stuck without music?"

I think on it for a second. "The speaker requires electricity. If the power grid fails, I won't be able to use it anyway."

"Okay, then I'll get you a backup generator or whatever."

"They're really expensive, you do not have the cash for a generator." I help at my mom's job for big events every now and then to earn a bit of money. I've been saving for over a year, but it'll probably take me three more before I can afford any serious equipment. Even when I finish Camp Doom, it'll never truly be complete until I have the generator. It's my prepper holy grail. The metaphorical cherry on top of my disaster sundae.

"Fine, then I'll get a job in the campus dining hall and send back money to you every month so that we can buy a generator. It'll be very Cold War of us."

I frown. "Well, if we—"

Mac throws up his arms. "Por los clavos de cristo, Niarah, just get the damn speaker."

We glare at each other. Weird Salesman takes our standoff as an opportunity to quietly nudge the speaker toward our cart. I look at him, indignant, while Mac just grins. Men. Always conspiring with one another.

I suck my teeth and reach for the speaker. Mac groans in relief. The machine is heavy enough to double as a weapon, so even if the power grid fails, at least it won't be a total waste of space. A pleasant surprise.

Back in Camp Doom, I set up the speaker. It's awesome. Much more powerful than the tiny Bluetooth pocket thing I usually carry around. It's not like the sound quality is better—in fact, it's worse—but the bass is louder and the whole thing vibrates when you turn it on. Maybe people in the early 2000s were onto something.

"Wanna pick the playlist?" I ask Mac.

"Nah, you go."

I fiddle with the aux cord. "I don't know if you'd like what I like."

He shrugs. "Try it and we'll see."

Can't say I didn't warn him. I turn up the volume and put on one of my favorite songs. It starts off slow with acoustic guitars that gradually morph into staticky electric ones. The drums are in the background at first but slowly rise to the front. The singer hums a subdued tune for the first minute before slipping into a growl. When the singer suddenly starts screeching at the top of her lungs, Mac drops the bottle of rug cleaner.

He laughs at his own jumpiness as he cleans up the mess. "I should've known this would be your style."

"Shut up." I pick up the roller to continue painting the door. I wasn't planning on painting at all, but Mac found out about the paint recycling program at the hardware store down the street and was able to get a couple of gallons of leftover white for free. I admit that the fresh paint brings out the colors of the yard through the windows.

"I don't understand a word she's saying," Mac says.

"Who cares?" I can feel her voice in my chest. It's splitting my eardrums. That's enough for me.

Mac watches as I hum along and pluck at an air bass, flicking tiny specs of paint on the floor. "Go ahead," he says, smiling. "Sing along."

"What?" My arms drop to my sides. "No."

"Do it."

"No."

"Why not?"

"I can't sing."

"All due respect, but neither can she." I'm about the hurl the roller brush at Mac, but he holds his hands up in defense. "Not an insult! This song goes hard. But you could do this."

"Not everyone can just 'do' this. It takes training. These singers—"

"Fine, I'll start." And without a moment of hesitation, Mac opens his mouth and starts bellowing like a banshee.

I rush over to slam my hand over his mouth. "Someone will think you're getting murdered."

He pokes my stomach and I bend over, accidentally freeing his mouth. "So what?"

He keeps screaming along and there's no stopping him. He uses his water bottle as a mic and thrashes around like the lead singer in Bad Brains. It's ridiculous. It's embarrassing. And, after the bridge, it's enough to get me to join in.

Mac passes me the hammer that we've been using to hang the wall hooks. I take a deep breath, then let out a warm-up snarl. The chorus crashes in and my voice crackles and singes at the edges. Mac takes his hair down and jumps around like a lunatic. A one-man mosh pit. I use the hammer as a mic for a few bars before a new idea strikes. Time to pivot this tool to its highest and best use: smashing a hole through the rotten wooden crate in the corner.

I swing the hammer through the crate like a divorcée with a vengeance. The motion ignites something deep in my chest. I breathe fire. I've never broken anything like this. On purpose. It feels incredible. I savor the weight of the hammer in my hands and keep crashing it down against the box again and again. The wood splinters and shatters. Dust flies everywhere. Some gets in my mouth and I don't care. I think of school. I think of Syracuse. I think of how fast this summer is slipping by. I hit and hit and hit. When the pieces get too small to smash, I stomp on them. Jumping and kicking and screaming alongside the music until the song dries out. When the final note comes and goes, my hands hurt. The early calluses from this summer are tender. My shoulder hurts, too, but not as much as my throat. I don't know how those Midwest screamo singers do this all the time. I should probably drink some tea before I tear the lining of my esophagus. If I lose my voice, then what would happen if—

"Damn."

I drop the hammer. I forgot that Mac is here. How did I forget that Mac is here?

I glance at the pile of destruction at my feet. "I got carried away." I adjust my shirt and feel the sweat beneath my arms.

"I can see that," Mac says. "The angriest music for the angriest girl." A smile tugs at the corner of his mouth. "Come here. You have a wood chip in your hair."

I cross the room until I'm standing right in front of him. I always forget how tall he is until we're close like this. I like the feeling of being shielded by height. From this angle, I can see the clean lines of his jaw and the rogue freckle to the right side of his Adam's apple. The familiar smell of something herbal and earthy lingers on his shirt. He picks the debris from between my braids, slowly. Slower than necessary. I hold my breath.

He motions toward the hammer but doesn't step away. "You should smash things to your scary music more often."

"Maybe I will." Every day, I carry around this underlying resentment at being told what to do, how to behave. This music releases some of that pressure. Even if I don't do it myself, it feels cathartic to listen to someone scream or tell the authorities to fuck off.

"Perhaps Camp Doom shall double as a rage room?" he suggests. The floorboards creak beneath us as he shifts closer. I match his movement. The loose fabric of his shirt brushes against mine.

"Perhaps." We face each other in charged silence for far longer than should be legal in moments like this. After an eternity, he reaches for my hand. I thread my fingers between his. "We should clean that up. . . ."

"We will," he says. I float my free hand to his waist and draw him closer. The look in his eyes makes all the air get stuck in my lungs. "We will."

I feel his hand start to sweat. He retreats for a moment to wipe his palm against his jeans before returning to reestablish his grip even tighter. I chuckle at the earnestness of the motion and he does, too. It breaks some of the tension in the room. But only momentarily.

"Is this okay?" he whispers as he runs his thumb gently along the back of my hand. His touch is soft. He watches our hands intently while my heart attempts to escape my rib cage.

I nod before I'm even aware of it. "This is okay."

My chest rises and falls, barely controlled. He swallows and all of the sudden we're both certain of what's about to happen. Anticipation skewers my senses, leaving me dizzy. As he leans in, his chain spills out of from behind the collar of his shirt, hovering in the air between us, absorbing the built-up electricity like a lightning rod. Our eyes flutter closed.

I count the seconds until I feel the featherlight brush of his lips against mine. He pulls back to gauge my reaction. He looks nervous all over again. But in this moment of hesitation, I can hear his uneven breath, feel the warmth of it on my skin. I melt back into him, pressing my lips to his with a heaviness that steals the air from our lungs.

My hands snake around to tangle in his unruly hair. His grip on my waist tightens. I hear something like a relieved sigh in the back of his throat, and it makes every part of me feel like lava.

I pour my feelings into his mouth. He drinks them down. We kiss in the middle of a half-built doomsday shelter. Our tiny shout into the void.

LET ME TELL YOU ABOUT MAC (AGAIN)

LET ME TELL YOU ABOUT MAC (AGAIN)

LET ME TELL YOU ABOUT MAC (AGAIN)

LET ME TELL YOU ABOUT MAC. WHAT I'VE learned about him over the past month and a half.

Mac is always on time. Perhaps the most punctual person I've ever met. He always arrives exactly at 9:30 a.m. on Camp Doom prep days with a level of accuracy so precise that I wonder if he actually gets here even a few minutes earlier but waits in his car, watching the clock, before coming inside.

Mac keeps at least thirty tabs open on his phone's internet app at all times because he googles almost every thought that crosses his mind.

Mac enjoys turning raspberries upside down, fixing them onto the tips of his fingers, then plopping them into his mouth one by one.

Mac collects compost from the houses on his block to reduce food waste. He has one of those tumbling bins that he uses to mix the trash with dirt. When it's ready, he donates the soil to the community garden.

Mac genuinely believes that a better world is possible.

From ages eleven to fifteen, Mac struggled with depression. Like me. His aunt and uncle's house way out east burned down in a fire—one of the many during a particularly bad drought year. They only lived in that faraway house in the first place because they could no longer afford to live in the city anymore. After the fire, they came to live with Mac's family. Mac's aunt and uncle joked about being California "climate refugees" and even though Mac understood that they were only making jokes about the situation because they had no other way to process the trauma, the joke still made him mad.

Mac was twelve when he had his first asthma attack. The doctors explained that his condition was environmentally produced, which is medical talk for the air around his house poisoned him. The city puts all the toxic industrial plants in neighborhoods like his old one where the residents are largely poor, immigrant, Black, brown. Apparently, other people got sick, too. This also made Mac mad. So mad that Mac hit someone at school. And then another. One day, he broke a window for no reason at all. Luckily, he found Color Outside. Mac stopped punching people. But he was still sad, and mad. Then one day, his older brother's college roommate came to visit and offered to teach him how to surf.

Mac was not a natural at surfing. It took him over a month before he stood for the first time. But he kept at it. He liked the way the waves would create a soft vibration in the board that would race from the soles of his feet right up to his heart. Mac realized that surfing helped with the sad and the mad, then one day—with his feet dangling in the cold ocean water on either side of his board—he noticed that the water didn't just make him not feel sad, but it made him feel happy. More than happy—*euphoric.*

Mac is one of the few guys I know who unironically and unabashedly use words like *euphoric*.

When the sun begins its descent after passing the high noon mark, Mac likes to lay out on a rock in the sun like a salamander.

Mac is sincere.

Mac says my name more than he needs to because he claims he likes how the syllables fit together in his mouth.

Mac might be the best friend that I've ever had.

I had a dream that I fell asleep in Mac's car while he drove us on a windy coastal road during golden hour.

Mac makes summer make sense.

TESSERACT

TESSERACT
TESSERACT

THE KISS HAS PROVEN TO BE AN ISOLATED INCI-dent, but that's okay. I think we're both working up the courage to try it again. Or maybe it was a one-time thing? I'd understand if it was. Who knows if I was even any good. How does anyone know if they're any good at kissing? Either way, it wasn't terrible enough to scare him away because I've seen Mac every day for the past two weeks.

Sometimes, we'll hang out with Andrew and Sage. Andrew will peer pressure Mac into driving us to some obscure hole-in-the-wall restaurant out east that he swears has the best soup dumplings in California. Sage will insist that we stop at various thrift stores along the way.

Sometimes, I'll hear Mac's car roll up out front and he'll be alone. We'll drive off-road to hidden trailheads that lead to sweeping canyons, cactus-covered mountains, or abandoned bridges from back when Southern California was full of mining towns. Other times, we'll go back to the stairs with the view and talk all afternoon. But there are also other days, three so far, when he'll come by at night. We'll slip into Camp Doom, sitting on floor pillows, and share stories in hushed voices beneath the faint glow of a battery-powered lantern as to not draw attention from my mom back in the main house. On these nights, we tend to get too honest. This worries me. How freely the conversation flows in the dark. But these nights also help with my insomnia. Somewhere along the way, Mac has become my melatonin—the medicine that allows me to actually sleep. I'm grateful for the relief, but I worry about developing a dependency.

One night, Mac's chair creaks against the wooden floor beneath him as he sets down a thermos. That's another thing about the night visits—Mac keeps bringing over giant thermoses of tea. I keep telling him that I could make tea inside for us, but he doesn't want my mom getting suspicious, so he brings it himself. It's kind of silly to use camping gear in my own backyard, but once I stop fighting it, I start to see the charm. It reminds me of elementary school—make-believe and adventures.

"My turn to ask a personal question," Mac says.

"After I get this right." I fix my tongue between my teeth as I struggle to weave a piece of yarn into something more secure. Mac and his dad used to go fishing, so he's full of practical knot-tying skills. He's been teaching me a new one that I've never tried before.

My attempt falls apart as soon as I tug one end. "You're overthinking it." He scoots closer. "This end goes over this one," he instructs softly as he guides my hand in his. We finish the knot, but he leaves his hands on mine.

"Can I ask my question now?" The calluses beneath his fingers brush against my knuckles.

"I'll allow one question," I say. I may even allow two if it means we get to keep sitting like this.

"Why are you really building Camp Doom?" he asks.

"You know why. I want to be prepared."

"Yeah, but for what?"

"Global oil crisis leading to massive food shortage. Earthquake. World War Three. Civil unrest. Zombie situation. Alien situation. Tsunami. Financial collapse. Crop changes. Radioactive disaster. Tornados. Sea level changes. Untenable wildfires. Other effects of catastrophic climate change . . ."

"Okay, yes, I'm familiar with all the ways that we can all die, thanks," Mac says. "I mean, like, we know that those things can happen. I guess I'm curious what makes you feel like you need to prepare."

I understand the subtext of his question. He's asking about me. My past. Why I'm like this. If I've always been like this. The reality is no, I haven't always been this paranoid. When I was little, I don't know if I can say that I was the most carefree kid alive, but at least I felt at home in the world. To be honest, I can hardly remember that feeling anymore. Comfort is an echo to me now.

I consider lying to Mac, brushing off his curiosity, but I settle on a half-truth. A bread crumb. "An emergency can strike at any moment and . . . I don't like feeling helpless. I felt helpless once, during a time when things at home were bad and . . . having a plan helps."

I mentally prepare a defense of my feelings. Anyone else might take this moment to psychoanalyze me, press further, or start a debate. But not Mac. Instead, he just nods and stares up at the skylight, wisps of clouds sweeping through the cobalt night sky above us. Luckily, Mac doesn't push. I like that Mac doesn't push.

I'm about to tell him this when my phone shudders with a text message.

INTERRUPTION

INTERRUPTION
INTERRUPTION

< Unknown Number and Me >

Unknown number: I found this photo of us when you were little. Are you around this summer? I'd hop on the next flight to Los Angeles if that means that I could see you. We really need to talk. It's urgent. Please. I'm sorry. Love, dad

MEMORIES
MEMORIES
MEMORIES

I DELETE THE MESSAGE, BUT NOT BEFORE I SEE the attached photo.

Me and my dad at a petting zoo. I am six years old. I am riding a hay-colored pony as he holds my back. We are wearing matching cowboy hats. His eyes are mine. My gap-toothed smile beams at the camera. He gazes at me with affection.

I look so happy. It hurts so much.

THE COLOUR IN ANYTHING

THE COLOUR IN ANYTHING
THE COLOUR IN ANYTHING

DEPRESSION ENVELOPS ME LIKE A WEIGHTED blanket, heavy and soft to the touch from repeated use over the years. The mornings pass quickly, but the afternoons drag on, taking forever to turn into evening. Hours and hours pass without event. I'm stuck like this for days. Three, maybe four. I lose count. Sometimes I sit in front of the TV, not watching it but listening to the sounds and feeling the lights burn my irises. Or I pick out the knots at the ends of my hair. I let Bruce sit beside me. He lies calmly, without expectation for me to play with him, in that intuitive way he does when he knows that I'm not feeling well. I wait until it's dark outside, for I've been waiting all day to go back to bed. No showering. No tears, either. I cried about my father once before, but I don't do that anymore.

I had my first Big Sad when I was ten. I missed school for a week and Mom wanted me to see a psychiatrist. As soon as she brought me into their office, though, I felt better. I didn't end up having anything to tell the therapist. The same thing happened when I was thirteen: I was out of it for a few days, then I bounced back. One day I was not fine, one day I was. There's been an annual episode ever since, so today's event is right on time. I've managed to convince my mom that I never stay like this long enough to warrant any serious intervention. Everyone has their bad days, and I'm no exception. So, she allows me to mope. Or "get it out of my system," as she calls it.

When Mac, Andrew, and Sage keep texting me, I tell them that I'm out of town and turn off my phone. Mac must've known this was a lie because he drives by the house to drop off a breakfast burrito. He doesn't linger outside, which I appreciate. I wait until his car pulls away, retrieve the food, eat it, then return to bed.

I hate summer. Everyone acts like summer is the greatest thing to ever happen even though it happens every year. The days are too long. The sun never sets until it's too late. It's hot and all the houses in LA are old—pre–global warming—so none of them have AC. I wipe the sweat from my eyebrow and roll over. I hate summer. It's the worst time of the year to be depressed.

I don't know why I get like this. Other people deal with what life throws at them and manage to not sink into a comatose state of debilitating sadness. I must not be as strong as other people.

I never know how long it will last. But I know it always will pass. In the meantime, all I can do is wait. Wait for it to subside or for the kink in my back from lying in bed all day to become unbearable enough to motivate me to leave my room.

After a few days, I sit up to inspect my body. My back feels fine. I sleep for another day.

From Mx. Ferrante

To Niarah Holloway

Subject Checking In

Hi Niarah,

I hope you're having a fantastic summer. How's the capstone project coming along?

Sincerely,

Mx. Ferrante

—

At Xavier High School, helping future leaders reach their fullest potential is our greatest passion!

Go, Bulldogs!

MINE
MINE
MINE

"NIARAH, DID YOU BARF IN MY PLANTERETTE?"

Mom has this fancy plant pot she loves. After not eating for over a day, I scarfed down a pint of Ben & Jerry's at midnight, but I ate it too fast. The gobs of cookie dough were simply too gobby. The bathroom was twenty feet away. The planterette was right next to me. It was either me or the fern. I did what had to be done.

"No, Mom, I did not barf in your planterette," I lie.

She pushes my bedroom door open another inch.

"Did something happen?" she asks. Her voice is timid. I don't think we're talking about the pot anymore. Unclear if this is good or bad.

"Not, like, something *has* to happen for your feelings to be . . . valid. But did anything happen that put you in this slump?" She probably rehearsed that part. There's a hint of concern in her voice that I understand to be of the father-related variety. She doesn't know, but she suspects.

It would be easy to tell her that he's been reaching out. To tell her about the photo he sent, and how it felt like such a low blow. Very easy.

I don't know why I don't tell her.

Maybe it's because I want to protect her. Maybe it's because I feel protective of my depression and I want it to be mine and mine only. If I can keep it all to myself, the sadness can morph into something that I can possess. And if I can possess it, then maybe I can control it. And if I can control it, then maybe I can dig myself out of this pit of dread.

I printed out the photo that my dad sent. I don't know why. I stared at it for a while, then shoved it out of sight. I shift around in my bed. I imagine the picture, smushed beneath my mattress and the bed frame, drilling a sharp pain into my side.

The princess and the pea. The sad girl and the family photo.

I close my eyes. "Nothing happened."

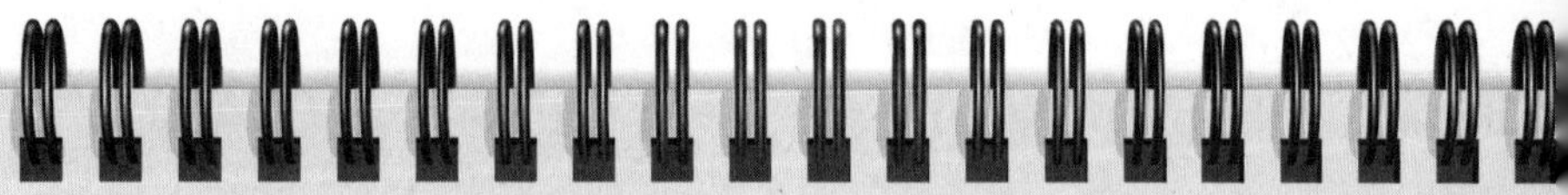

SURVIVAL TIP #31: STAY POSITIVE

It's easy to spin out and find yourself in a dark place when prepping, so it is important to keep your mind and body in sound shape. Don't lose sight of the ways in which prepping activities can help you maintain a healthy lifestyle, no matter what!

1. Exercise is good for your mood.
Whether you're hiking or growing your own food, exercise is great for your mental health. It helps reduce anxiety and increase your overall sense of well-being. Exercise is an awesome way to clear your head after a stressful day or work out any pent-up frustration about your overwhelming existential dread and family issues!

2. Fresh air improves your mental well-being.
Spending time outside can help lower your risk of depression, improve your mood, and increase your creativity. Exposure to natural light helps release the hormone serotonin, which can reduce feelings of paranoia, loneliness, and isolation. Definitely don't turn your bedroom into a cave and refuse to leave for days on end!

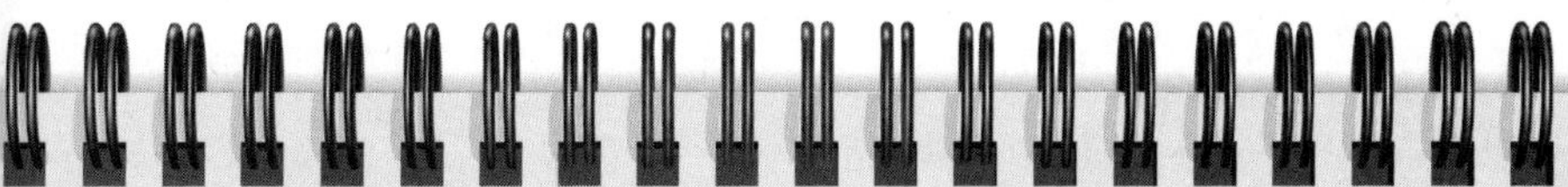

3. Being prepared reduces stress.

Many people find it helpful to do something with their hands, like cooking or building, when they're stressed out. Prepping includes many similar practical, physical activities. Try not to let too many days slip by doing nothing at all, otherwise you may find yourself demotivated!

SEROTONIN
SEROTONIN
SEROTONIN

I HAVEN'T MOVED OR LEFT THE HOUSE IN DAYS. I can't do anything.

Mom commands me to go sit outside in the sun. Vitamin D or whatever. When I drag myself into the backyard, there's a tiny plant in a pale yellow pot.

I reach down and grab the Post-it from its stem.

NO SUDDEN MOVEMENTS

NO SUDDEN MOVEMENTS
NO SUDDEN MOVEMENTS

PEOPLE DON'T USUALLY KNOW ME ENOUGH TO miss me. I search for signs of forgery in the note. Is Mac serious?

I'm lazily stirring honey into a cup of ginger lemon tea when Ox walks in. "Wow, hi," he says. He stares at me, startled.

I pretend like I haven't been a ghost for the past week, avoiding every common area of the house. "Hi."

"Your mom's picking up dinner tonight," he says.

"Cool." I lick the remnants of honey off the spoon and toss it in the sink.

"Do you . . . want to watch a movie? Y'all had that old screen forever, so I finally went to Best Buy today and got a proper TV worthy of movie night. I built a new console for it, too. Twice the size of the old one." He's talking too much, but I'm glad that he doesn't acknowledge the past few days. After a beat of awkward silence, he smiles. "No pressure?"

Mac's note burns a hole in my pocket. It gives me a little caffeine kick. "Maybe just the beginning of something," I say.

Ox shows me the new TV and it is in fact huge. The TV of my dreams. I could drool in front of this thing for hours. He puts on an old Stephen King adaptation. Bruce jumps onto the couch and barks his approval of the film choice. My mom comes home and tries her best not to act too excited when she sees us in the living room. She places the grocery bags down slowly, as if moving too fast will scare me away. I kind of laugh at her a bit, which she notices and laughs back. She joins us. I stay for the whole movie. My brain starts to thaw.

INSIDE OUTSIDE

INSIDE OUTSIDE
INSIDE OUTSIDE

< Mac and Me >

Me: you bought me a plant.

Mac: for health and good luck

Me: i'm not good at keeping plants alive. what happens if I kill it on accident? is that a bad omen?

Mac: in some cultures, if a plant dies, it means that it's absorbing all the bad energy in a room and cleansing the plant owner. it's a good sign

Me: so, if I keep it alive, it's lucky. if I kill it, it's cleansing?

Mac: yup

Me: sounds like fake news to me

Mac: please just take the plant. it's pretty

Mac: . . .

Mac: did something happen?

Me: not really.

Mac: is there anything I can do to help?

Me: no. thanks tho.

Mac: well can I come over tonight?

Me: no, I decided to paint the rest of the outside of camp doom so the fumes are bad. it needs to dry before we go back in

Mac: maybe we can hang out inside the house then? play video games

Me: no, my mom is home

Mac: i could finally meet her. i'll wear my nice shirt.

Me: no meeting my mom, no coming inside, remember?

Mac: right. sorry.

Me: i'm sorry. i just don't want that. ok?

Mac: no worries

Me: are u free tomorrow morning tho?

Mac: what do u have in mind?

SO IT GOES

SO IT GOES
SO IT GOES

THE PACIFIC OCEAN AT 8 A.M. DARK, FOGGY, restless. Cold. As in it's-the-dead-of-summer-but-you-still-need-a-wet-suit-if-you-want-to-feel-your-organs cold. But also, alluring.

Mostly terrifying, though.

Anticipation creates a traffic jam in my lungs, causing my breath to skip and staccato. I'm overtaken by the overwhelming urge to pee, even though I went two minutes ago. It's that feeling before stepping onto a roller coaster and the moment before the referee blows the whistle rolled into one. Is it too late to back out?

"There's nothing to be afraid of," Mac says as he lines up two surfboards on the sand.

"There's actually a lot to be afraid of," I shoot back. Drowning. Shark attack. Shark attack that leads to drowning. Tsunamis. Poseidon's fury. I asked Mac to take me surfing, but now that I'm here, all I can think of are the many ways that this could kill me. The waves crash menacingly against the shore, affirming my case.

Mac scans my face, attempting to diagnose my true Fear Level.

My fingers and toes tingle as I bounce on the balls of my feet.

"We don't have to if you don't want to," he says after careful review.

I don't want to try to surf. But I also don't want to *not* try. A few weeks ago, I would have never found myself in this position: pacing back and forth on a quiet beach, wearing a wet suit and preparing to try something new. But it's not a few weeks ago anymore. I'm starting to think that who I am today has more in common with who I'll be in the future than who I've been in the past.

"Let's get in before I change my mind."

Mac claps encouragingly and I don't bother trying to muster a smile through the nerves. On the sand, he demos how to pop up on the board. He explains for the fourth time how to know when to go for a wave. I have a rough understanding of it all. Or at least as much as I'll ever have while still on dry land. I've had enough of Tutorial Mode. I grab a board and head toward the sea.

It takes forever to paddle past the point where the waves break. Mac is patient, gliding alongside me, making sure that I make it out okay. The waves aren't too intense—Mac checked beforehand to make sure that the ocean was at least mildly beginner friendly today. Still, I'm already exhausted by the time we get out into the deep.

Once I'm no longer being pummeled in the face by waves, I start to relax. Mac pulls our boards together, his legs straddling his own board while his hands grip mine. We float alongside each other. Even through the wet suit, I can see the faint outlines of the taut muscles on his arms. He looks up at me through wet hair, smiling wide. "You made it out here. That's more than most people can do." He releases one hand from my board to give me a high five. I smile and return the gesture, but let our palms linger against each other. When Mac uses his thumb to trace a tiny circle on my knuckle, I don't move away. His lips part and I can tell he's about to say something. Something real. I cut him off.

"Show me," I command. I untie our hands. "Let's see you do the thing you love so much."

He looks uncertain. "You sure you'll be okay out here without me?"

I nod. "I want to watch you."

A coy smile spreads across his face. "Aight, then."

He lets go of my board and drifts a few feet away. He lets two perfectly fine waves pass. Is he nervous? Wait, no, it's not nerves at all—it's patience. He closes his eyes, listening to the ocean. After a few more minutes, he hears what he's been waiting for.

He slides onto his stomach and paddles hard as the water beneath him builds. He uses the strength in his arms to push himself up to stand. The wave opens at last and Mac's there, perfectly timed, to ride it. He cuts right, hurtling fast, but somehow with enough balance to wave at me. I wave back, wildly, as he whips the board back over the now-dying swell. Exhilaration dances in his eyes. Sheer joy. I never do things that make me feel like how Mac looks right now. But I want to.

When the next wave comes, I don't think. From the corner of my eye, I see Mac flailing his arms in panic, telling me no, but I don't listen. I paddle like hell, hurtling myself forward. My arms ache from exertion, but I don't care. The wave builds and climbs and roars and bursts before I'm ready.

The force of the sea slaps the back on my neck, banging my head against the board.

I flip. I flip. I flip. I flip. I—

Lose track of time. Of space. Of my body.

Salt water chokes the air from my lungs as I go under.

LIVING, BEING

LIVING, BEING

LIVING, BEING

SAND HAS FOUND ITS WAY INTO THE CORNERS of my eyes. I use water from Mac's bottle to flush it out. I can't stop coughing. The dizziness makes me want to hurl.

"What the hell, Niarah?" Mac picks seaweed from my hair.

"You look s-so mad right now," I wheeze.

"No, I don't," he replies, face fixed into an undeniable portrait of anger as he concentrates on wiping away the trails of sand caked to my forehead.

"That wave was huge, why didn't you wait for me?"

"I didn't want to wait for you." I cough again.

He sucks his teeth. "You're normally all risk averse. That's, like, your whole thing. Had I known that you'd pull some dangerous shit like this, I wouldn't have left you alone."

He has a point, but all I can say in response is that I used to think of myself as risk averse, too. My own words make me smile. I *used* to. Past tense. Not anymore. I start to laugh, and Mac gives me this horrified look. I laugh even harder.

"Are you concussed? Holy shit, you're concussed." Mac's looking at me as if I'm in the middle of a mental breakdown. But I'm actually experiencing the opposite—a mental breakupward? Is that a thing? A moment of hysterical joy and freedom that cracks open something inside of you and brings your spirit higher and higher?

Mac's eyes dart around like he's wondering if he should call for help. Poor guy. He's so worried. I'm such a bad student. Oh well. I keep cackling.

"No more surfing today. We're done." He unzips the top half of his wet suit before proceeding to examine my head for potential cracks or bleeding. He plunges both hands into my wet, tangled hair, grasping the base of my skull as if to make sure that it's still attached to my neck. I grab his wrists and pull his forehead against mine. His heavy hair falls forward, surrounding us like a curtain, blocking our peripheral vision. All I can see is him. All I can smell is the ocean. All I can hear is his staggered breath, my beating heart as I don't let him go.

"Mac. I'm okay." I use my thumbs to draw little circles on the tops of his hands. His veins and bones feel fragile beneath my touch. "That was fun."

"That was not fun. Not for me." He relaxes his grip but doesn't move, keeping his forehead pressed against mine.

I slide my hands from his wrists, down his forearms, and up his biceps until I arrive at his shoulders. His skin a shade of brown that glows from within due to so many days spent outdoors. I understand now the definition of *sunkissed*. It's Mac.

I trace my index finger along his cheek. His jaw stiffens beneath my touch. He swallows, finally catching on.

"How do you feel right now?" His voice comes out low. Hazy.

The ache in my arms from swimming feels good. The warmth

from the sand beneath my legs feels good. I touch Mac and he feels good.

I continue tracing his features, from his chin to his brow to the bridge of his nose to the soft pad of his bottom lip. He presses a lingering kiss onto my finger. It's the slightest touch, but I feel it everywhere.

Nothing matters. Everything is temporary. But pleasure? Maybe this is the antidote. Maybe I can get used to this.

Mac slips my hand into his. He squeezes it, then brings my wrist to his mouth. He plants a deeper kiss right where my pulse starts to race. Suddenly, I'm aware of every cell in my body, vibrating beyond control as electricity rips through my skin. Mac watches my reaction with heated eyes.

Falling for Mac is still off-limits. Developing any attachment would be foolish. But a little bit more of this? Of feeling good? If it helps me forget about everything else, then why not?

A knowing smile tugs at the corner of his mouth. He knows what I'm thinking. I want him to know. I close my eyes.

We can keep things light. A friends-with-benefits thing. Maximize all the pleasure, forget the pain. That's how to get through it.

I open my eyes and there's Mac, gazing back at me, looking like everything I've ever craved and everything I've never known all at once. I stare as he draws his bottom lip between his teeth.

"Come here," he whispers.

I lean in and taste the ocean on his lips. The world around us blurs at the edges.

We kiss like it's urgent.

We kiss like it's the only thing we were ever meant to do.

We kiss like it matters.

THREE CHEERS FOR EXISTENTIAL DREAD

THREE CHEERS FOR EXISTENTIAL DREAD

THREE CHEERS FOR EXISTENTIAL DREAD

MAC AND I GRAB FISH TACOS NEARBY FOR lunch before heading back to the beach to join everyone else for the Color Outside ocean cleanup activity. We split off into pairs with giant trash bags and waxy gloves. Andrew and Mac get caught up discussing a conspiracy theory about some weird cantina restaurant in South LA, so I end up alone with Sage, picking up faded bags of chips and plastic bottles with giant tongs.

The silence between us is comfortable now. It's sort of nice to be near someone who makes space to listen to and observe the world. After we clean up a solid stretch of sand, Sage pulls a water bottle from their backpack. The all-black canteen is covered in stickers, but one in particular catches my eye. Surrounded by bright purple and teal, the word *survivor* is etched in bold.

Survivor of what?

I glance at Sage, trying to guess. As if it's that easy—to look at someone and know what they've been through. I have enough home training to not outright ask what the sticker means, but Sage catches me staring anyway. I avert my eyes.

They rummage through their bag and pull out a stack of identical stickers, held together by a worn-out rubber band. They release one from the stack and try to pass it to me, but I hold up my hands.

"Sorry, you don't have to give me one. I was just looking—"

They flap the stack of stickers, as if to emphasize how many they have, then shove one into my palm anyway. I flip the glossy rectangle over. Sage's name is stamped onto the back. "You make these?" I ask.

They nod.

"Why?"

Sage smirks, then takes another sticker from the stack. They rip off the protective backing, then slap it onto the nearest trash can between several scrawls of graffiti. I laugh. "Cool." Sage smiles, like they already know.

The water bottle placement feels too in-your-face for me—maybe I can put mine somewhere more discreet? Sage looks at me, a question in their eyes. I rub the waxy finish and sigh. "The sticker's dope, I just don't know where I should put mine. I don't really . . . I don't know. It's not like I'm a survivor or anything."

Sage looks up at the clouds. "We're all survivors of something."

I don't know what to make of that, but I try to let their words sink in. An easy silence carries us back to the group. We're the last ones there.

"That's the messed-up thing about it," Andrew practically shouts. Waiting for the sunset, a big debate is underway. Mac fills cups with aguas frescas from giant jugs in the cooler that Andrew brought and passes them around. Everyone our age in

Color Outside crowds together, Andrew's magnetism drawing us closer. "There's this expectation for people our age to make a change. Come together like the Avengers and save humanity. And graduation has, like, really set that in for me, you know? That feeling—no, not feeling—that *weight.* That things are bad and if I'm not doing anything to make things better, then I'm bad, too."

"The other day after that Supreme Court decision dropped, my mom looked at me and said, 'Your generation has a lot of work to do.' I wanted to explode," a girl with green hair laments. "Like, why us? What if what you're leaving behind is too much?"

"I want to get a job, but all the ones that I want don't pay," Mac says.

"I want to get a job, but all the ones that I want don't matter," someone else adds.

"I don't want a job at all."

I wasn't planning on speaking up, but I find myself clearing my throat. "Save the world, save the planet, all while being productive members of the economy. It's bullshit." I've been quiet all conversation, so everyone turns to me. I try not to recoil from all the eyes on me. I get nervous, but Mac nudges my shoulder, so I keep going. "Everyone wants us to just stroll into this labor force that clearly doesn't give a shit about us. As if we haven't already seen enough to know how fucked these systems are." More people nod, really nod. I may not know how to talk about half the things that Sage, Andrew, and Mac do when they're together, but this? Existential dread and impending doom? The pressures of society? All the little dumpster fires everywhere? This is my shit.

"Well, fuck that," Andrew says. "This summer, we're not doing any of that." Everyone claps with that wild energy that I'm starting to realize only comes when you have a group of friends riled up together on a summer afternoon fading into night.

Sage locks eyes with me as they raise a cup and motions for everyone to do the same.

"What are we cheersing to, then, Niarah?" Andrew asks.

"Here's to . . ." I'm anxious again, but Mac doesn't let it get too bad because he leans into my shoulder. "Here's to being useless to capitalism?"

The whole group repeats it and takes a drink. Soon the group shifts back into an easy energy—the circle breaking off into new, separate conversations. It's a small moment, the toast, but it sticks in my mind. It warms me from the inside for the rest of the day, long after the sun has set.

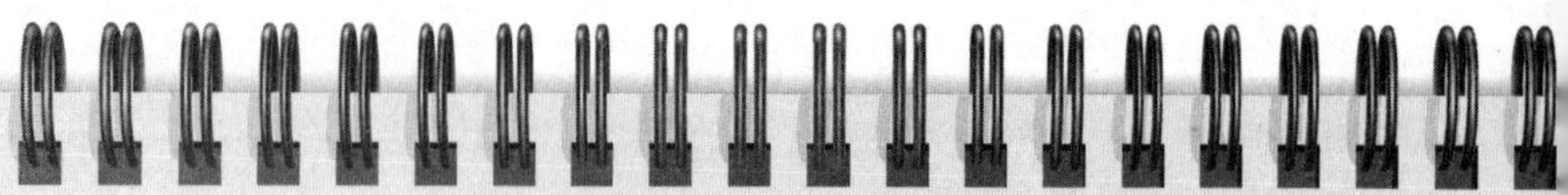

A PREPPER'S APPROACH TO A SUMMER CRUSH

Dealing with a summer crush is no different than dealing with the imminent destruction of humanity.

The first step is to accept the inevitable: The end is coming. The end of the Anthropocene (aka the period during which human activity has been the dominant influence on Earth's environment) is in sight. There will come a day when your friends—maybe even the first friends you've made in years—will leave you behind.

The second step is to prepare. You might be blissfully happy now, but you can't let spending time with your summer crush eclipse your prepping projects. When your crush is gone, you'll still have this. You pretty much only have this.

The third step is to resist the impulse to make plans.

Lastly, having prepared for inevitable disappointment, the final step is to act accordingly. Embracing the truth that nothing lasts forever means that one should not get attached. The best survival mechanism to survive a summer crush is to fortify the appropriate emotional walls. Create a homestead around your heart, and defend it diligently against

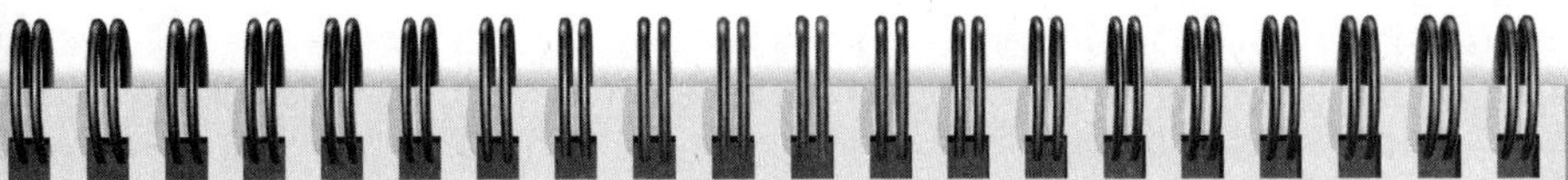

anyone who tries to make their way in. People come and go, but in the end, it'll only be you left alone.

In the meantime, have fun. Surprise yourself by how much fun you can have. But remember—

In the end, it's always only you.

HOME IMPROVEMENT

HOME IMPROVEMENT
HOME IMPROVEMENT

MOM AND OX STAND BY THE SINK DOING THE dishes. They trade places, smiling at each other, looking all doe-eyed. It's like watching two lovesick kids play House. I'm surprised that Ox doesn't get down on one knee right here and now. The whole picture makes me feel weird. Kind of happy, but also claustrophobic. I clear my throat, interrupting their domestic bliss. My greatest talent.

"Niarah," my mom says brightly. "Have you been in the living room yet?"

"Yes, I have been in our living room? In the house where we live?"

She nudges Ox. "Show her."

"Show me what?"

Without a word, Ox exits the kitchen. I glance at my mom. She bobs her head at me excitedly. There's a hardwired malfunction in my brain that whenever my mom gets too excited about something, it immediately makes me decidedly un-excited. We are the two opposing scales held by Lady Justice. She smiles, I frown, and suddenly The Avatar can restore balance to the world.

Reluctantly, I follow Ox. I find him standing, arms crossed, in the center of the room. Slowly, he steps aside. My jaw drops.

A giant custom-made storage cabinet stares right at me. It's wood with hand carvings up the side, stained in a deep black. I rush forward to examine the details. It's beautiful, but more important than that, it's practical. Filled with utilitarian bins and hooks to hang items from the sides.

"For Camp Doom," Ox says. "We're glad that you got out of bed. Got some fresh air."

I'm appreciative, but I also can't believe that the bar for me is set so low that I'm now being rewarded for merely leaving my bedroom. What an honor. I am my ancestors' wildest dreams.

"You didn't have to do that," I say. I'm at a loss here. "I don't deserve this."

Mom smiles. "You deserve a lot more than you think."

STOWAWAY

STOWAWAY
STOWAWAY

INCLUDING MAC, I'VE ONLY EVER HAD THREE crushes in my life, and I could never imagine actually dating any of them. The first crush was a charming narcissistic anime villain, so he was unattainable due to his limited existence as a fictional cartoon. The second was a girl who lived down the street back in Syracuse. She was six years older than me, so she was practically a grown woman. I found her beauty so terrifying that I could never talk to her. One time, in fifth grade, I was walking down the block at the same time as her, and when she waved at me, I turned the corner and hid behind a neighbor's apple tree until I was certain she was gone. Later, I went home and wrote her name across my journal forty-seven times. And now there's Mac. A real, age-appropriate person, in the same dimension as me.

I want to call him, but it's past two a.m. I don't even have a reason to call him. I just want to hear his voice. Pathetic. I kick off my covers and start pacing.

I feel crazy. If someone could see my thoughts, they'd think I'm a creep. Building out a fantasy over a boy who is leaving in four weeks. He didn't even tell me when exactly he was leaving, but I stalked the UC Davis academic calendar to figure out when he realistically has to move in. I did this after I spent an hour meticulously combing through his tagged photos online until I found one that Andrew posted for Mac's birthday and entered our birthdays into an astrology app to test our compatibility. See? Crazy Girl shit. I don't even believe in astrology.

One morning, when I brought us iced tea from the refrigerator during our break, he was looking at me funny. We kept making each other laugh while we were drinking, and I kept asking him what was up, but he wouldn't answer. I left to bring the glasses inside and when I came back out, Mac was crouched on the ground, holding a fallen tree branch the length of a wand. He must not have heard me coming because when I asked what he was doing, he nearly jumped out of his skin. He used his boot to kick around the dusty ground where he had been kneeling. He laughed awkwardly, pretending that it was nothing, but I caught a glimpse of it beforehand. In the dirt, he had drawn a lopsided heart.

My stomach hurts. I need some water.

I walk downstairs to the kitchen and fill a tall glass that will inevitably make me have to pee in the middle of the night. I down it in seconds, then fill another to go. But as I'm about to head back upstairs, I notice something in the window.

A soft light glowing from inside Camp Doom.

But I know for a fact that I turned the light off earlier after Mac left.

Intruder alerts sound off in my brain. My brain cells scurry around at the sudden commotion, trying to find the protocol for what to do now. A shadow crosses the window. There's definitely someone inside. On one hand, it could be a burglar. On the other hand, it could be a serial killer. Not great options. I could wake up my mom, but I don't want her going in Camp Doom, either. Or I could wake up Bruce to come with me, but he needs his beauty rest. Or I could call the cops, except just kidding because ACAB. So, I'm left with no choice. If I can't protect Camp Doom during normal times, then how could I expect myself to do it in a disaster scenario? I pull a frying pan out of the cupboard, put on my Crocs, and dip outside.

My heart is a jackrabbit, skittish and thumping against my ribs. I can do this. I can investigate. I'm not going to confront anyone—just assess the situation from a safe distance.

My shoes squish into the grass, wet from the nighttime dew. Each step elicits a wet fart noise. Maybe that will scare the intruder away.

I creep as close as I can to the window without stepping in the cactus that I planted there—I'm both annoyed and pleased that my defensive gardening works so well. I use the frying pan as a kickstand and press it into the wall as I stand on my tiptoes, straining to peek inside. I can see the outline of a body, a swoop of hair, and then—

"FUCK."

The frying pan slips and I tip forward into the cactus bush. A spike gets me right in the belly button.

"Hello?"

Time to run. I scramble to my feet and start for the kitchen door.

"Wait." The voice speaks in an urgent whisper. And suddenly, my fear dissolves.

I turn back to Camp Doom and find a drowsy Mac hovering in the doorway. A drowsy, shirtless Mac.

As I struggle to remember how to speak, his eyes finally focus on mine and register my shock at: (1) the sight of him, here, at this hour, and (2) the sight of his shirt draped across the futon rather than on his body. He rushes over to retrieve the shirt. "I can explain," he says. His curly hair falls in a messy curtain across his eyes. He tucks a wisp back behind his ear so that he can see me better. The sight of arms in motion beneath the porch light knocks me off-balance. I spin around.

"What are you doing here?" I direct my question to the moon, trying hard to fight the urge to sneak a peek back as he gets dressed.

I listen to the sound of fabric against skin as he tugs the shirt over his head. "Can you come in, please? We can talk inside," he says. I hesitate. "You can turn around now," he adds, a hint of a smirk in his voice.

I walk inside. My eyes zero in on the sleeping bag in the center of the room.

"Mac . . ."

"I'm so sorry." He blurts out the words like they're on fire. "I should've asked first. Please don't be mad." He knocks his fist against his forehead.

I rush forward. "Hey, hey." I uncurl his clenched first. "I'm not mad. I'm just . . . surprised. And confused."

Embarrassment radiates from him in waves. "I—I know. I'm sorry."

"So . . . you've been . . . sleeping here?" I ask. He nods, eyes avoiding mine. "For how long?"

"Just this week. And not every night."

This doesn't make me feel any better. "Are you in danger?"

He grits his teeth. "No."

"Are you in trouble?"

"It's nothing like that, I promise." He drops his hand from mine and sits on the sleeping bag on the floor.

I join him. "Then just tell me."

He sighs. "My family is . . . complicated."

"Okay. So is mine. Continue."

He finally meets my eyes. He looks so sad. It almost takes my breath away.

"This summer is a weird time at home. And I've been finding it hard to . . ." He pauses. "It's just—" He pulls his knees to his chest. "It's hard to explain."

I've been there. I know about how hard it can be to talk about home. But still, I find out he's been camping out here and I'm worried. This isn't the type of thing that I can just let go. I care too much. When did I start to care this much?

"Actually—" Mac sits up straight. "Do you want to come over for dinner tomorrow?"

"What?"

"Wait, no, not tomorrow. Tomorrow's Monday. But Tuesday?"

I've never been to Mac's house. It never occurred to me that I would ever go to Mac's house. "Is this invitation an attempt at dodging the question?"

"I'm not dodging. I'm requesting to answer it more thoroughly at another time with more context," Mac says. "It'll all make sense. Trust me. I'm not walking you into a minefield, I swear. My parents are nice. They'll love you. Andrew and Sage will be there, too."

"Now I'm even more confused." He can't stay at home, yet he wants me to go over there?

"Come and I'll explain then." His fingers play with the seam of my shirt sleeve. "Please?"

I don't know if it's curiosity or concern that makes me say yes.

WARM WELCOME

WARM WELCOME
WARM WELCOME

ANDREW IS ALREADY HERE WHEN I ARRIVE. HE'S cooking something wild in the kitchen, buzzing about as if it's his own home. A black bandanna holds back his dark hair as he stands over a cauldron of boiling red liquid. The clouds of chili singe the corners of my eyes.

Mac's brother Gael floats into the room. He's much older—probably somewhere in his mid to late twenties. He's tall and skinny with long loose curls that hang down his back, at least a couple inches longer than Mac's. He hovers by Andrew's side, inspecting the stove. "You're cooking it at too high of a temperature," he scolds.

"Gael, chill. Food is my line, drinks are yours," Andrew barks back.

They go back and forth like siblings. Andrew really is part of the Torres family unit.

"You have to watch the temperature in here, sweetheart," a woman says, rushing to Andrew's side to let some air in through the window over his head. She moves with urgency, but her voice is soft, like Mac's. She gently fans the chili-scented air above Andrew's concoction while placing a supportive hand on his shoulder. A linen house dress sweeps the floor at her ankles. Andrew feeds her a spoon of his recipe. She tastes it slowly, closing her eyes to savor it. "It's wonderful," she says. I can see where Mac gets his gentle demeanor from.

She looks up and spots me standing in the doorway. I give her an awkward half wave. She rushes in for a hug.

"I've heard so much about you," she hums.

I smile at the thought of Mac telling his mom about me.

Sage slides down the hallway in their socks to meet us. They give me a quick side hug.

Mac emerges in the curved doorway right behind them. "Sage, I don't want to debate with you," he says. And yet, Mac immediately continues a debate about how the ocean is much scarier than space while Sage shakes their head.

Mac's wearing another signature flannel, but this time it's a soft pink. Baby-blue Hypland x Naruto sweats and pale yellow Nikes complete the look. His clothes are technically what I've come to recognize as the typical Echo Park streetwear aesthetic, but the pastel color palette screams *Powerpuff Girls*. It's as though someone took the archetypal skater and dipped him in sugar, spice, and everything nice. The effect is . . . pleasant.

The front door opens again, and a striking couple enters the room. The man is short and muscular with a strong jaw and brow line. The woman has high cheekbones and a tall forehead, her hair coiffed in a neat updo clipped with one of those vintage wooden claws. They look exactly like Andrew.

Before I can finish taking them in, Mr. and Mrs. Pha stride

straight toward me. "Are you okay with a hug?" Andrew's mom asks.

"Sure?"

She grins and folds me in close. She smells like fresh laundry and expensive candles. "I'm honored to meet the new addition to Andrew, Sage, and Mac's crew."

I don't know if I'm a full-blown new member yet, but the thought still makes me happy.

Andrew's dad shakes my hand firmly before dapping up Mac's dad and putting down a case of Red Stripe beers. Mrs. Torres skirts over to her friend and the two immediately launch into a rapid-fire, hushed-voice keke. Andrew's little sister runs in, screeching like a banshee. Gael's daughter follows, catapulting headfirst into a pillow fort on the couch. Both girls are inexplicably dressed as Miles Morales Spider-Man. From the kitchen, Andrew yells something at Gael, demanding tongs, *now*. Mrs. Torres puts Sade on the speaker.

"Welcome to Tuesday Dinner," Mac says, holding his arms open to the chaos. His eyes crinkle with affection as he watches his family race around the room. I take note of the way that love looks on his face.

PLANTS AND POST-ITS

PLANTS AND POST-ITS
PLANTS AND POST-ITS

"MARCO, GIVE NIARAH A TOUR. DON'T BE SHY," Mrs. Torres says over her shoulder before disappearing into the living room with Andrew's mom.

"I'm not being shy," Mac says shyly.

"Pero not your bedroom," Mr. Torres calls out.

"Don't be a prude, Ricky," Mrs. Pha chides.

Mac draws a sharp inhale. "Ma, please get your people under control." He gives me an awkward, frazzled look and we laugh. "They're a lot."

"They're sweet," I reply. Sweeter than I'm used to from a family unit.

We begin our walk-through of the house. The home is beautiful—classic Spanish-style architecture. A terra-cotta–colored wall here, a deep teal there. Hand-painted tiles line the stairs. Mac pauses to point out a picture from a family trip to Chiapas, a childhood art project on the women of *Hidden Figures* for Black History Month. He makes obvious, boring statements, like "This is the living room" and "This is the bathroom." Each time, he casts me a small smile, acknowledging the banality of it all.

Eventually, we pass by a door covered top to bottom in vinyl stickers. "Wait, wai-wait—" I grab the sleeve of his shirt as he attempts to breeze by. He glances at my hand holding his sleeve. "Is this you?"

"Want a quick look inside?" he whispers. He asks me like it's a Top Secret mission, fixing his fingers into a gun as if we're about to storm a villain's lair. I join him, assembling my own finger gun. He cracks open the door to his own room slowly, creeping in, before kicking it down in dramatic fashion. "Hands where I can see them," he shouts once we're inside. His willingness to completely commit to a bit is infectious.

I strike a spy post alongside him and whisper-shout, "All clear." I only feel a little bit embarrassed as I do.

I would sit, but Mac's bedroom is a mess. It looks like a library and a greenhouse had a baby, but someone strapped a bomb to said baby and it exploded, bursting its essence all over the room.

"You didn't mention you live in a jungle," I say. There are plants everywhere. Long, dangling leaves in hand-painted pots hanging from the ceiling. Delicate sprigs of wispy, wavy green things bursting from macramé planters on the wall. At least a dozen succulents crowd together on a floating shelf above his bed.

He shrugs. "I like plants."

"I can see that."

He has two floor-to-ceiling wooden bookshelves that are completely full—so full that there are four different stacks of extra books lined on the floor towering like mini Leaning Towers of Pisa. Even more novels and art magazines line the surface of his desk. But while the indie comic anthologies and graphic novels look well worn, many of the novels and nonfiction books look completely untouched. I grab one and notice that it still has a receipt hanging out from behind the front cover.

"Do you actually read these?" I ask. A tiny horror strikes my chest that maybe Mac's one of those people who wants to appear like he reads a lot but has actually never read a book in his life.

"I've read every single book that I own," he says proudly. "I don't even buy the books until I finish them."

I raise an eyebrow. "How can you finish a book before buying it?"

"It's hard to sit still and read a book the normal way, but I love audiobooks. I listen to them at one point five speed while I'm walking around outside. I didn't learn to read well until much later than other kids, so I was always jealous when I'd go to friends' houses and see their book collections." He grabs a hardcover copy of *Braiding Sweetgrass*, tracing his finger down the embossed spine. "Whenever I finish an audiobook, I buy the physical copy so I can keep it on display." He returns the book to the shelf and runs a hand through his hair. "I don't know. I guess it is kind of weird."

"Not weird at all." There must be over a hundred books here, and each audiobook is probably at least nine or ten hours each. I try to imagine having the patience to listen to a thousand hours' worth of reading. And honestly? Couldn't be me. I'm a shameless skimmer, plus my brain couldn't handle listening for that long.

Office Depot needs to give this young man a sponsorship, since he's apparently their number one customer. Little colorful squares appear on books, on walls, on windows, on the faces of commemorative Dodgers bobbleheads. Each one containing checklists like the one in his car, but also little quotes and lines like the ones he's given me.

"You take notes while you listen to the books?" I ask.

"When I hear a line I like, I write it down. If I don't, I'll forget it."

I run my fingers along the posters layered on top of one another on the wall, careful not to disrupt the many tiny Post-its that cover it. A note with a tiny star on it catches my eye, but Mac lunges forward and rips it from the wall before I can read it. "Some of the notes are personal." He gives me a shy smile as he tucks the crumpled note into his back pocket. I could've sworn that right before he took it away, I saw my name written in his lopsided handwriting. He blushes and I try not to notice.

"Which one's your favorite?" I ask.

He points to a book that has something about dismantling patriarchy on the spine.

"Of course you picked this one." I mimic his voice. *"'Look at me, I'm Mac, just out here dismantling the patriarchy, no big deal.'"* I roll my eyes. "That's a good line. You point out this book whenever you have girls in your room?"

"First off, I never have girls in my room." He gives a smile backed with a bit of heat. My face warms in response. "Second, the dismantling-patriarchy thing isn't just a line." He holds up another book by an author named bell hooks. "Patriarchy forces this idea of domination as power. Like, 'If I can dominate this thing right here, then that's how I will get power in this world.' Once I learned about that, I started to see everything different. The US is obsessed with domination as power. You can see it everywhere. The school-to-prison pipeline, the criminal justice system, the extractive fossil fuel economy." He's getting worked up. We don't usually talk about these things. It's easy to forget that the guy's book smart when he's typically knee-deep in dirt, crawling around the bushes while affectionately naming roly-polies.

"Our Earth is dying because we're trying to dominate it," he continues. "And we do those same things to ourselves: try to dominate our emotions instead of seeing them for what they are."

I guess I try to dominate my emotions, too. Where does that impulse come from?

"Anyway, that's what Imma study in college," Mac says, plopping down onto his bed. "How all this stuff intersects with nature. Dismantling patriarchy, tackling the mental health crisis, centering Indigenous Traditional Ecological Knowledge, finding solutions to climate change. It's all connected. We gotta quit our addiction to domination. Surrender and submit to the earth. Listen to the land and see what it needs to heal. Then, maybe, we can heal, too."

I don't know how to respond to all of that. I never know what to say when people get too sincere with their optimism. I could never be earnest like him. Luckily, he doesn't pressure me to keep the conversation going. His bed creaks as he sits down on the edge. He scoots over for me to join him.

"So, what's the big secret?" I ask. His sheets are a soft linen, warm against my fingers. "Your house is awesome. Your parents seem great, so do your brother and your niece. What's so complicated?"

"Well, the problem is . . ."

"Fooooood's ready," Andrew calls from the kitchen.

Mac flinches at the interruption, rising to head back to the dining room. "To be continued?"

THE SOCRATIC METHOD

THE SOCRATIC METHOD
THE SOCRATIC METHOD

DINNER IS KIMCHI SOONDUBU JJIGAE MADE BY Andrew, with beef bulgogi tacos á la Mac's dad's influence (there's also a tofu version for Mac's vegetarian ass). Mac's brother Gael serves a Yakult soju cocktail for himself and the other adults. He makes a nonalcoholic one for the rest of us.

"The theme is Los Angeles synergy: Mexican Korean fusion," Andrew announces. "For our special guest, who's still new to the city."

My ears feel hot. "You guys didn't have to make a special dinner for me."

"Of course we did. Mac insisted on it." Mrs. Torres grins.

Mac shoots his mom a cutting glare. "You mentioned that you don't 'get' LA yet, so I thought we'd at least introduce you to some of the food." He keeps his eyes on the saltshaker as he mumbles.

Mac's niece lets out a theatrical "OOoOOoo," but he doesn't seem to mind it coming from her.

Andrew, Mac, Sage, and I take the seats on one side of the

table, while Mac's and Andrew's parents plus the little girls take the other. Gael rounds out the end of the table, and when I look around, I stare at everyone for a minute, slightly stunned. I can't remember the last time that I've sat down at a full table for dinner. It feels . . . warm.

Once everyone's plates are full, Mac's and Andrew's parents talk to me for a bit about how the best tacos in LA are at a hole-in-the-wall in Boyle Heights, but if I'm more interested in tamales, then there's a fantastic place downtown that Mac has to show me, and about how Mac didn't always like outdoors stuff, and it's okay to not be comfortable with the nature stuff at first because white people have made people of color feel unwelcome in those spaces, and did I have any other big plans for the summer—"She's building something amazing," Mac interjects—and how great it is for young people to work with their hands, and they don't even once ask me about why I suddenly moved in the middle of high school or what exactly I'm building this summer, which is unexpectedly nice.

But Gael is more curious than the others. "What does your mother do?" he asks.

This is an easy one. I got this. "She works at a museum."

"And your dad?"

A pang of anxiety ripples through my chest. I don't want to talk about him. Not here. I want this moment for myself. I want to enjoy dinner, not open up a whole line of new communication with Mac and his entire family.

"My dad is . . ." I search my inner dictionary of vague phrases. "He's not with us anymore."

Everyone gets quiet. Mac sets his fork down and looks at me. "I'm so sorry. I had no idea."

"It's okay. It's been a while."

Mrs. Torres shakes her head. "Losing a parent must have been terrible."

What? I didn't say—

Oh no.

My own vagueness spits back in my face. I grit my teeth. "Uh—"

"We don't have to talk about it," Gael says. "I'm sorry. I wouldn't have brought it up had I known."

I nod. Mac gives my hand a very tiny and very unearned squeeze of moral support. My stomach fills with worms. To be honest, I've fantasized about doing this before—telling people that my dad is dead so that I don't have to explain that he's actually just a bad person. I know it's a twisted, gross thing to think about, but I can't help it. Death is the ultimate conversation ender. When it comes to family, all I ever want to do is end the conversation. There must be something seriously wrong with me. Tonight is an accident, but the fact that I've considered this before . . . I must be sick.

Andrew and Sage lean over to pat my shoulder. Everyone gives me a sad smile. This is bad. But it's not terrible. I'll correct Mac about my dad after dinner. In private. Sure, it'll be weird to explain to everyone else later, but I'll cross that bridge when I get there. I shove a big spoonful of soup into my mouth. It burns my throat. I'm a lot of things, but I never knew I was a liar.

Either because of the awkwardness of the past minute or in spite of it, the dinner conversation picks back up at rapid speed, sending everyone down another tangent. Two blinks later, Mac's parents start packing everything up.

"Daniel and Frankie are probably wondering what's taking us so long," Mac's mom says.

Frankie? Frankie. I've heard the name Frankie before. That's Andrew's little brother. And Daniel? It takes me a second to remember him, too, but then it clicks. I lean over to Mac. "I didn't realize Daniel wasn't here." His little brother. "Where is he?"

Everyone around us gets quiet. Andrew's parents stand to help clear the table. Clearly, I've said the wrong thing.

Mac grabs his keys. "I'll tell you in the car."

BROTHERS AND FATHERS

BROTHERS AND FATHERS
BROTHERS AND FATHERS

MAC DOESN'T DRIVE ME HOME. INSTEAD, WE park at the lookout above Elysian Park. If you close your eyes, the buzz of the highway in the distance sounds like the ocean from up here. He cuts the engine. I try to keep my voice as gentle as possible. "So, Daniel?"

He whispers his brother's name in a voice that cracks with pain. Then he takes a shaky inhale and says, "He's in the hospital." My mind pieces together snippets of past conversations. His standing appointment on Monday nights, allusions to health issues. "He kind of lives there these days."

"Andrew's brother, Frankie, is his best friend, so on Tuesdays, they play video games. After the rest of us have dinner at the house, our parents go to the hospital and eat again with the boys. The hospital case worker suggested Family Dinner to 'maintain a sense of normalcy' for me." He stares down at his hands, curling and uncurling his twitching fingers. "But it's not normal. We're missing Daniel."

I swallow, trying to grasp the full scope of Mac's family life. "So, on Tuesdays, you and your parents are at the house, and Gael and his daughter come, too, but on other nights . . ."

"I'm alone," Mac completes my sentence in a voice so quiet it hurts. "We rotate other nights with Daniel. I sleep there on Mondays."

We're silent for a beat. What am I supposed to say now? I want him to know that I care, and that I'm listening, but my words are insufficient. I don't know how to comfort someone like this. I've never had the chance to try. "That must be hard on you all," I say at last. Not poetry, but at least it's something?

"I mean, it's the hardest on Daniel, obviously. I get lonely or whatever, but he's in a fucking hospital, so that's that." He leans his head against the steering wheel. "Our house is too big to be there alone. It freaks me out. Camp Doom is smaller. Cozier. And . . . you know." He shuts his eyes. "I like knowing that you're nearby. It makes me feel less—" He sighs. "Sorry. That sounds weird."

Sounds human to me. I brush my hand through his thick hair. "I've been sleeping better recently, too. I think it's because of you." Mac drags his head up to give me a weak attempt at a smile.

"Is Daniel . . . ?" I don't know where to start. Is he in a lot of pain? Is he going to be okay? Is it appropriate for me to even ask?

"We don't know. It started off with asthma, but then it got more complicated. Body spasms. Heart palpitations. He needed to sleep in a chair at night because nosebleeds started coming on so suddenly and severely that one night, he woke up choking on his own blood."

My chest tightens at that image. The messiness and the horror of it all.

"Last year, he got the cancer diagnosis. This summer he's trying a new treatment. He'll be there for a while."

For all the complaining I do about my life, I've never had to deal with anything like this. Loved ones battling diseases. Being at the mercy of profit-driven hospitals. The sound of a sniffle pulls me back. Based on the way Mac's clenching his jaw, he's trying hard to fight off the raw emotion gurgling through his veins. I don't think he's winning.

"It's my fault he's there." Mac shuts his eyes so fiercely that he might pop a blood vessel in his forehead. His shoulders bunch up, arms clench around his sides. His knees tremble violently. He is a black hole imploding in on itself.

I tread as carefully as I know how. "You said he has cancer. I—I don't think that could be your fault."

"It is, though." His fingers jerk into painful-looking fists. "There was an oil extraction site across the street from our old apartment. When I was younger, I thought it was fun to sneak in there after dark. The oil wells looked cool, so it became this thing, you know, to, like, break in and hang out or whatever." Another sniffle. He chews his lip. "Daniel never wanted to go. He liked his books, staying inside. But I would always drag him with me. I didn't like being alone."

He twirls the fidget spinners on his rings. The buzzing sound is ominous against his ragged breathing. "I didn't know that every time we hung out there, we were breathing in all this shit that would make him sick."

"Mac." I touch his knee, but he doesn't respond. It's like he doesn't even notice. "That's the oil company's fault. And the government's fault. That's not on you."

"I literally dragged Daniel there after school. Every day. We lived close, but it's not like my parents or Gael got sick. I wanted to hang out behind a No Trespassing sign, and guess what? I got asthma. Daniel lost two organs and eight lymph nodes. You can't tell me that's not my fault."

My brain struggles to connect the cheery Mac that I've known so far with this tortured side of him. It's easy now to understand why he used to get into trouble. It's harder to understand how he ever stopped. If I were him, I'm not sure that I would.

Beside me, I can feel Mac holding his breath. But eventually, he must breathe. And when he does, when his mouth falls open, all that comes out is a ragged gasp. This is when he falls apart.

It's been a long time since I've seen someone cry. I had forgotten the way that tears saturate the air in an enclosed space. He shifts his face away from me, but I can hear all the choked, pained noises crawling from his throat. His sobs belong to him, but the sounds ache in my own chest like an old wound. I watch the tears gather at his chin. I want to wipe them away, swallow them away, hunt down the cancer that's hurt all these people and tear it apart with my teeth. He wipes his nose with his sleeve and I grab his hand. I don't know what to say, so I squeeze. Hard. He hides behind his hair, drawn between us like a curtain, but he lets me hold his hand. I'm grateful that he does.

LOPSIDED

LOPSIDED

LOPSIDED

IF THERE WERE OSCARS FOR NIGHTMARES, I'D win Best Picture every night. I've hardly slept since visiting Mac's house the other day. Snippets from the conversation at the dinner table, the ride home, won't stop churning in my brain, generously providing my stress dreams with even more creative material than usual. It's a miracle I'm still standing given that all I'm currently running on is two cups of instant coffee, the sugar from the bag of peach rings I had for breakfast, and adrenaline.

I climb the tallest of the rock climbing walls, which surprises everyone in Color Outside, including myself. Another jolt of mild-danger-induced thrill tickles my brain. I move on to free-climb an advanced wall against the gym employee's warning. I slip and hit the pads on the ground, ass first. It hurts but I feel strong.

Across the gym, Andrew gets put on probation for doing the Spider-Man thing, repelling upside down from the ropes, after being explicitly warned multiple times to *not* do the Spider-Man thing. I join him to sit cross-legged on the large table in the corner.

"Prepare yourself because this might be my best work yet," Andrew says as he uses the climbing chalk to draw whiskers on our faces—earning yet another angry shout-out from the adults in the room. We look at each other and can't stop laughing.

"We need a picture of this," Andrew declares, but when I reach for my phone, it slips from my hand, plummeting toward the floor. Before I can react, Mac dives after it. He retrieves the phone and sets it back on the table beside me.

"Hey, you," Mac whispers in my ear as he brushes by, continuing his walk to the water fountain. I try my best to contain my smile, though my eyes must've ratted me out because Mac looks back at me over his shoulder, beaming.

Andrew shoves my knee. "ARE YOU A COUPLE YET OR WHAT?"

"Shut up."

"I heard Mac told you about Daniel," Andrew says. "Pretty big deal."

I nod. It is a big deal. I know. Which is why I've been trying to avoid Mac all day.

My strategy has been working for the most part. I stood at the back of the line when he stood at the front. When he and Sage volunteered to help climbers belay, I escaped to the restroom. But I don't think he's getting the hint. Rock climbing is hard but trying to act natural around Mac is harder. I've spent 99 percent of my brainpower over the past couple of days thinking about correcting him about the whole thing with my dad. I've rehearsed a million different ways of telling him that my father isn't dead. All I have to do is explain that I choked and apologize for the miscommunication. I'm just waiting for the right moment.

I hear my name being called from near the water fountain.

Mac waves a hand, motioning me over. My stomach swirls with nerves. "What does he want?" I mumble.

"You, obviously," Andrew says before unceremoniously pushing me off the table.

I try to shove Andrew back but he slips away, cackling. I'll get him back later. For now, it's time to face Mac.

It's hard to keep my breathing steady as I walk to the water fountain. I'm going to tell Mac about my father right now. Get it over with. Except what if he gets mad? What if he thinks I lied on purpose for attention? Or what if he thinks I'm, like, evil or seriously disturbed and doesn't want to talk to me again? Fuck. Why is admitting when you've made a mistake so fucking hard?

When I finally reach Mac, before I can say anything, he fishes a folded piece of paper from the back pocket of his jeans. "I've been tasked to deliver a message to you."

I blink twice. "Wait. What?"

Mac bobs back and forth on his feet. There's a sweet, earnest-excited smile tugging at the corner of his mouth. I grab the paper, noting the ink stains on the edges. "For the survival guide?"

"Maybe," Mac says, smirking. "Open it."

DANIEL'S TIP FOR BEING ALIVE

Yo, don't listen to anything Mac says. That foo don't know shit lol.

Anyway. The famous Niarah. Nice to meet you.

Mac says you're a gamer, too? Gamer to gamer, here's my theory on the apocalypse:

The best part of playing the iconic Legend of Zelda: Breath of the Wild game is the beautiful landscape, right? Runnin' around Hyrule when everything's so nice and green and lush? Well, the landscape is only that pretty is because it's after the apocalypse. The villain had to turn everything into ruins for Hyrule to regrow. So, maybe destruction isn't always negative because the world's supposed to go through cycles of rebirth to allow for renewal?

Hence, my tip: Play the games, watch the movies, and listen to the songs that have something interesting to say. Take it from someone with lots of free time and lots on my mind these days. As Yoko Ono said, "Art is a way of survival."

Mac's an idiot but he's aight. Looking forward to meeting soon

—Daniel

CALAMITY

CALAMITY
CALAMITY

DANIEL. OKAY. MAC TOLD ME ABOUT DANIEL, but he also told Daniel about *me*. Mac wants me to know his brother. The brother who he cried over. This all feels very real. Very intimate. Very much not what I deserve given that I'm literally lying to him about my own family. I start to sweat. Mac fidgets with his rings. I should say something. Anything. I skim the note again and clear my throat. "Your brother's so much smarter than you."

"Yeah, but I'm taller." He stretches his arms above his head for emphasis and winks. I flick his side and he crumbles.

Daniel's note vibrates in my hands. My stomach churns. I've met most of Mac's family, I've communicated with his younger brother, I've been inside his house, seen his room, heard his secrets. Meanwhile, I've done what? Kept things from him? Forbidden him from getting too close?

"Aren't you going to add an addendum to Daniel's tip like you did to my first one?" Mac asks.

"Nope."

Mac crosses his arms. "Why not?"

I smile weakly, half teasing, half guilty. "His is actually good." I fold the paper and put it in my pocket. "I should, uh, get back to keeping Andrew company while he's on Time-Out. Make sure he doesn't get bored and burn the place down."

Mac nods twice. "Yeah. Sounds good."

I practically run away, but if Mac notices my anxiety, he doesn't comment on it.

"What was that about?" Andrew asks once I reclaim my seat beside him.

"Nothing." I let out a nervous laugh before throwing chalk on Andrew's face. He tosses it right back. Some of the powder lands in my mouth and I gag, pulling theatrically at the hem of his new shirt to wipe my tongue, which makes him scream bloody murder.

"You two! Get out of here, *now*," the gym manager barks at us.

Honestly, hallelujah. It's a relief to be kicked out. Any excuse to not be near Mac right now. Not until I can get my shit together and come clean. Andrew loops his arm with mine and keeps cackling as we're commanded to collect our things and wait outside.

"They're so *strict*, my god," Andrew complains as he pushes open the glass doors into the summer heat.

"This is a glorified jungle gym, yet they're acting like it's a war zone," I agree.

As soon as we slump against the bench on the wall, Mac pops outside, too. Great. Lovely.

"You two are a very bad influence on the group," he says in fake anger.

Andrew sets his hands into prayer position and bats his eyes. "We're oh so sorry! Please take pity on us, supreme leader of the super-serious nature club."

Mac shoves his shoulder and sits down between us. The pressure to tell him the truth adds to the heat in the air. I break out into a fierce sweat.

It's then that a car pulls up to the curb. The entire parking lot is practically empty, yet it idles directly in front of us with the windows shut.

"Should we run?" Andrew asks after a beat. "This looks sketchy and I'm not in the mood to get kidnapped. It's way too hot for that."

I laugh. "I don't think—"

But then my voice runs dry.

The car door pops open with a soft click. From behind the wheel of an unassuming gray sedan, a ghost emerges. I drop my phone again.

We should've run.

A voice that I haven't heard for a long time calls my name.

I bolt upright. Andrew and Mac are quick to do so, too, matching my energy. I take off, speed-walking out of the parking lot, toward the street.

"What's going on?" Mac asks, his brows knit together.

"I just want to talk," the man calls, following us.

"Should I call someone?" Andrew asks, his concern mounting with each hurried step.

"No." We hit the sidewalk and I turn right, hoping that if I get far enough away, the ghost will give up. "I don't know why he's here," I mumble.

"So, you know him?" Mac presses, unsure whether this new information should make him feel better or worse.

After four years of not seeing or speaking to him, I'm not sure if I can say that I know my father anymore.

"You guys should go back," I tell the boys, but they don't

listen. I tuck behind a corner, relieved to see that my dad's car has stopped following us.

"Niarah, what's happening? Are you okay?" Andrew asks, but I wave him off. I'm too busy trying to steady the erratic beating of my heart. Mac looks worried as all hell. I'm able to collect myself back to my baseline, only for a moment. The car pulls up again, this time with the window down.

"Can you take this? Please?" My father's arm stretches out the car window, shaking slightly as a brown envelope flaps between his fingers. I can't help but gawk at him. The sight throws me. He looks older than I remembered. His hair has gone completely gray, his eyes a bit more sunken. The laugh lines around his mouth have solidified into hard-ironed wrinkles. He also looks softer. His eyes are pleading and apologetic. Sitting in the beat-up car, he looks gentle. I seethe.

"What are you doing in LA?" I shout, then hold my breath.

"Work," he says.

Oh. I'm relieved he isn't here for my mom, but also . . . annoyed. I hate that I'm annoyed that he doesn't even pretend like he's here for me. Not like I want him to be. I frown. I hate this. I hate it all.

He shakes the envelope again. "Please."

Andrew stares blankly between me and my father, not entirely sure what is happening, but not wanting to interfere. My father sighs and presses the envelope into Mac's hand. Mac stares at him, then at me, and then I see it click. Mac's eyes widen as he drops the envelope. It floats to the floor like fallen leaves from the oak tree in front of our old house back in Syracuse.

My father puts the car into drive. "I'm sorry, Niarah." He takes off without another word. Gone again.

We all stare at the envelope on the ground. It landed in a small puddle from a leaking fire hydrant a few feet over.

"Are you . . . okay?" Andrew asks tentatively.

"I'm fine." I bend down, retrieving the envelope. I thought it'd contain guilt money, but when I shake it, I can tell it contains something much more complicated.

A letter.

I bite the inside of my cheek.

"That was your dad." Mac doesn't phrase it as a question because he doesn't have to.

My hands are cold. Shaking despite the heat. "Yes."

"But you said . . ." Mac's face contorts with equal parts confusion and hurt. "You know what? I can't deal with this right now." He tosses Andrew his car keys. "Drive her home. I'm walking."

"It's, uh, kind of a funny story, actually—" I reach for Mac's shoulder, but he dodges me.

Mac scoffs. "You're unbelievable."

Half of my brain spins at the letter in my hand, half at the lie that has caught up to me.

An acidic vine of bile creeps up my throat.

Andrew steps forward. "Hey, you don't look—"

I throw up on my shoes.

HE'S FINE

HE'S FINE
HE'S FINE

THE MATH IS SIMPLE. MAC IS A REAL PERSON IN my life who I've upset. My father is a figure from the past, unworthy of my time or attention. It's easy to choose where to put my focus. After the rock climbing run-in, I called Mac immediately. I've called him twenty times in the four days since.

"He's not answering me," I tell Sage.

"Don't worry. He'll be here," Andrew says.

The three of us stand by the entrance to the concert venue, watching hordes of people slide through the metal detectors.

"You don't think he's still mad?" I ask. I grip the strap on my clear tote bag. With the venue's bag policy, I couldn't bring my usual Jansport. I hate see-through stuff, but this ridiculous plastic thing is better than nothing. I keep the letter from my father in my pocket, though. I haven't opened it—not sure if I ever will—but I also can't bring myself to get rid of it. I've been carrying it around with me everywhere, letting it burn a hole in my pocket. My own little bad luck charm.

"Oh, no, Mac's definitely still mad. We didn't tell him that you were coming," Andrew explains.

Right. I guess I wouldn't want to talk to me either. What type of freak lies about a dead parent? Especially to someone who's worried about their own family member actually dying?

I feel Mac's presence before I can even see him. It's a weird thing that's started since we've gotten close—I know the cadence of his step, the sound of his voice, anywhere, even in a crowd. I force on an uncharacteristically broad smile when he breaks through the crowd at last, walking up to us with his hands in his pockets.

He looks good tonight. Black jeans and a vintage black varsity jacket. A clean white tee with his chain peeking out from the collar.

When Mac sees me, he sucks in a terse inhale. He starts spinning his rings as he turns to Andrew, glowering. "You literally promised me that she wouldn't be here."

I shift awkwardly, trying to ignore the malice.

"Yeah, well, I lied," Andrew says.

Mac looks to Sage for backup, but Sage shrugs. When he cuts his eyes to me, I wave, like an idiot.

"Hi," I say.

He grumbles out a hi in response, but keeps walking. "Let's get inside or whatever."

I hesitate, momentarily doubting the Trap Mac into Hanging Out With Me plan, but Andrew nudges my shoulder. "Give him a minute. He'll be fine."

BEEF

BEEF

BEEF

ONCE INSIDE THE VENUE, MAC STILL WON'T talk to me. He's pissed. Really pissed. I start to get that familiar spinning feeling. The one where my mind starts to race after everything's been going too well for too long. The past few weeks were incredible before I messed it all up. I've been waiting patiently, bracing myself, for it all to inevitably fall apart. And now it finally has.

There's a tickle in my throat. I feel sick. Is it Covid or is it anxiety or is it depression or is it a cold or is it my period or is it dehydration or is it stress or is it my diet or is it karma or is it boredom or is it existential dread or is it cancer or is it—

"Shots?" Andrew raises the flask of whisky that he snuck in, its metallic container glinting beneath the artificial lights.

I yell yes right as Mac mumbles no.

"What? So you're a lightweight now?" Andrew jokes.

Mac frowns. "I don't want to spend every night of the summer drunk." He points to the stage, where the sound crew is setting up a drum set. "We should just, like, chill tonight."

Andrew sticks his tongue out. "We'll put it up for a vote, then. All those in favor of staying sober and wasting a perfectly good opportunity to get shitfaced at a show with your best friends the last summer before three of us leave for college, raise your hand." Mac's hand shoots into the air. "Okay," Andrew continues. "Now, all those in favor of drinking this gorgeous, smoky, delicious Japanese whisky that I went to great lengths to steal from my parents' liquor cabinet?" Andrew, Sage, and I all raise a hand.

"That settles it, then," Andrew says.

Mac pulls the collar of his jacket up over his face as he kicks his feet up on the divider in front of us.

"Don't mope," I tease.

"I'm not moping," he shoots back, crossing his arms.

"Ignore him," Andrew says, unscrewing the flask. "Mac's the one who got the fake IDs for us this spring, but now he always gets like this whenever things start to get fun."

"When I got the IDs, I didn't know that it meant we'd be getting drunk or high *all the time*."

Andrew sucks his teeth. "We don't get drunk or high *all the time*."

"Well, *you* do."

"Hey," Andrew barks.

"MAC," Sage interjects. They stretch out their arms between the boys. Sage pushes Mac back down with a firm press to the chest. "Chill out."

The tension in the air is unbearable. I've seen them bicker before, but never quite like this. Andrew doesn't look at Mac as he passes me the flask, slamming it down on the bench a little too hard, so that a few drops of liquor splash out. Why'd Mac have to ruin the vibe? If he was going to just get mad at us, maybe he shouldn't have stayed.

"You can still drink if you want to," Mac mumbles.

"I know that. I don't need your permission," I say, too defensively. This makes Sage and Andrew laugh. I seize the moment of levity, then throw a swig back. The whisky burns my throat and makes my gut churn. I try not to gag. Shots are terrible.

"You really don't have to drink that," Mac whispers.

"I thought you were mad at me."

He rolls his eyes.

"Nothing matters," I grumble. "Might as well drink and enjoy."

"Hedonists have more fun," Andrew chimes in from across the bench.

Mac frowns. "Look, I don't want to tell you what to do with your body—"

"Good, then don't." My jaw clenches as we glare at one another. Now he's getting on my nerves. "Look, I'm finally having fun for once. I would've never done something like this a few months ago. This is me healing."

"This is you numbing. There's a difference."

I down another shot. "Whatever."

The concert starts. The opening band is solid. Not really my style of music, but Sage and Andrew are loving it, so I lean in. The whisky helps. After a few songs, though, I start to get thirsty. "I'm going to the snack bar. Anyone want anything?"

Andrew lists off a string of snack options that Sage gives either a thumbs-up or thumbs-down. I try my best to remember the ones that they agree on. Mac says he'll go on his own after the opener finishes their set, which isn't necessary since I'm already going, but whatever. He can pout all he wants.

I wander over to the snack counter. It's stocked like a movie theater with all the essentials. I'm not sure what to order. My stomach feels weird from the drinking. If I hate how liquor tastes and how it sits in my body, then why do I keep accepting every shot? Water would be wise, but then again, they also sell blue slushies. Who am I to resist a blue slushie? I get one plus a soft pretzel for Andrew and Sage. I'm about to head back to my seat when I hear a familiar voice.

"I didn't know you left your house." I turn toward the sound. "Miss us?"

Corey and Xander. The assholes from school. I ignore them and keep walking.

"Why are you in a hurry? The main set hasn't started yet," Corey says. He reaches for my shoulder. I shove his hand away. It smells like artificial butter and sweat.

"Get out of my face." Corey and Xander are blocking the tunnel back to my seat, so I walk back toward the snack bar. Mac said he'd get his own food during intermission. Maybe he'll be there. I pick up my pace while Corey and Xander continue lurking.

"Wanna know how many new followers I gained after our last video?"

As if thinly masked bullying videos being passed off as "pranks" make the faceless strangers of social media actually care about him. Never have I met a boy so proud of his cerebral shortcomings. I walk faster now, but their footsteps follow close behind.

"Were you born this crazy or was it more of an acquired thing? Too much internet, too few friends?" I ignore him, but he keeps running his mouth. "It was you who egged my car, wasn't it?" I bite my tongue. "Morgan said she saw you do it."

Where is Mac?

I almost reach the corner, but then I feel the strap of my tote bag drag down my shoulder. With a harsh, quick pull, Corey yanks the bag from me. I drop the pretzel and almost the drink, too. "You still walk around with all your doomsday shit?"

My free hand clenches into a claw, cracked at harsh angles ready to cut. "Give it back."

"What you got, girl?" Corey opens my bag and aims it toward Xander so he can film its contents. "Let's see. We've got an unopened jar of peanut butter, a compass, a flashlight, and—aw—even a family photo." He rubs his thumb across the photo of my mom and me that I carry around, the one that I picked for the very first go bag I made for us when I was trying to get her to leave my dad.

This is when I lose it.

I glare at Xander hiding behind his phone camera. I shoot daggers with my eyes that are sinister enough to make him pause. He clears his throat. "Hey, Corey, maybe you should chill."

But Corey doesn't shut up. And Xander—despite his words—doesn't stop filming. So, I decide that it's on me to shut Corey up. By throwing the entire slushie at his face.

I toss the drink, then run. But I'm not quick enough.

Meaty hands slam against my back.

My chin hits the floor hard. I swipe my tongue over my teeth to make sure that none got chipped in the fall. I'm okay. I can smell the mix of Clorox and tobacco and Pepsi baked into the filthy floor and I'm pretty sure that there's gum under my knee, but I am okay.

In front of me, though, I see Mac's black sneakers appear. He stands at the end of the hallway several feet away, holding a blue slushie of his own in one hand while balancing a tub of kettle corn and a box of Sour Patch Kids in the other. His stance is wide.

"What's going on?" Mac's voice comes out low and harsh, yet Corey looks almost happy to see him. More audience.

"You heard about how she carries this kit around all the time, right? For the end of the world?" Corey's laughter is cut short by the sound of snacks hitting the floor. A pool of arctic-blue slushie splashes the black canvas of Mac's Vans.

My eyes follow up his legs until I see his hands, now clenched into two tight fists. The floor is sticky beneath my palms. I start to move. "Mac," I say. I'm on my knees when he takes a step toward Corey. His eyes are faraway, nearly unrecognizable in their darkness.

"Mac—" I say his name again, but he's not listening. Now he's moving fast. Too fast. I'm nearly on my feet. I'm yelling now. "MAC."

Corey scoffs, his voice the crackle of television static. "Yo, Niarah's crazy ass started it, so—"

And that's when Mac punches him. Right in the mouth.

IT COULD ALL BE SO SIMPLE

IT COULD ALL BE SO SIMPLE
IT COULD ALL BE SO SIMPLE

MY MOM ONCE TOLD ME THE STORY OF THE moment she knew that my father was The One. Back before things got crazy, before I was born. They were at a bar and some creep tried to grab her waist. My dad saw, snatched the dude by the collar, and threw him across the counter. He proceeded to climb over the broken glass to beat the guy in the face, repeatedly, until two other men pulled him off. Mom's eyes glistened when she told me that story. She said that when he punched that guy for her, she had never felt more safe. She told him that she loved him for the first time ever that night.

Only five years passed between that night when my father hit that man and the first night that he hit her. I always wondered how my mom never saw the abuse in her marriage coming. How she could've been so blind to the possibility of it. But tonight, when my heart leaps at the sight of Mac throwing a punch, when I feel myself fall for him even more at this first witness of violence, for a very brief moment, I understand my mother.

THE WAY BACK

THE WAY BACK
THE WAY BACK

COREY HITS THE FLOOR BEFORE I CAN EVEN stand up straight. Xander screams. Corey's blood mixes with the blue slushie spill on the floor, creating a sickly purple. In one hit, Mac broke the guy's nose. A security guard appears and shouts. Mac tugs the sleeve of my shirt, urging me toward the emergency exit. I'm trying to figure out what to say, what to do, but it's all happening so fast. Corey's holding his nose, trying not to cry. I stare at my tote bag on the floor between us. Is it too late to grab it?

The security guard is closing in, so Mac grabs my hand now, pushing open the door and sounding the alarm. Outside, he starts to run. I run, too. We make it to his car before anyone catches us. Mac tears open the passenger-side door for me, nudges me inside, shuts the door, then strides over to the driver side. He turns on the car, hits the gas, and starts driving without a word.

My stomach churns. Mac is seething. We do not speak. No radio. Windows up, so we can't even hear the sound of nighttime traffic out the window. As he drives, he alternates between flexing his hand and gripping the steering wheel so tight that his knuckles turn pale. He refuses to look at me. We ride together in frigid silence until he pulls up in front of my house. I'm uncomfortable but not angry. If anything, I'm overwhelmed. I never thought I'd see this side of him. I never thought seeing it would make me so confused. I reach for his hand, but he shrinks away.

"I don't wanna bond this way," Mac says quietly, his hands still fixed to the steering wheel.

I recoil. "In what way?"

"Over violence."

This pisses me the fuck off. I open the car door, climb out, and slam it. I hear Mac do the same right behind me as I barrel for the backyard gate.

"What?" Mac asks.

I whip around. *"'What'?"* Like he doesn't know why I'm irritated. I scoff. "Oh, I get sooo tired of this."

"Of what?" he asks, voice shaking. I try to open the yard door, but he presses it shut. "*Of. What.*"

"Of this game you play where you're so much more mature than me." I fling open the door again and stomp into the backyard. Mac's footsteps follow me.

"I don't know what you're talking about," he says.

"Yes, you do. You don't get to ignore my texts for days, go all White Knight at a concert, then act like *you* didn't just start a fight."

"I didn't start a fight. I ended one."

"Oh, well, in that case, let me go get your championship belt for such a clean knockout. Should I hold your hand up above your head? Let you wave to the crowd, Creed?"

"That's not fair."

"What's not fair is you acting like that was my fault." I reach for the doorknob to enter Camp Doom, but Mac steps in front of me.

He buries his hands into his hair and tugs, letting out a frustrated groan. "I never said it was your fault. I was just saying . . ."

I get a flashback of minutes before: Corey on the floor, holding his face, screaming at Mac on our way out. Mac yelling back—louder than I've ever heard him before. Less of a yell, more of a roar. I couldn't believe how his voice seemed to shake the glass doors. I couldn't believe how much it reminded me of my father.

A weary laugh escapes as I shake my head. "My father and Mac. Two men who know how to throw a punch."

Mac freezes. "What did you just say?"

I shove past him, opening the door to Camp Doom. "Nothing."

I plop down on the futon, pull out my phone, and start scrolling. Mac watches me, annoyed.

"Thanks for the ride home," I say as a means of kicking him out.

He doesn't budge. "Look. I'm—" He opens his mouth, but hesitates. He bites his lip. "I'm sorry. I'm really sorry." His voice comes out soft. The shift in his tone makes me look up at him.

He's standing in the doorway still, arms wrapped around his waist. "I hit Corey because he laid his hands on you. It made me . . . furious." He steps forward, standing above me. His face is cast in a shadow as he's backlit by the light above. "I'm not going to promise that I won't intervene if I see someone step out of line with you again. But I won't escalate things. I didn't have to hit him. But I guess a part of me wanted to. Badly." He opens and closes his fist, examining the fresh bruise on his knuckle. His words hang in the air between us. "Sorry. I'll go."

He turns to walk away, but I grab his wrist. He gazes down at me, his eyes uncertain.

"Sit." I pull him down gently to join me on the futon. He resists at first, but then leans in. "Sorry for slamming the door. I don't want to argue with you."

He sighs, pressing his face into his palms. "I know you don't like that I hit him. I don't like that I did it, either. I've been in this dark place before, mentally. I used to live here. But I don't anymore."

"Then where are you now?"

"Nowadays I'm searching for a form of hope that isn't bullshit. Everyone always says be happy because you only got one life or whatever, but that's never been enough for me. Like, Daniel, he's the best person I know, and guess what? He's sick. And he's not just sick, he's suffering. And there's no reason for it. There's no point to it at all."

I flinch. This sounds like something I would say. Not Mac.

"Life isn't fair. Some people suffer more than others. I know you think I'm all optimistic all the time or whatever, but I have a really hard time connecting to the cookie-cutter, bumper-sticker-brand-of-capital-H *Hope*. But ever since last year, I've been trying to find my own way to not live in despair because that shit, that will destroy you. You fall into a giant pit of dread and you get stuck there. Eventually, you fuse with the pit and suddenly you're pulling other people down with you. Or you're knocking them down." He looks away, bringing his knees to his chest.

"Am I a pit? Am I bringing you down?" The corners of my eyes start to tingle.

"No, no, no." Mac rushes toward me, crossing the futon in one swift motion. He drapes his arm on the back of the couch and brushes his thumb against the sleeve of my shirt. It's comforting without being overwhelming. "You aren't bringing me down. But I do wonder . . ."

I seize up. This is it. This is when he'll tell me that he doesn't want to see me anymore. I brace for the pain. "You . . . you wonder what?"

"If, maybe, you'd feel better if you talked about it?"

"Talked about what?"

"What happened the other day after rock climbing. What started your nightmares. Why you and your mom moved to California." He pauses. "Why when I hit a guy, you told me that I was like your dad."

Oh.

An invisible weight creeps into my chest, restricting my lungs' ability to breathe.

So, he knows. He figured it out.

The fear of being seen with such clarity makes me recoil into the pillow. Mac watches me patiently as I open and close my mouth five times in a row, each time searching for the right words. Where to begin. I've never talked about these things before—the thoughts that keep me up at night, the experiences that led to my constant state of paranoia. Why trust Mac with this information? Why trust anyone? Why would he stay after I explain to him the laundry list of mental illness and daddy issues?

Ultimately, it's the way he doesn't look away, doesn't backpedal, that makes me decide to talk. But when I open my mouth, I taste salt water. I bring my fingers to the corner of my lip and find it wet with tears. My tears. I blink again and feel it all rush forward. I try to apologize for crying, but instead, a starved, shocked croak echoes from my throat in place of words. I fold my face into my hands.

I feel Mac's palm, warm and steady, between my shoulder blades as I heave.

TOMORROW

TOMORROW

TOMORROW

THE SUN IS RISING BY THE TIME I FINISH LET-ting Mac in on the secrets of my life. A nine-hour-long conversation. The longest I've ever had. Dawn creeps in through the skylight, painting us in pale orange light. Bleary-eyed from lack of sleep, we squint to stay awake for a little longer.

When he finally stands to leave, sneaking out before my mom wakes up, he takes a Sharpie to the wall. I watch him as he leaves a note:

A form of hope that isn't bullshit.

"See you tomorrow?" he asks.

I nod. He leaves and I go to sleep, looking forward to tomorrow.

FLOAT ON
FLOAT ON
FLOAT ON

"THIS SONG NEEDS TO BREATHE." OX TURNS UP the volume and rolls down all the windows. Salty ocean air whips through the car, tousling our hair as we hurl down the Pacific Coast Highway. His speaker system is so intense that my water bottle vibrates in the cupholder. The bass and the drums give me chest compressions. It lulls me into a state of something like relaxation.

There's a unique pleasure in putting someone onto a new artist. Ox let me pick the playlist, so I put on Haru Nemuri. He's never heard her before, so after she wails at the end of "lostplanet" he asks me to run it back. We listen to the singer scream and thrash as we snack on the salmon onigiri and grapes that he packed for the drive.

Surf Day With Ox started off as a joke. I was complaining about how I wanted to surf again, but my friends think I'm a liability after the last time. Ox offered to take me himself. It seemed like one of those classic promises that adults make, when they vaguely suggest doing something nice for you but never follow through. Last night when he told me to be ready at seven a.m., I was surprised. Who knew that a man with a cobra tattoo is good at keeping a promise?

I hiss when the ocean splashes against my ankles. There's an icy bite to the water that I enjoy. It wakes me up.

I eat shit on three waves in a row. In a weird way, I love it. Getting tossed around, having to swim hard to make it back out past the break.

I hear Ox's voice over the waves after my fourth wipeout. "Are you drowning?"

"No."

"Good. Come back, then."

Unlike Mac, Ox doesn't freak out when I keep failing. He gives me a few pointers, but isn't too overeager about it. Maybe if I try hard enough at surfing today, I'll be so tired tonight that I'll actually sleep well. That'd be amazing. Why haven't I tried exhausting myself more before?

"Want to try the next wave?" Ox asks me.

I shake my head. "Too tired. I kind of like floating." Out here, the smell of seaweed overpowers the scent of the salt water. I like it.

"Then we shall float." He leans back on his board.

Ox isn't that bad. I bet he and Mom would be having the best summer ever if I wasn't here. They'd probably eat out every night at restaurants with low lighting and menus in foreign languages with no translations because they're both adventurous and like new experiences. Meanwhile I'm reluctant to try a new flavor of my favorite cereal.

Ox pulls a stick of gum out from the pocket on the shoulder of his wet suit. He folds it into his mouth slowly like a sheriff in an old movie lighting a cigarette. "I'd offer you one, but it's nicotine."

"How do you know I'm not a smoker?" I ask.

"Are you?"

"No."

"Good. Don't start. It's terrible. I only started after I got sober. I felt like I had to replace the drinking with something else, but that was a mistake. I don't think the cigarettes helped."

There's always a weird moment when an adult talks to you as an equal. My brain lags behind. Why is he being real with me? "What did help?" I ask after a beat.

"This." He draws a circle in the water with his fingers. "AA didn't really resonate with me, but connecting to nature did. There's something about being outside, doing something physical. I find it constructive." He looks like a seal lying on his board like this. A very content seal. "How's Camp Doom going?"

I lie down on my board, too. "It's going."

"Let me know if you ever need help."

"Thanks, but I'm good. More help is kind of contradictory to the whole self-sufficiency goal." It's already bad enough that Mac is helping. "When shit hits the fan, we'll all be on our own anyway."

Ox chuckles. "Have you ever seen a documentary about Hurricane Katrina?"

"What?"

"Hurricane Katrina. The big one that hit New Orleans in 2005? The government failed to protect people. First responders were slow to react. It was a true catastrophe. So many people died. But you know what always stands out to me?" I shake my head. "The people helped one another."

A shadow of a fish darts beneath our boards. "What do you mean?"

"When it felt like the world was ending, and the state only cared about protecting the rich, neighbors made rafts to save one another. They gathered resources, found boats, and rescued as many people as they could. The news is racist, so the media tried to portray everyone as looters, but many people broke into abandoned department stores to salvage fresh clothes for those who needed them. Food, infant formula for babies, all that. It was a horrific time—a true crisis—but people pulled together and helped one another out during and after the storm."

We're both quiet for a beat.

"Why are you telling me this?" I ask.

"Sometimes people find solidarity in disaster. When you care about the people around you, human society might not be as bleak as you think."

The water stirs beneath us and he bolts upright. He breaks out into a wide smile and nudges my board forward. "This is a good one, you got this."

I consider protesting, but the wave is right. Not too big, not too small. I start to paddle. I push up. I crouch. I stand.

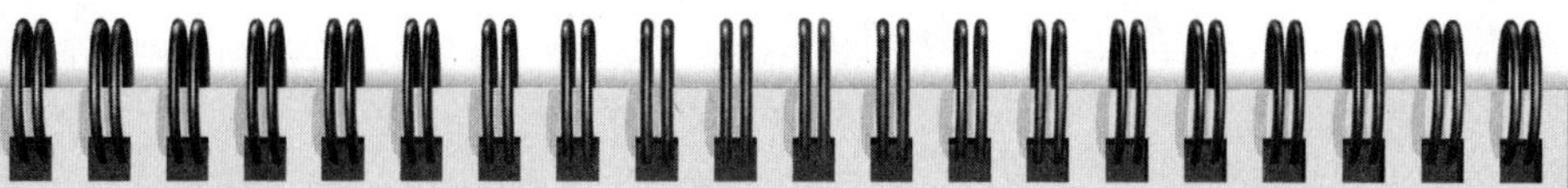

SURVIVAL TIP #35: THE RULE OF THREES

A mantra in the prepping community on survival is the rule of three: You can survive three minutes without air, three days without water, and three weeks without food.

Never test the limits of any of these or else you'll wind up dead.

TESTING THE LIMITS

TESTING THE LIMITS
TESTING THE LIMITS

HIKING TRAINING WITH MAC IS HARD, AND I'M still worried about whether I can keep up on the trip. Luckily, though, training has gotten a lot more engaging.

On our third "water break," Mac leans me against a tall tree. He flows his tongue into my mouth in rhythm with the kiss and I get dizzy. It's all sensations. His thumb on my neck, his chest against mine. After the first few moments of moving softly and slowly, something gives between us. Everything that has built up all summer rushes forward. My hands find his forearms, lean and dotted with faint goose bumps, then glide up his biceps, strong and shaking beneath my touch. I'm acutely aware of the thinness of his shirt and mine. Such faint pieces of fabric are all that stand between my skin and his. The thought makes my torso tremble as he grips a hand against my hip and—

"Time-out." I pull away. The sensation of breathing on my own once again sends my lungs into a brief shock. I press my hand to my chest to catch my breath.

Mac watches me, chuckling softly as he rubs a thumb across his swollen lip. "I like it when you call time-out. It's cute." He takes a swig from his bottle, downing it greedily. "You're cute."

"Just cute?" I grab the bottle from him, finishing the remaining water.

"Bonita, hermosa, linda, maravillosa, inteligente, sexy—"

"Okay, that's enough, thank you."

Mac looks at me and hesitates before saying, "You know, I got into UCLA, too. Maybe I wouldn't mind staying out here for school."

"Mac." I return the bottle to his backpack and pull out two granola bars. I hand him one. "Don't be insane."

"UC Davis has been feeling really far recently." He takes a bite, so big that half the bar disappears. "And it's not all about you. I like home. I like being near Daniel. I like . . . your company."

"You just said it's not about me."

"Yeah, well, people lie." He finishes his bar and tosses the trash into his bag. He dusts off his hands and touches my waist.

"Remember what we said about keeping things light?" I play with the collar of his shirt.

"Yes, I remember what *you* said about it."

I lean away. "You said you were okay with that."

"I am." He sighs. "I really am. It's just fun for me to think about a version of this that doesn't end at the end of the summer. I know you said you'd never consider long distance, but what if—"

"Mac. Please." I let my head fall in exasperation against his chest. "Let's enjoy this, okay? For once, I'm enjoying living in the present. Actually being in the moment. No more talk about the future. Let me be here right now with you." I pull him closer. "The art of being present, remember? Isn't that your whole thing?"

"It's not my *whole* thing," he replies.

I run my fingers through his thick hair. "Thank you."

He nods. I inch closer and he glides his finger along the part of my collarbone that peeks out through the neckline of my shirt. "Is time-out over yet?" he asks with a smirk.

And then we're back at it.

The rule of threes is simple: You can survive three weeks without food, three days without water, three minutes without air. For the next several days, Mac and I test the limits of the breathing piece. It feels like the entire week passes with our lips pressed together before we come up for air. Further research is needed, but kissing could be good training to build up one's tolerance for breath regulation.

FLOWERS

FLOWERS
FLOWERS

MOM WATCHES ME FROM THE SIDE DOOR AS I tackle the garden surrounding Camp Doom.

"Am I hallucinating?" she asks.

I can't help but laugh. The other day, Mac said that my mom was right, and that I should add some flowers to the garden, too. So, I picked some bulbs up from the community plant swap around the block. Just a few.

"Don't get too excited. The primary purpose of the garden is still to cultivate edible plants."

She holds her hands up. "I'll take what I can get."

We haven't talked much in the past few days. She powers through an awkward silence. "Hydrangeas?" she asks.

"Yeah." The soil is warm between my fingers. "They're, uh, you're favorite still, right?"

Mom looks at me, pausing for a beat. "Yes. They are."

"Good." I continue working.

Mom lingers outside, sitting in the chair by the door. Soon, she brings out a Toni Morrison novel and reads while I garden. We don't talk, but there is a lightness between us. One that hasn't existed for a while. We stay like this, engrossed in our own parallel activities, occasionally exchanging a brief glance of mutual acknowledgment, until sunset.

SURVIVAL TIP #39: FLOWERS

Consider planting flowers. For morale.

Of course, flowers will do nothing to protect against the ravages of flood or famine, but they will be nice to look at. We all deserve a hint of beauty in our lives.

MY BRAIN + THE END OF THE WORLD

MY BRAIN + THE END OF THE WORLD

MY BRAIN + THE END OF THE WORLD

GROUP PREP

GROUP PREP
GROUP PREP

THE BACKPACKING TRIP IS ONE WEEK FROM today. Planning is more complicated than I imagined. There are permits to confirm, parking passes to complete, meal plans to be organized, mileage goals to be calculated. For Andrew, ironing out these details is clearly tedious. The boy's only contribution to the conversation is when he shouts that as Culinary Advisor of the trip, he has exclusive reign over menu design, which was already a given. But I love helping Sage and Mac with the boring details. Figuring out how much of which items to bring, and who should carry what to distribute weight among the group. I've spent so much time preparing for the mega catastrophes hurling toward humanity, but I've never prepared for something good before.

It feels nice.

Meanwhile, Mac sits next to me, his arms hovering centimeters away from mine. When Andrew is zoning out, engrossed in the episode of *Demon Slayer* playing on the television in the background, and Sage is busy googling something about water sources along the trail, Mac slides a hand onto my knee. I'm wearing denim shorts, so the feeling of his hand on my skin radiates warmth throughout my body. I look from his hand to his mouth, then back to his hand, then his eyes. His shoulders shake as he stifles a laugh.

Hi, he mouths to me.

Hi, I mouth back.

He drags his thumb lightly across my thigh. Shivers pulse through my skin like ripples of water surrounding a stone tossed recklessly into a lake. The intensity of the feeling destabilizes me, forcing a sharp inhale to catch my breath. He smiles at me as if he knows.

The most connected to my body that I ever feel is when I'm playing video games. Nerdy, I know, but true. The simulated stress on-screen and violent vibrations of the controller remind me that my body *can* respond to certain emotional situations (most often, virtual ones involving a samurai's open world quest to avenge his kidnapped uncle). But beyond an artificial arena designed to make me addicted to a game divorced from my own reality, I don't often feel like I'm *in* my body. I know that I *have* a body, but that's the extent of our relationship. Me and Body do our own thing, and we're both okay with that arrangement. We don't know each other that well and I'm not used to her reacting in tandem with my emotions. So, when Mac touches me, and my heart and my brain and my chest and my stomach and my skin all come alive at once, I'm speechless.

One kiss with Mac. I kiss oneeeee person and I'm already going soft. Jesus. The sickness will take you out real quick.

From the corner of my eye, I see Sage open a fresh document on their laptop. They change to all caps to get our attention:

So, we have a water filter and propane tanks and— WAIT, NIARAH, SHOULDN'T YOU BE TAKING NOTES, TOO?

I freeze. "Why?"

FOR YOUR SURVIVAL GUIDE? ISN'T THAT LIKE THE PRIMARY REASON WHY YOU LET MAC DRAG YOU INTO THIS?

"Oh, yeah. Right." The survival guide. Duh.

"She's coming because she loves us, she just won't admit it yet," Andrew says over his shoulder as he passes by the computer to get more snacks.

"Not true."

"Which part? About loving us or being stubborn?" Andrew teases.

Mac tosses me a smile and I blush. I take out my notebook. "I am taking copious notes. The survival guide appreciates you all contributing your wisdom to my research."

SURVIVAL TIP #42: WHATEVER YOU DO

Don't forget about the survival guide.

PRACTICE
PRACTICE
PRACTICE

I WAIT TWENTY MINUTES BEFORE SPLASHING water on my face and hyping myself up to go out to Camp Doom. Mac always texts me now to make sure I know when he's staying over. Most nights, I let him be. I know he needs the space. But sometimes, I sneak out there with him. Tonight, though, I have a specific plan in mind.

I grab the bag that's been waiting in my closet all week. I walk by my mom's room, making sure that she's asleep, before slipping out the side door. I knock and Mac answers immediately.

"Hi," he says. I think I detect a hint of nerves in his smile, but they could be mine. I shove my free hand in my pocket to mask its shaking.

"I, uh . . ." I trail off, suddenly regretting my decision. "I got you a shed-warming gift." I shuffle the plastic bag out from behind my back and pass it to him as quickly as possible.

"But . . . this is your shed?" Mac raises an eyebrow.

"Yeah, well." I motion for him to open the bag. He pulls back the plastic to reveal a navy-blue sleeping bag. He steps back, examining the shiny nylon puff. "I know you already have one, but this way, you won't have to bring yours back and forth. Or you could still use yours, too, but it gets kind of cold in here at night, so two might be better than one. Plus, I was planning on buying one for here anyway, so it made sense, but you don't have to like—"

"Thank you, Niarah." He cuts me off with a soft grin.

I hover by the door as he unzips the sleeping bag and lays it down on the futon. He plops onto it like a fish before rolling himself into a blanket burrito. His hair sticks messily out the end in all directions. I laugh and he beams back at me, one of those self-satisfied smiles when he's pleased to have gotten a real reaction out of me. I try to hold it back, but I can't, which only makes him smile even harder. He unwraps himself. "It's so comfy."

"Good." My voice comes out quieter than I had intended. It's that accidental drop in volume that seems to put us both on edge.

Mac's backpack is slouched on the chair in the corner. The sleeping bag is on the futon. It's funny how when someone's sleeping in a room, the space takes on a completely different energy.

I point at the new shelf from Ox. "Did you remember to earthquake proof that? Drill the little things in to bolt it to the wall?"

"Yes, I remember, but no, I haven't done it yet. I'll do it when it's light out."

"Promise?" I ask.

He laughs. "Yeah. Promise."

I nod and sit awkwardly in silence.

"So, what's up?" he asks.

"Um."

I don't remember who pulls who in first, but it doesn't matter because soon, our movements are so tangled up in each other that my sense of separation from him disappears. The futon creaks loudly as we tumble to its almost-soft surface. Gravity leaves me on top, and for the first time ever, I get to be the one to pull his shirt off over his head. Bells blare in my head: *Attention, Mac is shirtless. We repeat: Mac is shirtless. Not on a beach. Not because he's swimming. But because he wants to be shirtless for you.*

I want to put my hands everywhere, so I do. I want to trace the outline of each of his muscles with my fingers, so I do. It's weird what runs through your mind in moments like this. Like here's this gorgeous, out-of-breath boy beneath me, looking at me in this way that makes my blood turn into warm honey, and all I can think about is the fact that up until now, all our kissing has always been vertical. Upright and standing. Seated on the couch or in his car a few times. But never horizontal. I can't stop the sharp inhale of realization that shocks my lungs. I cough it out.

"What? What? Is everything okay? I'm sorry? Are you okay?" Mac asks, pulling away with wide eyes. "This is fast. We can slow down."

"No, no." I place my palms on his chest. I don't want this moment to pass. "I'm okay." I press against him, but—

"Niarah."

I can feel the moment slipping away. "Mac, it was a cough, not an aneurysm."

He touches the sides of my face with vexing tenderness. "Let's pause, okay?"

Here he goes. Mr. Vibe Check.

I push off him and scoot over on the futon, crossing my arms. "Fine."

He sits up. Vertical again. Woop-de-fucking-doo.

I stare at the wall because I can't bring myself to look at him. "I didn't want to stop," I say. I miss the feeling of his hands on me already.

He clasps his hands in his lap. "We're not stopping, just pausing."

"Same thing."

He takes a deep breath. I hate it when he does that. Take a deep breath like he's in control of his feelings or whatever.

Quiet settles between us. A full minute of uninterrupted quiet.

"This is me working on my intimacy issues," I blurt out at last. My words come out harsh. Defensive.

"We don't have to, uh, go all the way there to be intimate, you know. Like, that's one form of intimacy, but so is conversation, so is eye contact, so is sitting next to each other, listening to each other . . ."

"Yeah, yeah, I know. It's just . . ." Suddenly, I feel so young. I pull my knees to my chest. Is it so ridiculous to want more? "Do you not want to?" I ask in a near whisper.

"Of course I want to. Are you kidding me? I've thought about it, like—" He stops himself. He shifts the nearest pillow onto his lap. I raise an eyebrow and he laughs awkwardly, rubbing the hair from his forehead. "Okay, there's no noncreepy way to disclose how much I've thought about it, but trust me: It's been a lot."

This feels genuine. I decide to believe him. "Have you ever been with someone . . ." I hesitate. "Uh, horizontally before?"

Horizontal. I wince. What is it with me and *horizontal* today? I can't even bring myself to say the word *sex* out loud. Why would he want to sleep with someone who's still too awkward to even say such a little word?

"Sort of," he responds. "There was a girl sophomore year. We did some stuff, but didn't go all the way. She told everyone that we did, though. She had an ex who she wanted to make jealous. Ever since then the idea has been . . . stressful."

"Oh."

Mac begins to tap his foot, notices it, then forces himself to stop. "Have you ever?"

"What do you think?"

"I don't know. You're full of surprises." He looks at me, I look at him.

"No."

Another long silence. The air buzzes between us.

"Maybe we should just watch a movie," he suggests, which is ridiculous since it's already past two in the morning, but whatever. I shrug in agreement. Mac nods and pulls his shirt back on while I go through the very elaborate performance of retrieving my laptop, plugging in the charger, dimming the lights, and selecting a film, only to immediately disregard it all and initiate making out with him again before the opening credits finish.

The urgency that flooded between us earlier comes surging back. I move onto his lap and wrap my arms around his neck. He moans when the fabric of our sweatpants rub against each other. Holy crap. That sound. I make a mental note to hold on to that soundbite for later.

We don't stay in this position long because soon I'm lying on my back, pulling him down with me. His hand hovers over the waistband of my sweats before quickly retreating. "Do you w-want to keep going?" he asks. His voice is shaking.

"Not all the way, but, uhm . . ." I guide his hand back to where it had wandered before.

Mac's hair falls over his eyes as he bites back a nervous smile before untying the drawstring and moving into new territory. I'm nervous, but committed to a Can Do Attitude.

At first.

I give him a couple of minutes to try and make something happen, but I don't feel anything. Except for discomfort and pinching. I'm probably doing something wrong. Mac's been with someone else before, so it's probably me, right? I try to get out of my head. Tap into my body or whatever, like Andrew's always talking about. But nothing is working. I don't know how this is supposed to feel, but I don't think it's supposed to feel like this.

"Can we stop?" I ask.

Mac removes his hand immediately. "Everything okay?"

"I don't think this is my thing." I pull up my sweats and sit up straight. "Thanks for trying, though." Immediately, I feel stupid. Why am I thanking him? Why is he even talking to me?

"Uh, yeah. Okay. Of course." He sits up with me, shifting awkwardly as I reach back for the laptop. He clears his throat. "Well, uh. What do you like?"

I scroll through movie options. "The Fast and Furious film franchise, horror movies about intergenerational hauntings, anything with Nic Cage—"

"C'mon, Niarah." He gives me a look, dripping with sincerity.

I sigh. "Making out is fun, but the, uh, other stuff? Maybe it doesn't feel good for me like how it does for other people."

"If you don't want to do it, that's one thing, and that's fine. Of course that's fine. But sometimes, these things might need . . . I don't know. Practice?" His ears are bright red. Poor guy.

"You know I've never done this with someone before, I have no idea what I like."

"Well, what about . . . you know?" I wait for him to finish. He makes a weird motion with his hand and blushes. He raises his eyebrows at me, asking, *Still no?*

I shake my head back: *You lost me.*

His eyes fall to the floor. "I mean like, uh, when you're by yourself?"

"MAC." I don't masturbate. I haven't since I was younger. The day I realized what I had been obsessively doing, the shame hit like a freight train and I stopped.

"I'm sorry, I'm sorry. Too much?"

"Yes." This is 1,000 percent too much. I'm cringing so hard that every bone in my body could shatter any second.

"Heard." He holds up his hands. "Last thing I'll say, then I'll shut up—"

"Wait, what? You're capable of shutting up?"

"Aight, aight, you got jokes. I get it." He nudges my shoulder. "But if you ever do explore alone and learn some things about what you like and want to try again together . . . let me know."

"Let you know?" I repeat, teasing.

He grins awkwardly but doesn't back down. "Yeah, you know. Keep a dude in mind."

I press play on the movie, praying to finally end this conversation. "Will do."

THE POWER OF SUGGESTION

THE POWER OF SUGGESTION
THE POWER OF SUGGESTION

THE FOLLOWING NIGHT, I TAKE MAC'S ADVICE. The one about self-exploration.

The first time that I feel it—when I don't back away when the feelings get big—my whole body goes limp. I sink into my soul. Every subsequent second is decadent.

So, I take his advice again. And again. And again every night this week, until it doesn't feel like his suggestion anymore, but something of my own.

IN CASE OF EMERGENCY

IN CASE OF EMERGENCY
IN CASE OF EMERGENCY

I THOUGHT THAT I'D BE HAPPIER WHEN I COM-pleted Camp Doom. We finished all the steps: strengthened the walls, built another shelf for food storage, installed an outdoor water tank, filled the closet with canned goods, organized several bags of seeds, planted a garden, and lined the back wall with ninja stars and a couple of pocketknives, just in case. On one of the smaller walls, there are lines of hooks with cookware and strings of various lengths and widths tied in knots. Mac still has to bolt Ox's storage shelf and the rest of the furniture to the walls, but besides that, we're done. The twinkling Christmas lights and box of old poetry books that doubles as a side table were Mac's idea—"In case you have to stay here for a while," he insisted.

I didn't plan on painting the interior, but Mac convinces me when he finds a cool electric-cobalt-blue color for free at the hardware store. In perfect West Coast Gothic script, Mac stenciled in black *Welcome to Camp Doom* on the walls. Our matching gas masks bookend the text on each side. And right below in the center, a clear floating shelf awaits the final touch: the survival guide.

I only have to finish writing it first.

In my mind back in June, Camp Doom would be spartan—minimal. But now I can see Mac's influence everywhere. I like it better Mac's way. And that's what makes me sad. It's almost time for him to go.

Mac makes a big deal out of us finishing in a very Mac way by tying a red ribbon around the front door to cut for the Grand Opening. "I went to, like, four different stores for the super-big scissors, but I guess that's only a thing in movies," he says, handing me a very normal-size pair. He's wearing dark jeans and faded black Converse with a button-down shirt and black bowtie.

"You clean up well," I say.

"If you think I look good now, you should see me on a proper date night. Te lo digo, cariña, you wouldn't even *believe* what I can do to this hair with a little motivation." He runs his fingers through his messy waves, shooting me a theatrical wink.

"No dates. I told you," I remind him between laughs.

"Not even a little completion of Camp Doom celebratory date?" He lightly nudges me against the wall, leaning over me with a smirk.

"This is the celebration," I say.

"Fine, then I'll cancel this." He uses his thumbs to push my chin upward as he sinks down to plant a kiss on my neck. The touch sends shock waves down my spine.

"We invited Andrew and Sage. They're already on their way," I say.

"Then I'll tell them there was a change of plans." Another kiss, the other side of my neck. More shivers.

"Mac . . ." My voice comes out hazy. He has that effect on me now. And from the way that he presses against me when I say his name, I know that he likes it.

"C'mon. One date." Another kiss, long and teasing as he floats his hands up my hips. "Please."

In the Before Mac Times, I could've never imagined myself changing my mind about anything over something as frivolous as a touch. But in the Now Times where lips applied to mine with the right amount of pressure is enough to hot-wire my brain, all my walls stand less firmly than before.

"When?" I ask. "We leave on the backpacking trip tomorrow."

"When we get back."

Before you leave, you mean. I give him a small smile. It might be nice to say goodbye.

"One date," I agree.

BACKPACKING SUPPLIES

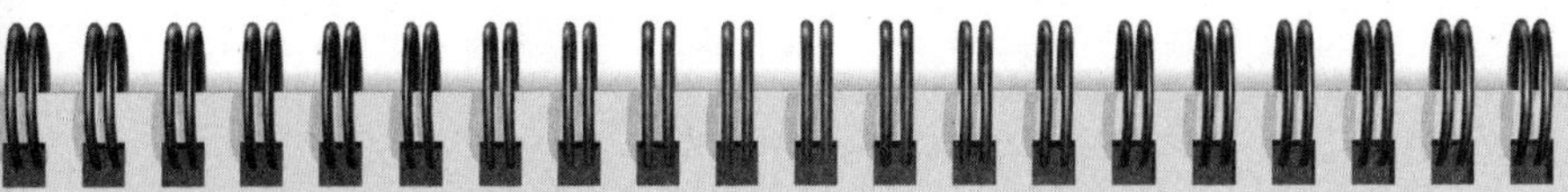

MAC'S TIP FOR BEING ALIVE #4

Less of a quote, more of a thought

Instead of trying to control nature (the external world), what would change if you knew that you were a part of nature, too? That you belonged to it?

See you tomorrow.

xx,

Mac

A GIFT FROM MOM

A GIFT FROM MOM
A GIFT FROM MOM

"THAT'S NOT A LOT OF STUFF," MOM SAYS AS we stare down at the items on my bed.

She's right.

I cross-check the contents strewn across my bed against Sage's packing list seven times. I don't want to forget something and end up having to construct a sleeping bag out of bushes or use a leaf as toilet paper. I've gotten used to the hikes, but backpacking? Still freaks me out. Which is tough because we're leaving in thirty minutes.

I have on the outfit that I'll wear for the next three days—a Dodgers hat, a breathable T-shirt and high-endurance sports bra, and a pair of insanely dorky yet functional hiking pants that zip off at the knees and convert into shorts, even though I'm certain that I will never take advantage of that feature. Although I imagine that somewhere in Utah, there's a middle-aged white man out in the woods, absolutely psyched to convert his hiking pants into shorts, that ain't gon be me.

Besides the clothes on my back, there's a sleeping bag and

sleeping pad, two pairs of wool socks, a long-sleeve shirt (what Sage keeps calling a base layer), a pair of long johns, a beanie, gloves, rain gear, and a warm jacket. I found a weirdly satisfying, collapsible dishware kit that contains a plate, bowl, and mug altogether, plus a fork and knife. There's a headlamp and a toothbrush. Two empty Nalgene water bottles. The envelope from my father. And that's it. For the next three days, these are the only items that I will carry.

I glance over at my laptop. This will be the longest I'll have ever gone without touching my most treasured item. It's nerve-racking, yet exciting. "What about the tent and stove and stuff?" Mom asks.

"The others took care of that. We'll divide up the group gear before we start hiking."

Bruce scurries over and tries to add his water bowl to the pile for the fourth time since he's been watching me pack. I laugh and scratch his ears. "I'll be home soon, bud. I promise."

"Your capstone is due the day after you get back from the trip. Are you all done?"

I've been too distracted to work on it much recently, but I can easily knock it out in one long cramming session once I get back. It's not like I've never procrastinated on a school project before. "I'll turn it in on time, don't worry."

She nods, but her eyes look distracted. She's clearly combing her brain for more questions, trying not to panic about me leaving. She and Ox leave for their trip in an hour, so she's been packing, too. "Did you sort out what to do about the backpack? I'm sorry you couldn't find one at the surplus store."

"Yeah, Mac's brother is letting me borrow his. He said it might be a little big, but it shouldn't be too bad. We'll make it work when they get here."

Mom nods. "Good, good." She hovers in the doorway. Stalling. "How far away are your friends?"

I check my phone. "They'll be here in five." I try to not notice how awkward my mom feels.

"I can't believe you're going *backpacking*," she says.

"Backpacking is an essential survival skill for the apocalypse."

"I don't get the feeling that you're only doing this for prepper research and PE credit."

Maybe she's right.

"Speaking of which. I actually, uhm—" Mom stops and starts again. She runs her fingers through her tight curls, then grabs something from behind the door. "I wanted to give you this."

She steps back, opening the door a little wider so that she can hold it up: a pale green 60L backpacking pack.

"Oh my god." I race over to the door, taking the pack into my hands. It's awesome. There must be a hundred extra compartments and pockets. This is the kind of bag that could be on the top shelf of a fancy REI outdoors store. The kind of bag that people who are real intense outdoor people would have.

"I found the bag, Ox sewed on the details." I turn it over and see that the front is covered in cool vintage embroidered travel patches from different parts of the world. "They're to motivate you to keep traveling. See the world."

Something catches in my throat.

"Mom, thanks, but . . ." I set the bag on the floor.

"I'm thinking of it as an investment in your well-being. In your future." She picks the bag up again and holds it up to my back for me to try on. It smells like nylon, the straps fit just right.

I can't speak. I can't believe how specific this gesture feels for who I am right now. This isn't the generic gift that I get every year—some variation of whatever parenting magazine says one should buy for their child at each given age—but something that actually fits me and my interests. Something that she noticed I needed, researched, then carried out a plan to give me at the perfect moment. The opposite of *Oops, sorry.*

I let the pack slip down my back before hugging my mom, tight. There are no more words to say out loud, but we both feel it—the reopening of something between us.

She rests her head on my shoulder, smoothing a handful of braids. "I want you to plan many more trips with many more friends. I—" Her voice cracks. "I want to see you keep looking forward to new experiences, baby."

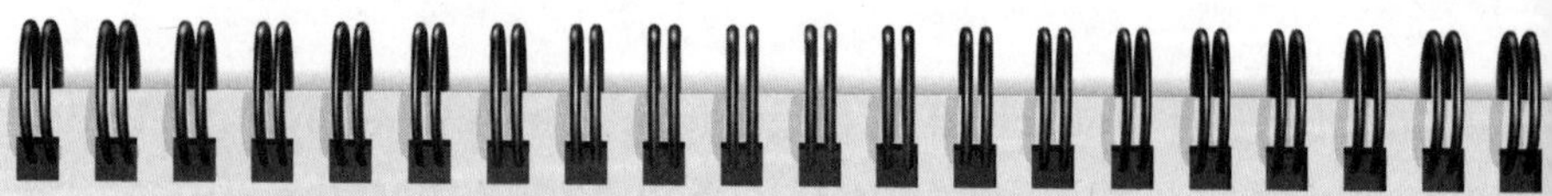

LAST-MINUTE TIPS ON HOW TO PREPARE NOT TO DIE ON YOUR FIRST BACKPACKING TRIP (AND MAYBE EVEN HAVE A GOOD TIME)

Practice different water filtration methods.

Test your gear beforehand. You might be confident that you know how to turn on your headlamp, but then you might realize it doesn't come with batteries. You will be glad you took the time to examine and test your gear *before* you were out in the middle of nowhere in the pitch dark.

Embrace the reality that very soon, you will have to dig a hole and poop in the woods. And that's okay. Because everyone will do it. You will do it. It will be fine. You will not panic, or cry, or attempt to not poop for four days because the idea of not having a toilet makes you want to die. It will be fine.

Learn to read a map, learn your mileage limits, and think about elevation gain.

Bring peanut M+M's or Nutella or trail mix; anything with chocolate and sugar.

Include a trip safety plan.

LNT: Leave no trace. Minimize your impact on the

natural environment you visit. Stay on established trails and don't litter. If you pack it in with you, pack it out.

Put your phone in a Ziploc bag, then double-bag it because if it gets wet, you will be pissed.

Do your own research, but ask questions and rely on friends with more experience.

Here goes nothing.

RICHTER SCALE

RICHTER SCALE
RICHTER SCALE

"YEAH, NOPE, I'M NOT GOING ANYMORE." I grip the column on the front steps of the house, my heart pounding so hard that it rocks my temples like a punch to the head with each beat.

"Niarah, it's fine," Mac says, extending a hand.

I smack his palm away. "Everything is most certainly not fine."

A quick rewind to forty-five seconds prior:

I'm outside, smiling with my new pack, all doped up on nice feelings from the little breakthrough with my mom, saying hi to everyone, minding my damn business, then *boom.* Mac's SUV starts to shake. Then the bushes shake. And then I look down and the ground is shaking, too. And all I can think to myself is: *Oh hell no.*

An earthquake? Today?

Nah.

I drop my bag and run to the front steps of my house even though I'm pretty sure that's the last thing I'm supposed to do.

Standing next to the car, all I could imagine was the emergency brake failing and the car rolling backward, flattening me out like a pancake. When the trembling finally stopped, I waved to Mac, Andrew, and Sage.

"Aight, it was nice knowing you. Y'all have fun on your trip now, you hear?" I turn to the house to take my ass back inside. If another earthquake hits, I'd rather be at home playing video games and hiding under a well-built concrete structure than out in the wilderness where some tree can fall and smash us to pieces.

"That wasn't even a big one," Andrew yells.

"Bro, the ground was *moving.* Don't look at me like *I'm* crazy when the earth's crust was shimmying."

Sage stomps over and grabs my sleeve. "Niarah. You have prepared for this trip all summer. You have overcome your aversion to hiking. You have purchased khaki pants that zip off into shorts. You are *not* backing out at the last minute." Sage gives me a scolding look that damn near takes my eyebrows off.

Andrew leans out the car window. "If you don't come, then who's going to drink all of these—" He pauses, looking up at my house to see if my mom is there. "Delicious, definitely not alcoholic beverages with me?"

"Natural disasters are literally one of the leading reasons why I prep. And you fools want to, what? Ignore what is an obvious sign from the universe that we should not be going on this trip?" I shake my head in disbelief. "What if an aftershock hits while we're in the forest?"

Mac shrugs. "What if it doesn't?"

"We should wait until there's absolutely no chance that another earthquake will hit."

"We're in California. There will never be a moment when there's zero chance of another earthquake," Andrew says.

I cross my arms. "I don't think we should risk it."

Mac leans against the column opposite me. "We're as well-prepared for this trip as we possibly could be. There's a risk in doing things, there's a risk in staying home. There's even a risk in crossing the street."

"We can't be frozen by all the risks around us, otherwise we'd do nothing at all," Sage says.

Doing nothing at all sounds pretty nice, to be honest. But then I glance at my brand-new backpack from my mom and Ox lying on the ground. I sigh. "You LA people are out of your damn minds," I huff, nudging off the column and pointing at Mac. "I'd take an annual, highly predictable upstate New York blizzard over a random earthquake any day."

He smiles as he holds the door for me. "Get in."

0.3 MILES INTO THE HIKE

0.3 MILES INTO THE HIKE
0.3 MILES INTO THE HIKE

I BREATHE IN, THEN OUT. A RABBIT DASHES across the trail. The trees smell like a fairy tale. It's all very cute for a minute. Until shit gets real.

Hiking with the pack is difficult. And by *difficult*, I mean excruciating. Way harder than I imagined. The straps of my pack rub against my shoulders. My steps are unsteady, and I find myself leaning forward to counterbalance the weight. My lungs wheeze. Back in LA, we stuck to well-maintained spaces. I'm not used to having to pay attention to my footing on a rough trail. The extra mental space required to do so makes it even more exhausting. Stray branches scrape against my thighs. I hear bees buzzing but can't see them, as if they're hiding, waiting to attack. How much farther is the campsite? Why did I let these people talk me into this? I must've been super desperate for friendship to end up out here.

"Have you looked up yet?" Mac's voice cuts through my inner rant.

"If I look up, then I'll trip." Actually, I've already tripped. Twice. I kick a particularly intense root for emphasis. "See? Death trap."

"Then we have to stop more. You can't spend the entire hike staring at the ground," he says. "Look where we are." He motions at the scene around us like a daytime television host and right as I'm about to tell him so, the beauty of the surroundings really does shock me. When did everything turn from a pale, sandy beige to this deep, ancient green?

"Break?" Sage suggests.

"Thank god." I sink down to the floor, not having enough energy to care about how dirty my pants will get.

"Should we play a round of waterfall?" Andrew asks. "We're crossing our first water source in a quarter mile and can fill up there." Andrew talks me through the instructions for a drinking game for water. It's weird and wholesome and half of us end up covered in water that we spit out after Sage makes a weird face that makes us laugh too hard with our mouths full. I shove two peanut butter energy bars down my throat, and at last, I feel like I'm not going to die (yet).

Mac identifies a rare bird, and we all watch the tiny creature quietly make a nest for a while.

Everyone waits for me to give the signal that I'm ready to keep going. Somehow, I'm able to stand again.

We keep hiking.

1.1 MILES INTO THE HIKE

1.1 MILES INTO THE HIKE
1.1 MILES INTO THE HIKE

BY THE TIME WE HIT THE FIRST MILE MARKER, I'm sweating like a pig. We all are. I unzip my pants into shorts.

You hate to see it.

2.3 MILES INTO THE HIKE

2.3 MILES INTO THE HIKE
2.3 MILES INTO THE HIKE

WE SEE A BLACK BEAR. AN ACTUAL, LITERAL, goddamn bear. Everyone panics—even Mac—but I read the backpacker's manual a million times, so I remember what to do. I make a lot of noise and the cub scampers off like the book said it would. Everyone applauds, impressed. It feels nice.

SETTING UP CAMP

SETTING UP CAMP
SETTING UP CAMP

TAKING OFF MY PACK FEELS INCREDIBLE. IT'S like New Year's Day, mixed with successfully copping someone's Netflix password, topped with finding an extra chicken nugget in the bottom of the bag all in one. A Top Ten sensation. I flop onto the ground, reveling in how light I feel. "Hallelujah."

Mac joins me on the dirt. "How you feelin'?"

"Soooo much better now."

"Don't get comfortable yet." Andrew opens his pack and starts unloading items. "You and Mac set up the tents. Me and Sage will organize the food."

"Can't we leave all the food in our packs?"

"If you don't mind enticing another bear and/or having everything be eaten by raccoons in the middle of the night, then yeah, sure."

Noted.

Mac and I assemble the two tents quicker than I anticipated. Turns out, they make these backpacking tools pretty efficient. We never discussed sleeping arrangements. Who's sleeping where? I toss my bag into the same tent as Andrew in a panic.

After the tents are ready, Mac pulls out a tarp to set up a rain fly to protect us from the elements. We pull it taut between two big trees and use rope to tie each end.

"What's for dinner, Chef?" I ask Andrew when we're done.

"Peanut curry noodles with sautéed vegetables and chickpeas."

"Sounds elaborate."

"It is." He lights the portable stove and adjusts the heat. "Who has the can opener in their pack?"

"I think I do?" I don't want to get up, though.

"Want me to get it for you?" Mac asks.

"Yes. So much. So lazy."

He smiles. "Aight, hold on."

I'm already so sore from today's hike. Leaning forward hurts. The backs of my thighs, my neck, my arms—everything.

"I can't find it," Mac calls out from inside the tent.

"It's in the pocket," I yell back.

"There are literally forty different pockets."

I groan and crawl into the tent. Mac's all hunched over, looking like an absolute giant. He fishes around my pack.

"It's in the inner pocket at the top," I direct him.

"This one?" His hand plunges into a deep pocket.

"Notthatpocket."

Mac pulls his hand out of the bag, revealing a small square box. He reads the label and turns red. "You brought . . . condoms?"

Okay, time to die. I snatch them from his hand and shove them back into the bag. "Condoms are an essential survival packing item. I have, like, ten packs at Camp Doom." Mac stares at the corner of the box hanging out of my pack. "They, uh, make amazing compact water containers that can hold as much as two liters of water if handled properly. They are, after all, designed to be watertight. The elasticity of latex condoms is SHOCKING."

Mac grins, so I keep stammering. "They have other uses, too. Like, need to keep fire tinder dry? Condoms."

"Niarah—"

"Have a medical emergency and need sanitary gloves or a tourniquet to treat wounds? Condoms."

"Niarah."

"Get stranded without food and need to build an impromptu slingshot to hunt wild animals? Condoms."

"Niarah." Mac grabs both my hands and settles them into my lap. "I am glad that you are prepared for the various emergency situations that may arise on a trip. It's fine. I won't think anything of it."

He grins and crawls out of the tent, but right before he zips it shut behind him, he makes one last comment: "I would be curious to see a condom slingshot in action, though. Trojans versus bears." He holds up the USC victory sign before letting the tent entrance flop closed.

COLD-WEATHER MAC

COLD-WEATHER MAC
COLD-WEATHER MAC

MAC APPEARS FROM HIS TENT WEARING WOOL socks with Birkenstocks. He slips a fleece jacket over his flannel and puts on a knit beanie. Back in LA, I've only seen him in summer clothes. Out here, though, with the cold mountain air, I get a glimpse of what fall weather looks like on him. He wears the season well. Too bad I'll never get to see him in autumn. I eat another bowl of Andrew's cooking and try not to think about how all good things come to an end.

BUOY

BUOY
BUOY

THERE IS SOMETHING IN MY BAG THAT I DIDN'T pack myself. It's a tiny surfboard keychain. I think it's from Mac at first, but when I turn it over, I see words carved into the bottom: *Float on.*

I think of Ox and smile. I hope they're having fun on their trip. Maybe next year, the three of us can go camping. I fall asleep thinking of the places we can go.

SETTLING IN

SETTLING IN
SETTLING IN

I SLEEP LIKE SHIT. ALL THE WONDERS AND romance of camping aside, the actual experience of sleeping on a thin pad in a tent in the woods? Not that fun. We went to our tents around midnight. At around three a.m., I had to pee, but when I peeked out from the zipper of the tent, it was *dark*. Like, SpongeBob-Rock-Bottom-Advanced-Darkness dark. And there were all these sounds. Could've been squirrels, could've been a serial killer. Who's to say? So, I kept my ass in that tent until sunrise.

When it's finally light out enough to pee, everyone else has already started to wake up. No roof over your head means you wake up when the sun rises. Your body automatically goes back to that primal clock. Would've been anecdotally cool if I weren't so exhausted.

Andrew boils water for a quick oatmeal breakfast while the rest of us break down camp. It's pretty intense to wake up at the ass crack of dawn, then suddenly pack everything up to move on so quickly, but there's a satisfying rhythm to it.

The Day Two hike feels different from the first. It's still hard and I'm sore as hell from yesterday. But after the first few miles (I can't believe I'm hiking *miles* now), I settle in. The weight of the pack feels grounding. Each step is purposeful.

"Holy shit," Andrew screams up at the front of the pack. He breaks off into a sprint.

"What? Is it a cougar? Ax murderer?" I clench the straps of my backpack, ready to fall to the ground, tuck my limbs under the pack, and play dead like a turtle.

"What is with you and this ax murderer thing?" Mac asks as he jogs to catch up to Andrew. Sage is in front of me, so I'm last to see it—I come around the bend in the trail that opens up to a clearing.

"Whoa."

LIFE IN HIGH-DEFINITION

LIFE IN HIGH-DEFINITION
LIFE IN HIGH-DEFINITION

THERE IS A MASSIVE, CRYSTAL-CLEAR LAKE. THE water is a shade of aquamarine that looks like it belongs more on the logo of a water company claiming to be "bottled at the source" than on an actual, real place. The forest surrounds the lake on nearly all sides, except for the bit in front of us where a short, rocky beach welcomes us to the water. I'm still trying to pick my jaw off the ground when I hear the first splash, then another, then one more. All three of them have already dropped their packs, kicked off their shoes, stripped off their top layers of clothing, and dived straight into the glassy water.

"I thought we had a ton of miles to cover today—do we have time for this?" I yell.

Andrew attempts a handstand, belly flops, then calls to me, "Backpacking rule number one: We always have time for swimming."

"Get your ass in here," Sage commands.

Mac splashes Sage, but they splash him back way harder, shooting water straight into his face. He laughs wildly.

I take off my boots and put my feet into the water. Goddamn this is cold. Maybe I could wait out here? Sit in the shade? The rocks are not smooth. They dig into the bottoms of my feet, making each misstep cost more and more in tiny pain. "These rocks suck, I don't want to have to walk back out!" I yell, but they don't hear me. They're all too busy enjoying the water. "Fucking hippies."

I groan and hold my breath. Time to go. I push forward and swim in the shallow water. Lakes are cold as fuck. It's that glacial water. Straight from the mountains. I dunk down. The freezing water shocks my lungs like an AED, leaving my scalp tingling.

It's so refreshing that every ounce of tension melts from my body.

Not bad.

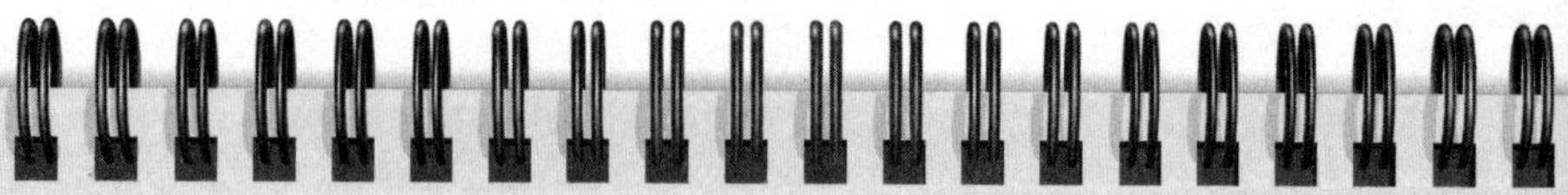

SURVIVAL TIP #46: LEARN TO SWIM

Earth is about 75 percent water. This makes swimming an essential survival skill.

Also, it is fun.

THE DEFINITION OF APOCALYPSE

THE DEFINITION OF APOCALYPSE
THE DEFINITION OF APOCALYPSE

APOCALYPSE. **ROOTED IN THE GREEK WORDS** *apo*, meaning "un," and *kaluptein*, meaning "to cover," *apocalypse* is generally regarded as something terrifying and negative. A life-ending event. The invitation of pain, then darkness. Before the trip, Mac sat next to me as we read the definition on my laptop screen beneath the fort of blankets. He asked me a question that rocked my core: "What if the apocalypse is an ending, but it's an ending to all of the things we actually need to end in order to sustain life on this planet?"

At its etymological core, *apocalypse* means "to uncover."

He went on, "What if things aren't getting worse, but just getting uncovered?"

To be honest, I never used to think of uncovering as something good, either. But then I learned of its potential sweetness. When Sage and Andrew head to the lookout to watch the sunset, and nobody is left at the campsite except for me and Mac, we tangle ourselves up on a blanket on the grass. Mac kisses me, I slide my hand up the gap that emerges between his shirt and his skin as he leans over me. We laugh into each other's mouths, not wanting to break the kiss, until he reclines, removes his shirt, and my whole body shivers at the sight. Light reshapes the curve of his spine, soft and bare. We're still taking things slow, but I luxuriate on this tiny step we've taken, this reveal of his body to me, of mine to him. How holy it is—the moments when an item of clothing comes off, and the trust and vulnerability that ushers in. Turns out, not all reveals are terrible.

What if life isn't getting worse, just uncovered?

ALL IN

ALL IN
ALL IN

POST-SUNSET, THE HILLS TURN INTO A shadow—dark grays and browns with a halo of periwinkle light at the highest elevation, orangey-pink sherbet colors at the lower points. The sounds of nature slip from the orchestra of birds' last conversations of the day to a chorus of crickets. An owl hoots—I never thought I'd ever hear an owl in real life—and being out here finally sinks in.

Mac and I fill the water filter from the stream while Andrew and Sage prep for dinner.

"About the, uhm, tents," Mac begins. He shifts back and forth on his feet, shoving his hands into his pockets. "There's something that I want to show you on our last morning. The only thing, though, is that we'd have to get up super early. So, I was thinking if you're down, then maybe tomorrow night we could . . ."

"We could . . ."

"Maybe share the same tent? So that you don't wake Andrew up in the morning?" Mac's shoulders pitch upward.

I love it when he gets like this. When the usual Mac confidence is replaced with this shy version of himself that cares so much. As if I'd ever reject him. I almost laugh out loud at the thought. "I would love to share a tent with you, Mac Torres."

ENDINGS

ENDINGS
ENDINGS

BY THE TIME THE FINAL NIGHT OF THE TRIP comes, part of me can't wait to get the hell out of here and shower. But another part of me secretly wants to stay here forever. No phones, no news, no traffic, no pollution. Just us.

Our camping spot tonight has a designated firepit and wood, so we're able to get a small campfire going.

"I'm sad this is ending. This summer," I say.

"Don't call it an ending," Andrew says.

"Why not? It's objectively true," I say. No sense denying it.

"Well, what if endings, true endings, don't really exist?" Mac interjects. He catches my gaze and holds it steady. "What if we let go of the idea of finite endings, and instead thought about transformations? Like, what if everything that we currently call an ending is actually just transforming to the next form? We might not know what exactly the next form is, but we don't need to understand it to think of it as changing into something else."

We're all quiet for a moment, but then—

"Yo, you've been listening to too many audiobooks, man," Andrew says.

Mac shrugs. "Maybe."

Andrew takes out his phone and fashions a makeshift speaker out of a coffee mug. We take turns adding songs to the queue. Our options are limited to the tracks that he has already downloaded, but the selection is strong nevertheless. We start with the type of radio pop garbage that we all secretly love to sing in the shower, transition to songs that were popular at least a decade before we were born, then flow into a string of deep house. I had never heard of deep house before Andrew, but now I know and love it. It's the type of music that will put you in a trance. It's the type of music that pairs well with the glow of a campfire.

I give Andrew, Sage, and Mac some privacy to enjoy this last moment together. They've been welcoming, but I know it's a bittersweet night for the original crew to know that they're all about to scatter across the state in just a few days. While the three of them slip into nostalgic Remember Whens and midnight confessions, I pull my father's letter from my bag.

I'm not afraid of the world like I used to be. He doesn't affect me anymore. I don't need to carry this weight around. I don't need to wait for an ending—I'm ready for a transformation.

I toss the envelope, still unopened, into the fire. The edges singe and curl. I watch it turn to ash, then return to my friends. Deep breath in, deep breath out.

Sage reads to us aloud from an old book of short stories. We sit around the fire, bundled up and listening as their voice, accented by the crackle of the burning wood, carries on from line to line.

For someone so sparse with their own words, they're an engrossing reader. Andrew wiggles beneath Sage's arm and dozes off. When no one is looking, Mac traces his thumb along my bottom lip. He looks at me all hazy eyed. If the world ended right now, I wouldn't be mad.

THIS UNIVERSE
THIS UNIVERSE
THIS UNIVERSE

MAC AND I LIE ON THE GRASS, LESS THAN TWO feet apart. Our hearts beat faster when we each realize that the others aren't awake. Just us.

I roll to my side and Mac rolls to his. It's so quiet, but I can hear his breath as it clouds the air between us. It's too dark to see his face, but I can feel his movement, slow and steady, as he brings a hand out from his sleeping bag up toward my face. His palm is freezing when it touches my cheek, but I couldn't care less. It's just the right temperature to cut the heat that his touch sparks through my body. I lean in and my lips fumble from his nose to his chin to the corner of his mouth, half-parted in an exhale.

"Wanna go on a walk?" I whisper.

"Yes."

And so we get up. Moving quietly to not wake the others. I reach into my pack nearby and pull out the tiny package. I grab a flashlight, he grabs our sleeping bags, then my hand. We walk to the lookout, fashion a new bed on the grass, then lie down.

I keep my shirt on when I show him what I taught myself about how I like to be touched. He's eager to learn. So eager that I don't want him to stop. He huddles beneath the sleeping bag as he crouches above my stomach. His kisses move lower and lower until everything that I thought I knew about touch is wiped away with one dizzying wave.

I tremble from the cold night air on my face, his hands on my skin, the warmth of my name on his breath when I climb on top. I pass him a condom.

"Is this what you want?" he asks.

I'm nervous. "Yes. You?"

"Yes."

And then we do the things you do when it's three a.m. and you're far away from home and beneath a sky full of stars and the boy with the beanie says your name so softly that you shiver.

DIZZY

DIZZY
DIZZY

I DREAMED THAT WE WERE STANDING TOGETHER in the rain. When I wake up the next morning, our sleeping bags are covered in dew.

I touch Mac's forehead and he opens his eyes slowly. Once his sight fixes on me, he smiles. "It's five a.m.," I whisper. "Should we get going? For your surprise?"

He sits up, stretching his neck. "Actually, we're kind of here already." He looks out into the canyon and I see everything that I couldn't in the dark last night—the forest bathed in pale light with the river running through it. It's so beautiful that my brain struggles to grasp the sight as reality. It's almost too grand to be real.

"I marked all the east-facing spots along the trail that were supposed to have the best sunrises. Enough elevation and a clearing of trees so that we could see it clearly."

"Oh." This is quite possibly the most Mac surprise ever.

"I'm sorry if I overhyped it, I don't have much planned—"

"No, no. This is perfect." We watch the sunrise. I listen to the birds. "I'm nervous to go back. Reenter the real world."

"Why?" he asks.

"What if another mass shooting happened while we were gone? Or a war? It'd make all of this feel so messed up."

He chuckles. "The world is messed up, so we're not allowed to enjoy ourselves?"

"Maybe? I don't know. You don't get guilty?"

"About this? No way." He kisses me softly. "Us being in love is good for the world."

Love. There it is. I didn't expect to hear him say it so soon. Or ever. It makes me a little seasick. Everything feels like it's moving a little too fast. I smile, give him a quick hug, and walk away to see if Andrew needs help cooking breakfast.

Physical Education Activity Log (page 3 of 3)

Student Name: Niarah Holloway

Date	Activity	Duration	Supervisor Signature
July 31	Miraculously not drowning while surfing	2.5 hours	Marco Torres
August 1	Trail leader on a group hike	4 hours	MAC
August 2	Super legitimate outdoor construction project	6 hours	M.T.
August 4	Plant garden	3 hours	Marcooooo
August 5	Beach cleanup to not upset the orcas	3 hours	M
August 9	Carpentry + construction project	7 hours	Mac Torres
August 10	Spider-Man training/"rock climbing" pt.2	2 hours	MMMMMAC
August 11	Sunset hike to secret spot with view	3 hours	M.T.!!
August 13	Complete outdoor construction project	8 hours	LETSGOOOO
August 14-17	Backpacking trip	70 hours	Marco *round of applause* Torres

Hours Complete / Number of Hours Required for Completion: 187 / 80 **hrs**

overachiever :)

GRAVITY

GRAVITY
GRAVITY

THE HIKE BACK TO THE CAR IS FINE—MUCH quicker on the downhill than the way in. Everyone's tired and there's that lazy energy that comes with the last few hours before the end of a trip. We were up too late last night, too early this morning. The energy is subdued as we throw our packs into the trunk. Mac sits with Andrew up front, sensing my need for some personal space after this morning, but besides that everything feels normal. Until we hit the highway. Until we return to cell phone service.

My phone goes off. Then Andrew's. Then Sage's. Mac's, too. We get a few texts, then a few more. Then a lot more. Unread texts, missed calls. The notifications pile in, faster than we can read. The collective roar of dozens of cell phone notifications firing hums like a beehive.

My stomach drops.

This isn't good.

FINALLY

FINALLY

FINALLY

THE SUNSET STRIP EARTHQUAKE. THE MAJOR shock lasted ten to twenty seconds and registered a magnitude of 6.7. The biggest that Los Angeles has seen in years. Its epicenter only a few miles from our neighborhood. Apparently, the quake before our trip was just the appetizer. The one that hit late last night was the main event.

It wasn't the type of earthquake that crumbled buildings, so there weren't many casualties, but the shake left certain older structures vulnerable.

My mom has left dozens of voicemails in the past twelve hours. I call her back immediately. I tell her we're okay and ask about how Florida went, but she talks fast and just says she's at the store, but will be back soon. She tells me not to go in the backyard until she gets home.

That is when I know.

Even so, that doesn't stop the small cry that creeps out my mouth when I finally see it: Camp Doom in ruins.

I yank open the door and flip on the light. My heart stops at the sight. My backpack slips from my grip, hitting the ground with a soft thud.

All the custom shelves and bookcases have toppled over, leaving books and shattered glass and dirt from the planters everywhere. The shelf from Ox was so heavy that it took out the coffee table, snapping it in half. On its way down, it must've toppled the food storage container because now the stockpile litters the floor, tiny nuts and beans all over the place. From the way the food bags are torn open, it looks like a family of raccoons crawled in through the broken window. The animals must've thrown the party of the century here, ripping and nibbling everything to shreds. Every wall, every shelf, every box . . . It's all destroyed.

All those weeks of planning, all those weeks of work, all gone. I will not cry. I will not cry.

My pocket vibrates. A text from Mac: *All okay?*

I'm still trying to make sense of it all—how Camp Doom could look so bad when the house looks perfectly fine—but then I see it: the drill on the table. Beside it, all the bolts and screws. Aka what Mac promised he'd use to earthquake proof everything.

He said he'd do it. He said I didn't have to worry.

I shut my eyes as my fists tremble.

This is all his fault.

AFTERSHOCK

AFTERSHOCK

AFTERSHOCK

WHEN I DON'T RESPOND TO HIS TEXT, MAC comes into the yard to check on me. His eyes widen as he takes in the room, quickly noticing the drill in my hand and the mess on the floor. He puts two and two together.

"Shitshitshitshit, wait. Wait, wait, wait. Fuck. I'm sorry, I'm so sorry. I forgot—"

"Of course you forgot."

Mac twitches, but remains calm. "It wasn't on purpose. I could've sworn I—"

"Could've sworn you what? Made a sticky-note reminder?" I start to pace. "*Do the one thing that Niarah asked me to do*. The one most important thing."

"Okay. Hey. I know you're . . ." He looks frustrated. Maybe the sticky note is a low blow, but I don't care. He takes a deep breath. "You know remembering those types of things is hard for me. And it wasn't like this was the 'one thing' you asked me to do. We did a lot here. There were so many things—"

"You're right. There *were* so many things. But guess what? Now they're all ruined. Ruined because of you."

"That's not fair." Mac frowns. "Look. I'm sorry, okay? This . . . this sucks. But, like . . ."

"But what?" Sweat starts to gather at my forehead.

He exhales. "The important thing is that nobody got hurt."

"What's that supposed to mean?"

"I don't know! Like, I know you're mad. And again, I'm sorry. But, like, Camp Doom . . ." He sucks his teeth. "I don't know. I just feel like it's not that deep."

"This was important to me," I say defensively.

"Yeah, I know. But that was before everything."

"So, what? You think that after fucking around with you for a couple months, nothing else in my own life is important anymore?"

"Whoa. No. I didn't say that. You know that's not what I mean." He crosses his arms. "I know Camp Doom was an important distraction for you, but—"

I scoff. "You wanna talk about distractions? This place was the opposite of a distraction—this was what was making me feel *safe*. If there's any distraction here, it's you."

Mac's eyes widen. "Is that all I am to you? A distraction?"

I roll my eyes. "It's not *all* you are."

The energy between us shifts, and I feel my anger slowly shift from offensive to defensive. Mac gives me a hurt look that cuts through my frustration. I try to recover. "I mean, that's part of it, obviously, but not the whole thing. We hook up and it's fun or whatever. And that's why I like it. I don't have to think about other stuff when I'm with you. But that's normal. Right? Don't you see me the same way?"

I take a step toward him. He takes a step back. "No. I don't.

I'm not hooking up with you because I want to use you as a diversion for existential dread or all the other shit we deal with."

"I'm not *using* you—"

"But you are! You just said you are." He grabs his neck in frustration. "TV is a distraction. Video games are a distraction. Building a fucking emergency shelter in your backyard is a distraction. But you and me? This is not a distraction." He stares at the ruins. "It *was* not, I mean."

I plunge my hands into my hair, frustrated. "I'm the one who's supposed to be mad here. All this shit is broken and—"

"Niarah, this is just *stuff*. Everything in here can be rebuilt or remade. I don't want to talk about a fallen bookshelf when you're out here telling me that our relationship is apparently bullshit."

"Relationship?" I ask.

His face twists. He starts toward the door.

"Mac, we talked about this before. We weren't going to get too deep. I don't know why we're even fighting about this right now."

"Do you seriously believe that? That you don't understand why I'm pissed that you compared me to a fucking emergency kit? After everything? After last night?"

I groan. "I'm using the wrong words, okay? You're not understanding me. If you knew how bad I feel all the time, you'd know how much it means to me that you've helped take my mind off everything."

He jerks his head to the side as he barks out a harsh scoff. "Well, I'm glad to have been of service to you." He storms through the door, slamming it shut. "I am not your coping mechanism."

GONE
GONE
GONE

MAC'S GONE BY THE TIME MY MOM GETS HOME. I hear her hurried footsteps rush toward me as I sit on the floor, surrounded by the broken fragments of everything that me and Mac had built together. She hugs me tight.

"Where is Ox?" I whisper.

"Niarah . . ." She wants to talk about my feelings, but I don't have room for that right now.

"No. I need Ox's help now. If we start rebuilding today, we can make new shelves before the end of summer. I can still finish before school starts."

She doesn't reply. When I look up at her, I see that she's crying. Something catches in my throat. "Mom?"

"Ox is not here."

"When will he be back?"

I walk into the house, straight to the living room. It's empty. My heart starts to race.

I repeat my question—this time, though, while fighting back the thread of anxiety crawling up my throat. “Where is Ox?”

“Sit down, Niarah.”

“What’s happening? Did something happen to him?”

“It’s going to be okay—”

“Where is Ox?”

“In rehab.” She raises her voice. It startles me. “He relapsed.” Mom lowers down onto the couch. I can’t move. “He’ll be there for a while.”

“Not forever though, right?”

“Of course not forever.”

“Okay, but then why is all of his stuff gone?”

“After he’s done there, I’m not sure if I want him to keep spending time with us.”

A flare of anger rips through my chest. “Did he hurt you?”

“No, no, of course not. Ox would never.” She pats my shoulder. “I wasn’t even there when it happened. It was before we were supposed to meet at the airport. I’m not sure if I want . . .”

“But it’s Ox. Mistakes happen. But he can come back.”

“I don’t know. I . . . I don’t know.”

Got it. No Mac. No Ox. Understood.

It was fun while it lasted.

I am exhausted. And because I don’t have anything left to say, I head upstairs. I touch her hand on my way out. “I’m going to lie down for a while.”

WE WILL GET THROUGH THIS

WE WILL GET THROUGH THIS
WE WILL GET THROUGH THIS

MOM CLIMBS INTO BED NEXT TO ME. I LET HER hold me like she did when I was little.

"I know that you and Ox had started to get close, but me and you? We will get through this," she promises.

I know it's inappropriate, but I can't help but think of that old disco song "I Will Survive." I have a quick image of me and my mom dressed in '70s attire, wiggling down a Soul Train Line.

I say "Okay" anyway and give her a squeeze.

She keeps holding my hand to comfort me, but I don't need to be comforted. If anything, I feel bad about not feeling that bad. Yeah, Ox had become important to me. More important than I had anticipated. But their breakup is probably worse for her than for me. The timing doesn't feel right to express these things, though. I stay quiet.

Eventually, my mom's breathing becomes regular as she dozes off into a nap. She must've been so upset waiting for me to come home. Poor woman. Moms really have it tough. They take hit after hit after hit, all for what? For their daughters to not want to hang out with them? My phone vibrates with a notification from my Reminders app: *Capstone Project Due Tomorrow.*

Fuck.

I'm still fifteen pages short and 100 percent not motivated to change that. I shouldn't have left this 'til the last minute. Will Mx. Ferrante really fail me? That would suck. But then again, I'd deserve it. Sophomore year wasn't even hard, I just couldn't keep up. Everyone else in class was able to pass, even the mindless idiots forged from plastic. But not me. I couldn't get my shit together. As per usual.

I roll over and drag the covers over my head. I pull out my phone and type into the search bar: *Will things get better?*

The first response that comes back is loud and clear: *No.*

Thanks, internet. Good talk.

My mom wakes up with a start. "Are you okay? You okay?" The frenzy in her voice tells me that she must've been having a nightmare. Like mother, like daughter.

"I'm fine, Mom." I pat her shoulder. "I'm fine."

MINOR IRRITATION

MINOR IRRITATION
MINOR IRRITATION

MOM AND I SPEND THE NEXT DAY HUDDLED together on the couch, watching reruns of her favorite old show, *Girlfriends*. It feels good to be there for her in her time of need. At night, she leaves to pick up dinner from my favorite restaurant, but twenty minutes later, she texts that it's closed, permanently. For whatever reason, this bothers me. More than necessary. This place had the best pad see ew I've ever eaten and now all of the sudden it's closed? There was always a sign in the window thanking customers for over thirty years of business. The thought of the one local institution that I felt connected to closing pisses me off. But whatever. Joke's on me for getting addicted to one spot.

Mom texts again, asking if there's another place that I'd like her to pick up from instead.

I don't care, I reply. And I really don't. If I can't have that pad see ew, then I have no opinions about what else to eat.

You sure? she asks.

I sigh. *Yes. I don't care.*

I'll say it louder for those in the back: I don't care. I don't care. I don't care.

SCREEN TIME

SCREEN TIME
SCREEN TIME

WHILE MOM'S OUT, I TURN ON EVERY SCREEN in the house. The television. My laptop. My phone. Her iPad. Even the Apple Watch that she never uses. I turn the volume on each device up as high as it can go.

I sit in the living room. Bruce nuzzles my side, but I can barely feel him. The sound from the screens vibrates the rug beneath my fingers. Somehow, on every single device, there are only commercials. There's one for plaque psoriasis, one for a subpar fast-food chain, and one for homeowner's insurance. None of them are funny, but you can feel the actors on-screen practically sweating as they try to make me laugh. I'd feel bad for commercial actors, but the regulars probably make tons of money. It's hard for me to feel bad for people with boatloads of money. Maybe that's harsh of me. I don't know. Either way, I hate commercials. But I don't let it get to me. Because I am fine.

I consider making myself a snack, but discover that I am glued to the floor. The devices are loud. My neighbors are probably irritated, but the sound is still too underwhelming. It's not deafening, which means that it's not loud enough. Because the thoughts start to creep in.

I'm no good with too many thoughts. I think about everything. All the responsibilities, all the failures, all the disappointments.

I think about how Mac told me that he loves me, but I didn't say it back because I don't know if I do. I don't know if I do because the only person I really love is my mom and even that love is hard for me to digest. My mom will be disappointed when she finds out that I didn't finish my capstone. It will be so embarrassing to repeat sophomore year because I couldn't bring myself to do a simple project. I should've been working on my capstone, but instead I built a doomsday shelter. Camp Doom wasn't even that good and now it's destroyed. Everyone thinks I'm weird. My only friends are moving away next week. I have zero faith that humanity isn't hurtling toward a violent end. People have it way worse than me, yet they're still finding hope. Other people, better people than me, are trying to make the world a better place. I never do anything to make the world a better place.

The thoughts keep coming. I put in my earbuds, praying that the targeted noise cancellation is enough to drown them out. All the good thoughts—the normal, healthy thoughts that miraculously had surfaced to enjoy a brief moment in the sun this summer—run away when they see the bad thoughts multiplying. The good thoughts don't even put up a fight.

HOW TO SURVIVE

???
Who knows.

SPIRAL

SPIRAL
SPIRAL

THERE WAS A TIME IN MY LIFE WHEN EVERYthing felt stable. Right as I got comfortable, right as I let my guard down, the person closest to me—my father—revealed his true self, and my world changed. Overnight. One day, we're this happy family. Next, there are shards of glass from broken vases scattered across the floor. I cut my foot on the wreckage and suddenly I'm bleeding.

If there's no safety at home, then I should look out the window at the rest of the world, right? Except no. Because out there isn't any better. It's worse.

I don't know how to make sense of a world that doesn't make sense—a life where disasters, of both the natural and human variety, lurk around every corner. I don't know how to put it out of my mind, or how to pretend to smile like the others. I don't assume that nobody else has existential dread, either. I know I'm not special. But when I see that other people deal with the same shit that I'm dealing with, if not much worse, yet they've somehow managed to be at least partially functioning human beings—capable of pulling themselves together every morning and making plans for summer vacation or college or five years from now—I get jealous. Then the jealousy makes me feel pathetic. Maybe I'm not trying hard enough to be okay. Could that be it? That I'm just not trying hard enough?

I don't always feel like living, which is why I hold on to the idea of surviving. But after having allowed new people into my life only to lose them, what's the point of any of it at all?

STATIC

STATIC

STATIC

I FEEL IT IN MY HEAD FIRST. STATIC CRACKLING between my eyebrows. It spreads from there, wrapping my head in a dark cloud. The feeling travels down my throat, choking it dry, until it hits its main target: my chest. My heart. The Bad Thoughts morph into Bad Feelings. They burrow into my core, collapsing inward for the briefest moment before exploding in all directions, painting every inch of my body with numbness and pain. Some people don't know that you can feel both at the same time—everything and nothing. But you can. I do. All the time.

I try to fight it like I've done before. I try to look for a tether to keep me grounded to this world. But I can't find it.

I do some sit-ups. Exercise can increase dopamine levels. Maybe if I went to PE this year, I'd have more dopamine stock-piled up. I crank out thirty crunches at high speed, then wait. I lie on the floor and nothing changes. Not for a while. Not until something inside of me cracks. I turn inward, following the trail to the break inside of me, hoping that maybe it's been forged to let some light in. But when I find the source, I gasp for air. The crack inside my heart is not here to help. No, no. It's here to signal something else.

I choke out. Tears have found their way into my mouth. How did I not notice that I am crying? How did I not notice that I am wailing? Wheezing? How did I not notice that I'm finding comfort in the moments of suffocation between my ragged breaths? That I'm wishing for the spaces to get bigger and bigger and bigger and—

I don't know why I'm crying. I don't know why I've ever been able to exist and not cry.

It's my dad, but it's not my dad.

It's my mom, but it's not my mom.

It's Ox, but it's not Ox.

It's my friends, but it's not my friends.

It's school, but it's not school.

It's this country, but it's not this country.

It's this world, but it's not this world.

It's Mac, but it's not Mac.

It's me, but it's not me.

A door is opened. My body moves. I find myself back at the stairs where Mac once took me. The ones that lead to the view that is worth it. There's a tall building nearby with a fire escape. I'm on the roof and the city looks beautiful. I open my phone and take a picture, but the camera can't capture the lights. It's the worst photo I've ever seen. All darkness and shadows. Nothing makes sense.

I'm so tired of being the person who's always looking over their shoulder.

I'm so tired of being anxious.

I'm so tired of being.

HONESTY

HONESTY
HONESTY

I TEXT MY MOM MY LOCATION AND ONE WORD.

Help.

RESCUE

RESCUE
RESCUE

SHE DOESN'T ASK WHAT I'M DOING UP HERE. She already knows. That's why she's crying. That's why she's gripping my shoulders so tight that her nails cut my skin. That's why she showed up with a paramedic team.

That's why I can't say anything. Not to her, not to the paramedic, not to anyone.

Physically, I am still on the roof.

Mentally, I am nowhere.

Patient Care Reporting

Patient Name:	Niarah Simone Holloway
Age:	16
Incident Date/Time:	August 21, 10:17pm
Reason for Call:	Suicidal Ideation

Incident Report:

Paramedics were alerted to a situation near Elysian Park and arrived at 10:17pm. Patient was observed sitting alone. She appeared numb and initially ignored attempts at communication. The team completed a physical as well as a suicide risk assessment. Once deemed to no longer be at risk of self-harm, patient was released to the custody of her mother with resources on how to seek further mental health support.

Prepared by:

Marie Blair

EMS incident reports contain protected health information as defined by state and federal law. This information must be kept confidential and comply with Fire Department Policies.

THERAPY

THERAPY

THERAPY

MY MOM DOES NOT LEAVE MY ROOM EXCEPT TO open the front door when the doorbell rings. She returns to my side within seconds. My old therapist, Shirley, hovers by the door. Who knew that doctors still made house calls? I nod to let her know that I want her here. She enters without a word and pulls a chair up next to my bed.

Shirley asks some questions. How long I've felt this way, when these feelings started. I don't have any straight answers. I ramble, but I don't cry.

"I thought that you were doing better," my mom whispers. Her voice catches. "I hadn't seen you this happy in years."

"Yeah," I reply. I don't know how to explain it, either.

Shirley asks more questions. We take lots of breaks.

"How often are you having these thoughts?"

"When it gets really bad, what do you do?"

"What scares you about these thoughts?"

I'm here, but I'm not here. That is, until her last question.

She asks for permission to hold my hand. I say yes. Her palms are smooth and smell of cocoa butter lotion and the gold rings that adorn her fingers.

"This is the most important question for tonight, Niarah," she says. I nod. "What do you need in order to feel safe?"

"I . . ." I've tried a lot of things to feel safe before. They didn't work. "I don't know." I don't know what I need to feel safe.

"Well," Shirley says, "we'll help you figure that out."

Hey,

I got your message. You're probably surprised that I'm responding. I guess I'm surprised, too.

You fucked up. Mom is so mad at you. I'm so mad at you.

I'm mad at you for so many reasons. You can probably guess the most obvious ones. But I'm also mad because I can't help but feel like me and you have more in common than I'd like to admit. "Self-destructive tendencies" is what the therapist called it. "Intrusive thoughts" is another favorite buzzword. She's good at her job or whatever, but I'm not sure what she expects me to do with these terms other than hold them in my mind and stare at them blankly.

Anyway. It's not like you have any real stake in my life at this point, so talking to you makes more sense than anyone else.

My mother doesn't trust me. My best friend doesn't want to be around me. I don't particularly want to be around me, either. I assume you can relate.

I know you've been trying to "make things right," but how? What can you do? What's your plan? With everyone that you hurt, but also, yourself? How do you actually think that you can fix your life?

Let me know.

Sincerely,

Niarah

Niarah,

When your letter came in, I couldn't believe it. I have so much to say, so much that I want to respond to, but first and foremost, I'm sorry for everything. Truly. I know I messed up, but I want to make things right. How I'll do that? I have no clue. But thank you for writing me and giving me an opportunity to figure it out.

It sounds like a lot has happened since I last saw you. I'm sorry I can't be there with you.

About your main question, though—about how to "fix" things—I have some thoughts.

Life isn't about getting rid of the fears but learning how to manage the anxiety. It's not about fixing life, it's about learning to live in it. Sometimes, a mental health crisis feels like standing on the edge of a waterfall. But oftentimes, it feels more like living in the ocean, constantly treading water. If we make our goal to be perfect, fit, happy, productive, at ease, and calm at every moment of every day, we'll drown. This is why we need to surround ourselves with other ways to stay afloat. Little life preservers. These floating devices can be as small as wanting to hear your favorite band's new album when it drops, or they can be as big as pets like Bruce who depend on you, or your connections to your community. Isolation hurts us when we don't take the time to nourish our roots.

What keeps us afloat is love. It's connection. It's friendship. And guess what you found this summer? All of that. So now, go nourish it. Love doesn't disappear overnight, so be honest with everyone, and see what happens.

I'm walking the fine line between trying to respect your mother's boundaries and letting her know that I'm sorry and I'm not ready to give up on what we have. I'm here now to do the work to make sure that I can continue to be the type of person she can trust. No matter what, though, I'll always care about you both. And you can always talk to me.

You're a good person. You're more than your intrusive thoughts.

Sending a hug,
Ox

PS: About your "best friend"? You're talking about the kid sleeping in the shed, right? Yeah, don't even try to deny it. We know. You think your mom wouldn't notice some wavy-haired teenage boy sneaking around her yard at night? Give her some credit. Anyway, talk to him, kid. Just like your mom, just like your friends, but don't be stubborn. Relationships can't heal without a little vulnerability.

THE DIRECTION OF LIGHT

THE DIRECTION OF LIGHT
THE DIRECTION OF LIGHT

"YOU KNEW ABOUT MAC?" MY VOICE IS HARDLY louder than a whisper, but my mom still hears it. She turns down the volume of the Jazmine Sullivan song playing on the speaker.

"Of course I did," she says without missing a beat. But then she freezes. Her eyes widen with surprise at the sight of me out of bed for the first time in a few days.

I sit on the frayed brown sofa. "How'd you know?"

"You ain't slick."

"I feel like I've . . . I don't know. I don't know why I let myself get so caught up. Now that it's over, I feel stupid."

"You're not stupid." She joins me on the couch. "You deserve friendship. You deserve to have someone be sweet to you. Depriving yourself of human connection isn't bravery, it's self-harm." Her words rip another crack in my heart, but this time, it's not the bad kind. It's the type of crack that lets some light in.

I sit back and look, really look, at Mom. Even before everything went wrong, Mom was always trying to stay close to me.

How many times has she insisted that my relationship with her is more important than any other one in her life? That I'm worth the effort that she pours into my life?

The plant that Mac gave me weeks ago sits in the corner. It leans toward the window.

"Phototropism," Mom says. I look up. She points to the lopsided plant. "The growth or movement toward light."

I chew on the word. "What's the word for the opposite? Growth toward darkness?"

"Skototropism."

"That'd be a really good band name."

She chuckles. "It would be."

Me and mom. Two plants in the same pot. One skototropic, one phototropic. A dimly lit doomsday shelter in the backyard of a house full of windows.

Mom grows in the direction of light.

I think I'm starting to appreciate her method of survival.

FINAL TIPS FOR SURVIVAL

I don't know if I want to keep updating this guide anymore, but I do have one last suggestion.

Try to focus on the things you can control:

- How you treat yourself and your body
- How you react to people and situations
- Where you give your time, energy, and attention
- How you speak to and treat others
- The people you choose to surround yourself with
- The content you consume
- What you do with your spare time
- How you ask for help when you need it
- How you express your thoughts
- Your perspective—learn to look at the world and not only see all the things you can lose, but also all the things you can gain

Remember: Life can be more than survived. It can be lived.

DISCOVER

DISCOVER
DISCOVER

MOM ASKS ME TO PRINT OUT A RECIPE ON HER laptop, which is a waste of paper (something that I didn't use to care about), but it's been a long time since we've cooked together, so I let it slide. The elaborate meal activity was my therapist's idea. I'm seeing her twice a week for the time being and she's having sessions with my mom, too. We're supposed to work on communicating more, but also spending low-stress time together, too. Hence why we're attempting to cook a salt-baked whole fish with fresh herbs from the Camp Doom garden. Given our questionable kitchen skills, I am anticipating ordering pizza later, but hey. We're trying. I wish I could tell Andrew, but ever since everything exploded with Mac I've felt like I don't have a right to Andrew's or Sage's friendship anymore. Their allegiance lies with Mac, not me. But I still imagine he'd be impressed with my culinary aspirations tonight.

Mom's laptop is on the table in the living room. The tab with the recipe is already open. She's in the kitchen, pulling out a baking sheet. All I have to do is press print. That's it. Except when I go to press print, she gets a notification. An email. From someone who . . .

Why is he emailing her?

I shouldn't open it. I don't even want to open it and yet somehow, I feel my fingers graze across the trackpad of the laptop. Her inbox springs to life. At the top of a pile of spam, an unread message shines. I know I shouldn't, but I click.

From Stephen Holloway

To Lorielle Dixon

Subject Niarah

Any updates?

—

Reply

From Stephen Holloway

To Lorielle Dixon

Subject Niarah

Thank you for taking my phone call the other day. I know that wasn't the conversation that you expected, but I appreciate you speaking with me. I've tried calling and texting and emailing Niarah, but she won't respond. I know that I have no right to ask you this, but I think it's important for Niarah.

Can you please let her know that I need to talk to her?

Niarah deserves to know that she has a sister.

—

Reply A     

HER NAME IS

HER NAME IS

HER NAME IS

I HAVE A SISTER?

I have a sister?

I have a *sister*.

"You knew?"

I hand her a printout of the emails from my father.

She winces once she sees. "Yes." She sets the knife back down on the cutting board. "He didn't tell me as soon as he should have, but he did tell me. A few months ago."

"A few *months* ago?"

I grab a lemon from the fruit bowl, desperate for something to squeeze. "How old is she?" I ask.

Mom hesitates. "She just turned two."

My heart stops. *Two.*

That's so . . . so young. Part of me expected that she'd be my age or older—the product of some affair that we never knew about. But no. She's a toddler.

I did not expect her to be a toddler.

Things are bad enough for my generation, but hers? My god. The world that she'll inherit . . . it'll be so much worse than mine. My blood boils all over again. How could my father be so selfish?

My mom mistakes my silence for curiosity. She continues. "Her name is—"

"I don't want to know her name." If I know her name, then she becomes real to me.

I dig my nails into the rind of the lemon, releasing a hiss of citrusy mist. The fibers of the fruit bury themselves beneath my fingernails, the scent overtaking the air. "He was such . . . He was . . ." My heart pounds in my chest. "He was such a bad father. Why would he, how could he ever, think that it'd be okay for him to have more kids? Him of all people?"

Having him as a father was no easy thing. I feel bad for the little girl. I feel bad for me.

"People . . . grow up. Even grownups keep growing up. He's been seeing a psychiatrist, you know. He's on medication now. And he's sober these days. I haven't seen him, but from what I understand—"

"He's a liar. Of course a liar would lie about becoming a better person."

Mom folds me into a hug. I let her.

"Do you want to meet her?" she whispers.

I pull away, abruptly. "Why would you even ask me that?"

"Well, she's your family, so . . ."

"We're not family. Blood doesn't make family."

"Fine. Maybe you're not family now. But you could be."

I squeeze the lemon so hard that my thumb punctures the skin, plunging into the core of the fruit. I hiss when the acidic juice stings the small cut on my knuckle from camping. I free my thumb and plunge it beneath a stream of cold water in the sink. As the water rushes, I sink my forehead onto the cool tile of the counter. Mom watches silently until she cuts off the water and hands me a napkin.

"No one's going to force the relationship, but you're the big sister." She retrieves the lemon, slicing it in half and squeezing its juice onto the fish. "It's up to you whether you want to be in her life or not."

I'm the big sister.

The thought sinks in heavy like lead.

GOODBYE

GOODBYE

GOODBYE

TODAY'S THE DAY THAT ANDREW LEAVES. OX'S letter rattles around in my brain. I rally to leave the house to see him off, shoving away my shame about what Mac might have told him about our final fight. But Andrew is happy to see me. We sit on the front porch of his house. Over the course of the past hour, I've already filled him in about my last few days. Mac, Camp Doom, the roof. It wasn't as hard as I thought it would be to tell him what happened. Maybe it's the fact that he's getting ready to leave, or maybe it's because he listens to me vent with no judgment, but I decide to keep talking.

"So, I found out my dad has another kid."

"Oh *shit.*"

"I know."

"Older or younger?"

"Younger. It's a girl. She's two."

"Goddamn."

"Yeup."

"You gon' meet her?"

"Nah."

"Why not?"

"It's all too . . . I don't know. It's all too fucked up. I don't want to have to deal with that. Plus, like, what do I have to say to a toddler? I don't even know what I'd bring to the table by entering her life."

"It might be nice for her to have someone to look up to," Andrew says.

"I'm not the type of person that anyone should ever look up to."

"Well . . . I look up to you."

"Really?"

"No. Of course not. Look at us—we're both a mess."

I shove his shoulder and we laugh.

"Felt like the right thing to say in the moment, though," he says.

I lean back onto the grass. "I don't want to be anyone's role model."

"Then don't. Just be her sister."

Quiet.

Andrew checks the time on his phone once more and sighs. "Aight. I'm callin' it. I don't think Sage is coming."

"Why wouldn't they?" I ask.

"Last night, I may or may not have confessed some . . . feelings. Unclear how it was received."

"I'm sorry," I say. Nothing's ever easy between friends. "Proud of you, though."

He gives me a weak smile. "Me too."

Andrew calls out to his parents inside and asks them for a ride to the culinary school student housing in Irvine after all.

"Be ready in ten!" his mom shouts back.

"Wanna smoke before you leave?" I whisper.

"Nah, I'm good. I'm taking a break from drinking and smoking for a while."

"Wooooooooooow. I never thought I'd live to see the day."

"Yeah, yeah."

"Why?"

"Last night, I was out of weed, but bored as hell after I finished packing. I tried to jack off, but it, like, didn't work, so I—"

I hold my hands up. "This is more detail than I anticipated."

He laughs. "It's been so long since I've done anything sober. I feel like my body's starting to forget how to feel good if I'm not somewhere on the spectrum of buzzed to fucked up."

"Hmm. All the interventions, everyone's warnings, and in the end . . . it's masturbation that scared you straight."

"It's a break, not a forever thing. The world is harsh. Sometimes we gotta dissociate to soften the blows. But I can't, like, live in that constant state forever. The goal is balance, or whatever. I don't know. I'm tryna figure my shit out, man."

I nudge against his shoulder. "I support it."

We keep talking until his parents come. A feeble attempt to ignore the growing strain of the impending goodbye blooming between us. When his mom pulls the car up to the curb to start loading in his suitcases, I try to think of something good to say.

"So, uh, thank you for . . . being—"

Andrew cuts me off, pulling me to his chest so quickly that it knocks the wind out of me. "Don't you dare do a big thing."

"Thank god." I sigh. "I didn't want to do a speech."

"I know, babe."

We hold each other for another long moment until his mom clears her throat. We separate, reluctantly, and I watch as Andrew shuts the trunk, giving me one last salute before opening the car door. The words *safe travels* are about to form on my lips when a blaring car horn rips down the street. We look up, but there's no one else there. Andrew shrugs, climbing in, but then the honking starts again. Loud and obnoxious like someone laying on the horn. I hear tires skid and smell the burned rubber before Sage's car whips around the corner. I watch Andrew's expression morph from shock to relief as Sage throws the car into park and stumbles out of the driver seat.

"Scoot over, Andrew."

For once, Andrew is silent. He can hardly contain the massive grin on his face. Sage gives me a hug and mumbles an apology into my ear, plus a promise to text me later. Andrew's parents smile as Sage climbs into the back seat.

"We'll see you soon?" Andrew says.

I put my hands in my pockets. "Yeah."

Sage narrows their eyes. "No. Say it."

"I will see you soon."

Andrew grins. "There we go."

I watch my friends drive down a street painted purple by the fallen jacaranda flowers. Sage blasts a song that I shared with them while Andrew hangs an arm lazily out the window, trying to catch the wind.

I was prepared for this moment to feel like a final goodbye, but Andrew's words have permeated my brain. I'll see them soon. I know it.

LOOKING FOR MAC

LOOKING FOR MAC
LOOKING FOR MAC

STRAIGHT FROM ANDREW'S, I WALK TO MAC'S house. The lights are off and there are no cars in the driveway.

I wait for a while, but after two neighbors side-eye me, it starts to feel shady lurking around. I pull out my phone to call him, but that feels desperate. I check the date. He's leaving tomorrow. So, I am desperate. I let my finger hover over his name in my call history, but I never tap the screen.

I spent the summer with Mac. We had fun. Now summer's over.

It's time to move on.

I pull out a crumpled receipt from my bag and leave him one last note.

VISITOR

VISITOR
VISITOR

BACK HOME, MOM CHECKS ON ME EVERY twenty minutes, like clockwork. She doesn't say much when she stops by until around nine p.m. She knocks on my door extra softly. "You have a visitor."

INSIDE
INSIDE
INSIDE

MAC IS STANDING IN THE DOORWAY TO MY room. Mom is beside him. He holds up the note that I left on his door.

Mom breaks the silence. "So, you're the mysterious kid who's been sleeping in my backyard."

"Mom."

"Honestly, Niarah, I don't know why you didn't introduce him to me like a normal person. What did you think I was going to do? Terrorize him?"

"MOM."

"I'm just saying."

"It's nice to meet you, Ms. Dixon," Mac says. He shakes her hand like a gentleman, and she practically melts. I try not to roll my eyes.

He's wearing old jeans and a plain white tee. No flannel today. His hair is pulled back, so I can see the worry lines on his forehead clearly. He grasps his elbows as he turns to face me. "Can I come in?"

Mom looks at him, then at me, then back at Mac. I nod to her first before I wave Mac inside. I don't leave my bed. Mom lets us alone, but leaves the door cracked open.

"So, this is your room," he says, staring at the largely bare walls.

"This is my room."

The walls are undecorated, except for one corner. There, a cluster of Post-its from Mac gathers in a swarm of neon pinks and yellows and greens. He sees the notes and smiles, but it's sad. He slips his hands into his pockets as he examines my bookshelf. My collection is much smaller than his, but he reads every spine. He looks at every pen, every video game carefully. I know that he's moving so intentionally because he's never been in here before, but I also get the feeling that he's busying himself because it's easier than looking at me right now. I don't want to look at myself, either. I haven't seen a mirror in days. Still, though, I want him closer.

"Come here," I say softly.

He looks up, meeting my eyes for the first time today. Without hesitation, he swoops forward, nearly collapsing onto the bed as he wraps his arms around me. The cotton of his shirt is soft against my cheek. The muscles in his arms flex as he pulls me tight. His hands move frantically from my spine to my neck to the back of my head to my shoulders. He touches me with the awe of someone who's recovered something precious.

"I'm so happy you're here," he whispers into my hair, matted and frizzy at the back of my neck.

I don't know if Andrew told him or Sage or my mom or whoever, but I don't really care. I'm relieved that he already knows so that I don't have to tell him myself.

"I know our last conversation was . . . bad. But I would've come by sooner had I known. I'm so—"

"I didn't actually do anything," I find myself saying. It's hard not to feel the need to defend myself, even when nobody gives me a reason to.

"I know. And I'm grateful." Mac lets go at last so that he can look at me. He takes a long, deep breath and scrunches his mouth to the side to prevent himself from crying. There's an unbearable grief in his eyes, but he doesn't comment on it. He swallows and clears his throat. "I really care about you, and I want you to know you can tell me anything."

"Did you get that line from that article about how to talk to someone who tells you that they're thinking of suicide? The one with the cute graphics?"

"Yes." His expression is difficult to read.

"I read that article, too. Good stuff. Very thorough."

A half smile from Mac now. Progress. He bites his lip. "I mean it, though," he says.

For a moment, I worry that he's going to ask for more details, but he doesn't. I forget that that's one of my favorite things about him: He doesn't push. I touch his face, and he lets his lips spill into my hand, leaving a featherlight kiss. "I know you do." I lean back on top of the covers to stare at the ceiling. Mac kicks off his shoes and joins me. We lay separately, but hold hands, letting the weight rest on top of my thigh. "Sorry that I wasted our last days together being a mess."

"Don't be sorry. You're not a mess." He gives my hand a squeeze. "Nothing you're going through changes how I feel about you."

Another line from the website, I'm sure. But again, I know

he means it, so I try not to be a smart-ass about it. I squeeze his hand back.

I crawl into a ball beneath the covers, my voice barely a whisper. "I can't tell you how much it hurts."

I hear a sniffle up above. "That's okay." A wipe of the nose. A shaky exhale. "I'm glad you told someone that it hurts at all."

"You don't have to stay," I mumble. It's his last night in LA and he shouldn't be wasting it here.

"This is where I want to be," he says, voice more serious than I've ever heard it before. "If you wanna get up, I'll help you get up. If you wanna lie here, I'll lie here with you. I'm here for you and always will be. It's that simple."

He folds on top of me and holds me close. We don't talk about how he's leaving tomorrow or about the other night. Instead, we talk about movies. Board games. Conspiracy theories. Vampires. Farming. If vampires could farm. Pointless, aimless conversation carries us into the night. Midnight strikes, but Mom must hear us laughing because she lets him stay. Pointless, aimless conversation carries me into another day.

RUINS

RUINS
RUINS

IT'S NEARLY 2 A.M. WHEN OUR VOICES START to trail off, turning into strained whispers.

"It's getting late," Mac says, though by the way he's looking at me, I don't think he wants to leave. I know that I don't want him to.

"Wanna see Camp Doom?" I ask. "One last time?"

I can tell he wants to protest the finality of it all, but he knows on some level that it's true. We slip out of my room down the hallway, through the yard, and into this place that we tried to turn into something special. We lay down on the futon, the only item spared from the wreckage of the earthquake. It looks as if the apocalypse happened all around us. I laugh.

"What?" he asks, a teasing smile on his lips. His hand rests along the seam of my shirt.

"Camp Doom in her final hours." I look around and spot memories in every corner. "I learned how to tie that weird fishing knot in here."

"You learned how to kiss in here." He smirks my way and I

shove a pillow at him. He leans in close, his forehead touching mine. "I fell in love in here."

I stare at him in the dark. This boy who still loves the world that raised him despite the troubles it's caused him. This boy who loves me. He knows that I feel the same way. I don't have to say it because I know that he feels it every time we touch. Every time we're together like this.

"I wanted us to end up together," he whispers.

"I wanted that, too."

"I still want it."

"We both need—"

"I know, I get it. And I respect it. I'm just sayin' I still want it. And I'm going to miss you. Can't tell you how much I'm gonna miss you."

Hours pass. When the sun begins to bleed in through the skylight, he gathers his things to leave at last. I walk him to the door.

My shaking hands drift up to cradle the angles of his face, the clean line of his jaw. I touch his lips. A faint blush creeps up his cheeks and he casts his eyes to the floor, the corners of his mouth quirking up to form a melancholy smile.

This could be the last time I ever kiss Mac Torres. I try to remember all the details of what he looks like right now, brown eyes gazing over at me on the last day of summer. Blue jeans, heavily worn and frayed at the bottom heel. The faint impression of the pendant of La Virgen beneath the fabric of his shirt. Faded white Vans with hearts drawn in Sharpie along the rubber edge. The dark laugh lines that appear to be holding up his cheekbones whenever he smiles with his teeth. Curly, disheveled hair that falls in heavy wisps over his eyes. Warm breath trickling out from full lips against my neck.

In the ruins of Camp Doom, we kiss one last time.

REST STOP

REST STOP
REST STOP

MY MOM IS DRESSED UP IN OUTDOOR RECRE-ation attire like it's Halloween. She looks like Girl Scout Troop Leader Barbie. I wear the same thing I wore on the backpacking trip, including the pants that zip off into shorts. Just in case.

Mom agreed to let us camp for one night on our drive to meet my sister. We're car camping because it's her first time and I insisted on bringing Bruce with us, but I'm excited to show her the stuff I learned on the backpacking trip, even though I act like it's no big deal.

I curate the music for the whole drive, switching between the albums *Kid A* and *In Rainbows*. It's not her usual style of music, but I'd be lying if I said that I didn't have an ulterior motive. When we pull over at the rest stop and she steps away to "make a call," my secret plan works. There's a shaky timbre in her voice as she speaks, but it's not the angry kind. It's the timid kind. I know she's talking to Ox. Radiohead is his favorite band.

Mx. Ferrante only gave me an extension for a few more days,

so I keep writing whenever we stop the car. Bruce nuzzles against my hip as I pull out my laptop and type.

Niarah Holloway
Sophomore Capstone Project
Mx. Ferrante's class

HOW TO SURVIVE BEING ALIVE
(AND MAYBE EVEN LIVE A LITTLE, TOO)

Dedicated to my younger sister, Raven—
I can't wait to grow up with you

Dear Future Self,

By now, you are twenty-six years old. Congrats on surviving this long. Sixteen-year-old you from the past would like to thank you. But first, I want to tell you a story.

It all started with the beginning of the end of the world.

One morning, Doomsday Girl woke up and realized the sky was falling. At first, she kept this knowledge a secret. It kept her up at night, dreaming of The End. So, eventually, she decided to do something about it. She decided to prepare. That way, she thought, she could have a sense of control. She'd feel less scared. She could protect herself and the ones she loved. But soon, others discovered her secret. She readied herself to endure their laughter, but instead, they listened. They didn't agree, but they helped her anyway. Then came the day that the earth rumbled. All of Doomsday Girl's hard work came crumbling down. She went crumbling down with it. It scared her how much she wanted to live. So, when the dust settled, she didn't keep her fear a secret this time. Her people kept her safe. Life in ruins is still life. The sky may fall one day, but how beautiful it is to hold and be held in the meantime.

Looking back, I still think that building Camp Doom was valid. There's the pain of society, then the pain of your own life, then these massive threats like climate change and it's all too much. Of course, mental health struggles often trace back to global, societal, and political struggles. Sometimes, I want it all to stop. This summer, I really wanted it to stop. There's no way for me to know if you still feel like this, too. I hope that you don't, but if you do, I understand.

We have a friend who's fond of quotes. It sort of rubbed off on me. I have a new favorite by this poet Alok V. Menon, who writes, "I am both the happiest and the saddest I have ever been." I feel this so deeply. I am both the happiest and the saddest I have ever been. I'm learning how both of these things can be true at the same time. How nothing's easier than it was before, but ever since this summer, I've started to notice the way that the light shimmers on the corners of every happy moment. How sweetness fills my bones when I spend time with people I love. My lungs keep on breathing, my eyes keep showing me beautiful and strange new things. My skin tingles with the memory of Mac, knowing that I can touch and be touched like that again. My heart beats in my chest, reminding me that I want to be alive. I haven't cured anything, but there's a shift happening.

What a brilliant, twisted miracle it is to survive oneself.

I wrote down everything that happened this summer. I did it for me, but I also did it for you. To remember how it felt, how it hurt, and how it started to get better.

I can't believe that I'm writing something this sincere. I've gone soft. It's embarrassing. But it turns out I like being soft. I've abandoned many of my old tools. Turns out cynicism is just another way of saying that you're scared.

I don't think that the world is getting better, but I don't think that's the point.

It's work. Real work to choose to stay here. I want to be present. Because when we're not present, we miss the miracles. We miss the cues for love, for change, for revolution. If you're reading this, sometime in the future, that means that you're still doing it—still choosing. And for that, I thank you.

Remember what Mac said, about how what if there are no endings, and instead only transformations? Until the next transformation, our job is simple: Be here now.

The world is always ending. We stay in love.

RESOURCES

Crisis Text Line
www.CrisisTextLine.org
Crisis Text Line provides free emotional support and information to teens in any type of crisis, including feeling suicidal. You can text with a trained specialist twenty-four hours a day. Text *HOME* to 741741.

Trevor Project
www.TheTrevorProject.org
The Trevor Project provides suicide prevention and crisis intervention services to lesbian, gay, bisexual, transgender, and questioning (LGBTQ) young people. It offers free, 24-7, confidential counseling through the following: Trevor Lifeline—toll-free phone line at 1-866-488-7386; TrevorText—text *START* to 678-678; TrevorChat—instant messaging at TheTrevorProject.org/Help. It also runs TrevorSpace, an affirming social networking site for LGBTQ youth at www.TrevorSpace.org.

988 Suicide and Crisis Lifeline: Call or Text 988
The Lifeline is a twenty-four-hour toll-free phone line for people in suicidal crisis or emotional distress. An online chat option is available at www.988Lifeline.org.

National Domestic Violence Hotline
www.TheHotline.org
Text *START* to 88788
1.800.799.SAFE (7233)
The Hotline is a 24-7 center that has access to service providers and shelters across the United States.

ACKNOWLEDGMENTS

The author recognizes the Gabrielino/Tongva peoples as the past, present, and future caretakers of the land, water, and cultural resources in the unceded territory of Tovaangar (the Los Angeles basin) where this story takes place.

Thank you to the following individuals who provided tools to my own survival kit, without which this book would not exist.

- Water, *Leslie Noble*
- Compass, *Jordan Adero*
- Crank-up radio, *Jasmin Ayanna*
- Sunglasses, *Jah Jua*
- Energy bar, *Yasir Jua*
- Iodine, *Jim McCarthy*
- Flashlight, *Rebecca Kuss*
- Binoculars, *Ashley I. Fields*
- Notebook and pen, *Zareen Johnson & Jessica Cruickshank*
- Walkie-talkie, *Danielle Parker*
- Emergency blanket, *Latrel Powell*
- First aid supplies, *Blair Thompson*
- Gardening seeds, *Alixx Lucas*
- Freeze-dried meals, *Max Mendelsohn*
- Matchbox, *Phaedra Frampton*
- Sewing kit, *Dianne Kaiyoorawongs*
- Cookware, *Emma K. Ohland*
- Work gloves, *Daksha P.*
- Whistle, *Linda*
- Emergency shelter, *"The Village"*
- Guidebooks, *bell hooks, adrienne maree brown, Anna Tsing, "Hard Times" by Paramore,* For The Wild *podcast*

Thank you to my community. You are my most important flotation device.